The Magpa c

written by

All characters in thi͟s ͟creat͟ed
by Daniel J. Barnes and all the characters in this
publication are fictitious, any resemblance to real persons,
living or dead, is purely coincidental.

All rights reserved.
No part of this publication may be reproduced,
or transmitted, in any form or by any means without prior
written permission from Daniel J. Barnes.

Magpa: Sorrow was edited by Amy Rollinson.

All Daniel J. Barnes creations, characters
(apart from public domain characters) and media are
owned by Daniel J. Barnes and must not be used or
distributed without consent.

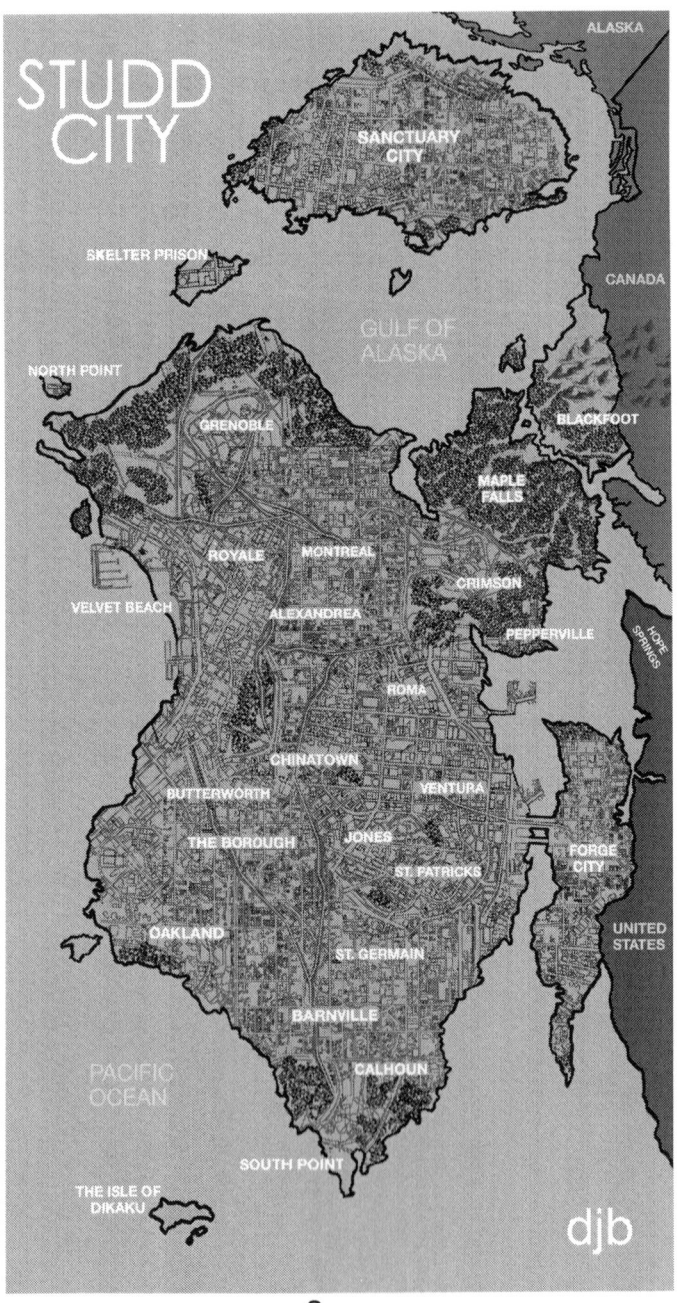

To Jess

MAGPIE SORROW

Thank you!!

One for sorrow,
Two for joy,
Three for a girl,
Four for a boy,
Five for silver,
Six for gold,
Seven for a secret never to be told.
Eight for a wish,
Nine for a kiss,
Ten a surprise you should be careful not to miss.
Eleven for health,
Twelve for wealth,
Thirteen beware it's the devil himself.

I

HOPE SPRINGS, OREGON 1693

The baby screamed hysterically as Jonathan Cartwright burst into the cabin and slammed the door behind him, crunching the rusted latch into place and frantically sliding the wooden bolts into their brackets.

"You need to leave, Nancy!" He screamed, his chest heaving with rapid breathes.

His wife Nancy stood dumbstruck in the middle of the decrepit cabin, cradling her child in her arms tightly, protectively.

"What is happening?" She mumbled, her eyes moist with tears, swaying the child from side to side to stifle his cries.

Jonathan ran to the window and gazed through the grimy glass in despair at such an overwhelming sight that met his eyes. His temples throbbed with anxiousness and his long fringe dripped with perspiration, fear had gripped and there was no reply for his bewildered wife. He slammed the inner window shutters into place. Shutters that Jonathan had painstakingly constructed on the insides of each window to their humble cabin to keep out the chill of winter, however these shutters would not be able to keep out what approached.

"Jonathan!" Nancy cried loudly to be heard over the

distressed child.

Again, he did not reply, as he scrambled across the cabin, tripping on a blanket strewn upon the damp floorboards, kicking a bucket out of the way and wildly flinging a chair onto the unmade bed. In his eagerness he knocked the family table causing the single candle that lit the room to teeter in the cradle of its brass holder, he grasped the candleholder and halted its sway, the flame flickering feverishly before returning to a gentle flutter.

"Jonathan!" She called again as he moved towards the other window and stared out it in horror.

"Jonathan? Answer me!" She screamed, matching tears of anguish streaming down her and her child's face.

"They are coming for you." He murmured.

"No!" She whimpered and as he stepped away from the window she could see them, dozens and dozens of torches quivered in the darkness, the amber light shimmering on the sharp metal of the pitchforks and scythes, tools that were now seen as weapons held tightly in the clammy hands of the marching mob.

"The Witch Finders!" She gasped.

"They have come for you, Nancy." Jonathan cried, slamming the shutter across the window and concealing the angry mob of Finders that rapidly approached their dilapidated cabin.

"You must go! Go now!"

"But Jonathan…" She weeped and gripped the child tightly, uncomfortably tight, "…but what of the babe"

"I will take him." He said, prising the child from her grip, "Come William, come to Papa!"

"No, my babe, my little…"

"It's the only way my love. They will not harm me or the babe." He looked at her with sorrow in his eyes and then gazed into the moist blue pools of his son's and smiled.

"But what of me?" She blubbered as she stood quivering in her rough, cotton nightgown, her face gaunt contorted with fear.

This season's crops had died, the ground had become frozen like stone and the community blamed witchcraft. The community blamed Nancy Cartwright.

"What will become of me?" She snivelled, knowing far too well what awaited her.

Jonathan said nothing and turned his full attentions on that of his son, kissing the mop of hair that hung in disarray on the child's head.

They were all hungry and it showed, but Nancy was ever so thin, dangerously thin with malnutrition, her hair hacked short into a style that resembled that of a boys, Jonathan had cut it that way with the use of a bowl and his hunting knife, but she had liked it. Now she stood quivering in her cabin, with her arms stretched out to her husband and child, candlelight bathing her in an eerie light that projected an almost birdlike silhouette on the walls.

"Please Jonathan, help me." She whimpered.

He embraced her, the child sandwiched between them tightly, for a moment this seemed to comfort the child and his cries of anguish ceased.

"Just hold me and tell me everything will be okay." Nancy said looking up at his stern but handsome face, tears welling up in his eyes and cascading down his chiselled cheekbones before snaking through the uneven patches of stubble that had set upon his face.

"Jonathan!" Nancy said again, "please!"

"I can hold you, but I cannot lie to you, Nancy." He sighed. "You must go if you are to be spared."

"But…"

"There are no buts or maybes my dear, if they find you here they will kill you."

Their moist eyes locked onto each other and there were no more words to be spoken, they both knew that his harsh words were the truth of the matter.

"Hold me a little longer." She snivelled all the while the sounds of stomping feet on the frozen ground came closer and the ghoulish cries of slander and murder filled the air.

Jonathan embraced her tightly and she rubbed her forehead against the uncomfortable, roughness of his chin and stroked the thick dark hair on William's head. In that moment there was nothing wrong, there was silence and she felt the warmth of her husband and child, she felt the love and the sorrow that seeped from her husband. She closed her eyes and reminisced of the wonderful times that they had spent together as a young family in their little home on the outskirts of Parliament Grove. She remembered cooking broth on the stove, watching Jonathan sowing the fields and working tirelessly to haul the vegetables by himself. Everyday he would work so hard and she would always greet him on his return with a cup of ale, a bowl of broth and some home baked bread. She remembered making love on a bed of straw and thin, coarse blankets rubbing at her flesh. The birth of William and feeding him for the first time, such blissful memories that she knew would never be replicated. This was the end, but she could not let go, she would not.

"Bring out the witch!" Came the growl from outside the cabin and the door rattled on its hinges as it was struck vigorously.

Nancy returned from her musing and the cabin rattled with the vigorous strikes from the angry Finders, who took tool and weapon and struck at the flimsy, wooden construction.

"Bring out the witch I say!" Came the voice again, this time with more aggression and venom. "By order of Judge Tobias Bittern!"

The mob of Finders echoed his sentiment with malicious calls of 'witch' and 'whore'.

"S-She has gone!" Jonathan called back. "Please leave me and the child in peace."

"Spawn child of a witch!" Came the angry reply and again heavy blows fell against the door.

Jonathan pulled himself away from Nancy and held the child closer.

"You must go, Nancy." He whimpered, and with that the child started to cry again. "It is the only way."

Nancy stood hugging herself and shaking profusely, she gazed at the front of the house and the glow from the Finder's torches cut through the gaps in the wall of misshapen wood panels. Outside the windows broke, the sound of glass breaking and then vigorous strikes bombarded the fragile shutters.

"They will soon be in!" Jonathan cried, "Go, now, leave us!"

"Jonathan..."

"GO!" He screamed at her and there was no love in his face, only fear and frustration. If she did not leave, both Jonathan and William would die too.

"Bring her out!" Came the cries.

"Drown her!"

"Hang her!" They spat with venom.

Nancy looked all around and noticed that the light from the torches were only at the front and sides of the cabin and had not yet reached the rear of their home.

She finally made for the back door and unlatched it.

"I love you both." She said.

"Just...go." Jonathan sighed.

"Give her to us, Jonathan!" Came the voice of Judge Bittern, "Give her to us and you will be spared."

"She has fled! She has gone!" Jonathan called back.

She turned to leave, but then stopped and sighed.

"I did not mean for any of this."

"I know."

She faced him and once more their eyes met, moist and full of sorrow.

"One more embrace?" She asked. "A last embrace and

then I shall leave."

"There is no time, they will be upon us any moment now!"

But his words fell on deaf ears and she bounded forward and embraced her husband and child, squeezing them tightly.

A shutter splintered and the ugly face of a Witch Finder appeared in the gap, his eyes grew wide and he called to the others.

"He lies!" He growled, "Cartwright lies! The witch is there still!"

The mob's cries grew louder, enraged at being lied too and they struck the cabin with relentless abandon.

"Go, damn you! Go!" Jonathan whined, pushing her away.

She gazed upon them one final time as the heads of tools erupted through the walls and shutters, bathing the cabin with torchlight and polluting the air with hate and bitterness.

Nancy burst through the back door of the cabin, the cold air striking her as soon as she exited. She ran barefoot across the frozen mud towards the gathering of leafless trees. Her frantic breathes exploded from her in thick plumes, gooseflesh rising from tight skin that seemed to cling to her bones. She stumbled and fell, grazing her exposed knees on the dried mud that had frozen in sharp unforgiving shards. She hissed with pain as she saw blood seep from her wounds, but the horrid cacophony that could be heard from the cabin was enough to spur her onwards. She moved again, tears streaming down her face, blood streaming down her shins, almost mimicking her sorrow.

But she did not look back, she could not. She made it to the edge of the large grove and froze, staring up at the dark behemoths of bark that blocked her way. Parliament Grove was a mass of contorted trunks and branches, locked in a tense, constrictive dance, with each branch seeming to reach for her like the boney hands of some fleshless wraith.

Nancy was cold, but an eerie shudder worked its way down her spine and again her body was covered in gooseflesh. It was not the wintery breeze that caused this reaction, but fear.

She stepped forward, branches snapping underfoot, causing her to wince with discomfort. Moist, dead leaves squelched between her toes, which was a strange, but not an unpleasant sensation. She was ready to walk through the trees into the darkness, into the unknown and never look back. But she was halted by a strange squawking sound, its pitch was disturbing and she shook her head wildly to try and rid her ears of such a horrid sound.

The squawking pitch did not stop.

Nancy gazed up and noticed a large bird, thick with black and white feathers, a streak of blue-green seemed to change tone as the creature moved along the branch above her. It was a black-billed magpie and its dark beady eyes shimmered at her playfully.

"One for sorrow." She whispered, she knew the rhyme and that seeing just one of these creatures brought with it grief and tragedy.

Suddenly her babe let out a bloodcurdling scream and she span around swiftly, almost losing her footing in the pile of rotting leaves.

"William!" She murmured and gazed in horror to see the cabin consumed by flames.

Any ideas of fleeing were now the furthest thing from her mind and she raced over the frozen ground she had already trodden, to make for her child. No longer did the winter breeze or the sharp folds of mud beneath her feet harass her, a feeling had swept over her, an instinct like no other, a mother's instinct to protect her child. As she reached the cabin and swung open the back door, an immense backdraft of raging flame forced her back, she stumbled and fell onto her rear as the quivering flames licked at her like Satan's tongue.

She gazed at the flames, eyes wide in horror as she looked inside and saw Jonathan standing in the middle of the cabin, gripping the babe closely as if to shield him from the flames. Tears ran down his face as he whispered to the babe and Nancy could see his lips flicker with lies, telling the child that everything would be okay.

The Witch Finders had remained at the front of the building and stepped back to witness the raging inferno.

"Watch for her men, watch for her." Called Judge Bittern, holding a mallet aloft and pointing towards the roof of the cabin that danced with a thousand flames.

"The witch's spirit will leave the flames and make to escape. Be wary of this."

The roof collapsed and Nancy watched on as heavy beams that were consumed with flame fell down upon her husband and son. The screams of the child was halted immediately and

Nancy let out a shriek that mimicked that of the magpie that had taunted her.

"Witch!" Came a call and one of the Finders appeared from around the corner of the cabin. "She is here!"

He was joined by other Finders who stood and gawped at her, their weapons gripped in their hands not knowing what to do next. Nancy scrambled backwards on the floor, as Judge Bittern barged his way through the rabble, his trusted mallet in hand. He stopped and scowled at her.

"Don't just stand there!" He bellowed. "Kill the bitch!"

They moved toward her slowly, stalking her, but Nancy would not wait for them to close the gap and swiftly she rose and once again ran toward The Grove.

"She is heading towards Parliament Grove!" Someone shouted in a cautionary tone.

"The Grove, it be cursed!" Another Finder bellowed.

"Pay no heed to such folklore men." Bittern announced, "The only unworldly being within its trees is that witch."

Nancy did not think twice about entering The Grove a second time and she burst through the leafless branches that scratched and tore at her flesh as she passed, as if The Grove longed to take her for itself.

With each stride she took she saw magpies skipping along the branches of the trees as if keeping pace with her. As she ran she could hear the snapping of branches behind her and the brutish calls. She looked to see dozens of flaming torches creeping through the mass of trees like floating spectres of fire. She turned away from the impending threat and focused again on the magpies that squawked at her, it was if they were almost guiding her along the way. She remembered the rhyme, the old nursery rhyme that was song by every child in this region.

"One for sorrow." She started, her breathes heavy from her vigorous dash across fallen trees and harsh foliage.

"Two for mirth." She murmured, her words were low but they made her feel less anxious about the situation and helped her forget that she was being chased by a mob of angry Witch Finders.

"Three for a funeral, four for a birth..."
Her mind wandered for a moment as she thought of her child now burning in their home. Tears fell again and she noticed that dwelling on this had slowed her considerably and she could hear the voices of The Finders more clearly, they were gaining on her. She focused again and moved faster continuing with her rhyme.

"Five for heaven, six for hell..." she whispered the last word and looked up and noticed that the magpies had settled at a clearing in the grove and called to her to join them, no longer would they pursue her. She turned into the clearing and ran through the thicket where an old well stood. Three feet of piled stones fixed into place, saw it rise form the clearing like a chimney that she had seen on a few homes within Hope Springs, belonging to those more fortunate to have such luxurious features on their dwellings.

She stopped dead with the final words of the rhyme echoing in the clearing, "Seven for the devil, his own self."

Nancy approached the well, slowly with caution, she could still hear The Finder's calls and the constant breaking of branches. She touched the cold rough texture of the rocks that made up the well's head. Gone had any structure or device that could lower a bucket in search of water, which led her to believe that this well was indeed barren and had been for a very long time. She gazed into the darkness that formed below her, a shaft of black moist stone with roots breaking out from between the tired old structure. The winter's moon appeared from behind a thick wall of cloud and illuminated the clearing, it was then that she saw the parliament of magpies that surrounded her, for every tree was consumed by them. She looked on and gasped at just how many there were, all of their eyes staring at her and squawking erratically as if she should know what to do next.

"I don't know what you wish of me?" She asked the magpies, they shrieked and cackled as if discussing with each other what she had just said. The moon's rays exposed several small rocks that had become dislodged from the well's head over time. She scooped one up and dropped it unceremoniously down the well. The rock span and turned and then disappeared into the darkness below. It seemed to fall for the longest time until there was a thud that echoed from below, the sound of the rock striking solid ground. As Nancy had presumed, there was no water left within the bottom of this well.

The magpies chattered again and she looked away from the black hypnotising hole that lay below her. As she leaned over it she noticed a narrow ledge several feet within its confines, she believed if she could climb down to the ledge then she would be able to hide within the shroud of the wells shadow.

She climbed over the circle of raised rocks and managed to grip the inner wall with her toes and fingers, holding tightly she allowed herself to hang, her toes wriggling as they frantically probed for the whereabouts of the ledge. After several stressful moments she found her footing and relief consumed her as she lowered herself down to the ledge keeping a firm grip on the inner wall. She maneuvered herself into the shadows and kept as close to the wall as she could. She listened intently, trying not to even breathe for it may give away her position. The magpies had become silent, but she knew they were watching, a bird that she never thought one would be able to trust. She heard the dripping of water coming from below, perhaps there were caverns beneath her still harbouring some moisture. She was soon brought back to the here and now as the voices of Witch Finders were close, uncomfortably close.

Nancy was motionless, listening to the Finder's gruff voices curse her name and her existence, she could see the tops of trees reaching for the moon as if to grasp it in its crooked embrace. The torchlight flickered above her and illuminated the gloom, she held her breath. The torches passed by and there was only the moon again to light the gaping hole above her head, she felt reassured when the voices started to move away with the glare of the torches and she breathed a sigh of relief.

There was a squawking sound that echoed around her and she looked up to see a magpie perched upon the well, its head tilting from side to side as it regarded at her. It cawed loudly again and slammed his beak into the rocks that made up the well's head.

"Damn bird!" Nancy cursed under her breath. "Get out of here!"

It shrieked at her and pecked again vigorously at the rocks, she repositioned herself and freed a hand to swat the bird away, it did not take kindly to the gesture and shrieked again at her, trying to nip at her fingers with its snapping beak.

"God damn you creature, be gone!" She said swiping again, this time the magpie flew away, but her flailing hand was suddenly gripped tightly at the wrist.

"No!" She cried, her voice defying her and circling around her in a terrifying echo.

The rough fingers of Judge Bittern gripped around her frail wrist tightly and he appeared over the well. His wart covered face lit unflatteringly by torchlight, revealed every crease and defect that sprouted from his evil face.

"Nancy Cartwright!" He hissed with venom and hatred and hoisted her up out of the shadows by her wrist.

"The witch!" Someone cried. "We have found the witch."

Nancy hung from his grip, kicking her legs frantically in a feeble attempt to escape.

"I am no witch!" She screamed.

"Oh, come now!" Laughed Bittern who had now been joined by his Finders, each one as ugly as the next.

"That is exactly what you would say if you were one."

The Finders laughed at her, salivating at what their leader had in store for their latest find.

"You are the cause of the bad winter and the frozen crops." Bittern announced as he shook her wildly, she could feel her shoulder burning with pain as if it would burst from its socket at any time.

"Please," She pleaded, "these words you speak are not true."

"Oh, but they are!" Bittern bit. "You have brought with you magpies to this land. We had never had their kind here before and we all now what bad omens accompany them."

"They are but birds, they have no meaning."

"Pah! A witch's tongue drips nothing but lies! You must be made an example of and pay the price for your devotion to Satan's dark arts."

"It is you that should be punished, not I!" Nancy cried, her wrist and shoulder howling from the pressure, he gripped her even tighter, tormenting her further for her blatant disrespect, his dirty nails digging into her flesh drawing blood which caused her to cry out in pain.

"We are the punishers of sin, witch, not you! Your kind are demons that live among us! Demons that will be vanquished by us, the whole and the true."

"You are the demon here, Bittern!" She seethed.
He glared at her.

"You have just burned an innocent man and a child!" She screamed and her words made several of The Finders look at each other, faces blemished with the guilt for being part of such an heinous act. Bittern showed no such blushes upon his grim face and continued to stare at her.

"How could you let a child burn to his death?" Nancy asked, tears cascading down her cheeks, she had stopped wriggling now as all her energy seemed to have gone, she had no fight left and the loss of her husband and child was too much to bear.

Bittern ignored his followers and their long guilt ridden faces and he smiled at her. It was a horrid smile, a smile that knew things, secrets that someone like Nancy could never know. He lowered her down and she grabbed a hold of the well's craggy lip and hung there, sighing with relief for her bruised joints and torn ligaments. She looked up at him with moist eyes of blue, her face covered with dirt, blood and tears.

"But Jonathan was a liar my dear. And lying is a sin is it not?"

"But..."

"And the spawn that would grow from the wicked womb of a witch and from the seed of liar, well, what kind of person would they grow to be?"

Nancy's eyes grew wide as she saw the Judge spin his hefty mallet in his chubby digits and knew what fate awaited her. She had seen that mallet fall on the skulls of fellow Hope Springs folk, Rebecca Wainwright, Janice Hodge and Emily O'Shea, all of them executed because they were believed to be witches.

"The verdict has been passed." Bittern growled and raise the mallet in the air.

"No!" Whispered Nancy.

"Guilty!" He held the mallet aloft before bringing its blunt head hurtling down on her fingers that gripped the lip of the well, her bones shattered under the impact and her fingernails dug into the rock and split free from their confines. Nancy screamed in agony and the sound carried down the well into the darkness as she hung, lifelessly by one hand.

"Guilty, guilty, guilty!" Bittern roared and with each word brought the mallet down upon her other hand.

That was all it would take and Nancy fell down into the darkness, her skull cracking on the inner wall several times as she twisted in the air. When she struck the unforgiving soil, her legs and arms were broken and contorted like the branches of a tree, she spluttered and coughed and internal blood spewed from her mouth, staining her chin.

"She is still alive, Judge!" Gasped one of The Finders.

"Of course she is still alive, she is a witch!" Bittern growled.

The man looked at him dumfounded, "What should we do?"

"We will make sure she never leaves here, let her rot in her damp grave at the bottom of a well." Bittern spat. "Now bring me some nails and boards."

Nancy tried to move but each movement caused her bones to crack. Her muscles spasmed out of control and her wounds seeped relentlessly. Her fingers were now misshapen and crooked like the legs of a crushed spider. And now the tears came, for she wept for her husband, wept for her babe and wept for herself.

The sound of hammering filled the well and carried around her as she lay in the pitch black cavern of nothingness, she looked up to the light at the top of the well, the torches illuminated the opening and made it look like a burning sun on a fine summer's day. But then the burning visage was eclipsed by long misshapen boards of wood as they were placed across the opening. Judge Bittern slammed the mallet down into long rusty nails to secure the boards in place. Soon there were enough boards across the top of the well to extinguish the light and even the sound of hammering and The Finder's voices had left and she found herself alone in the darkness with nothing but the cracking of her bones and the sound of dripping water for company.

She closed her eyes and controlled her breathing, shallow and long were her breaths and then there was another sound that greeted her ears and made her eyes flutter open. A shuffling sound as if several creatures were moving around her all at once, she felt something sharp probe her wounds and it made her grimace. She felt claws caress her flesh as these creatures climbed on top of her and probed her wounds vigorously, eating away at her flesh. Nancy managed to lift her head out of the soil and could just make out the shapes of a dozen birds skipping around on top of her broken body pecking at her flesh.

"Magpies!" She murmured and a strange smile caressed her lips, then it became a strange cackle of sorts that filled the damp cavern, causing the magpies to disperse, their tender ears irked by the pitch of the sound. She stopped laughing and all at once the magpies were back on her feeding at her exposed wounds once again.

She closed her eyes and once again began reciting the nursery rhyme.

"One for sorrow, two for mirth, three for a funeral, four for birth, five for heaven, six for hell, seven for the devil, his own self."

She repeated these words over and over quietly to herself, all while the magpies feasted on her flesh. Suddenly she stopped reciting the words and her eyes opened again to reveal vein infested whites as they slowly rolled back in her head. She convulsed, violently, pink froth of saliva and blood spewing from her mouth. Then came words from her lips that were ancient, words that were not spoken by any in these parts, the words of witchcraft.

The magpies fed eagerly and paid no attention to her convulsions or her strange words, for all words were strange to the ears of a magpie. Slowly her wounds began to swell and the loose flaps of skin draped itself over the feeding birds wrapping around them and tightening the way that a python might suffocate its prey. The magpies screeched in distress as they struggled in vain to escape. It was all to no avail and Nancy's flesh consumed the birds, flesh, bone and feather, they could be seen wriggling underneath a layer of skin like a sickening shadow puppet display. There was the sudden crunching of bones and her body started to contort again, taking on a very different shape. Her flesh became leathery in texture and her toes grew claws, splitting her feet violently in half. Her arms snapped back into place and her hands warped into fingerless stumps as the structure of her bones became wing like. She rose to her newly clawed feet and teetered from side to side like a newborn foal, then let out a shriek of pain as her spine snapped into a peculiar shape and she stood hunched over as black feathers started to sprout out of her flesh in random patches. Her arms that had now become wings covered with copious amounts of feathers that matched that of the magpies she had consumed. Beaks of magpies broke through her flesh and squawked loudly, only for her flesh to constrict around them again and pull them back inside her crooked and misshapen body. Her eyes were as white as marbles, shining in the darkness as her skull crumbled, the flesh of her face hung lifelessly, only for the skull fragments to reconvene and form a long beak that ran from the bridge of her nose and past her chin, a sight so grotesque it would be near impossible to put into words. But the most disturbing thing about her new appearance was her eyes that shone out from the deep sockets, human eyes set in this unholy beast of Satan.

She screeched and cawed, shaking her head from side to side as feathers continued to pierce her flesh, fluttering uncontrollably. The flimsy nightgown hung from her hunched and jagged physique, the cotton stained with blood and dirt and almost now shredded to pieces. A third claw burst out from her torso, sharp claws tearing away what was left of the nightgown and its fingers clicked its nails together as it formed between two lifeless sacks of flesh that were once full with milk and brought nourishment to a child, a child that's bones were now black and rested upon the charred carcass of his father.

She spread her wings wide and shrieked loudly, the sound was hideous and could be heard for miles, some say that it put a stop to The Witch Finders celebrations, in fact it put an end to The Finders altogether for no man dared step foot back in Parliament Grove for fear of what made that sound on that cold winter's evening. Whatever she had become it was obvious that she was no longer Nancy Cartwright.

PARLIAMENT GROVE 1987

The grove was covered with a plethora of fallen leaves, a riot of autumnal colours forming a carpet, just yearning to be crunched underfoot and Max Chambers did not disappoint. The boy jumped up and down in the leaves, his mittened hands scooping them up and launching them into the air, watching as they fell around him like gigantic colourful snowflakes. He smiled broadly, his chubby cheeks peppered with freckles and his mop of auburn hair made him fit in nicely with this time of year. He gazed at the leaves above, reds, oranges, yellows and amazingly some still green as if they were clinging on to the branches for dear life. The Grove was silent and Max watched as leaves finished their cycle of life and dislodged themselves from the branches, the same branches that had once helped nourish them and now discarded them, allowing to them to fall to the floor and decompose to feed the earth.

"Marco!" Came a voice through the trees.

"Shit." Max sighed, his moment to enjoy the silence and nature was over. He heard other children's voices call back with the preferred word of this children's game.

"Polo." He called.

"Ha!" He heard a girl's voice call. "I'm coming for you

Max, I can hear that you're close."

"Shit, Molly you barf bag!" Max grumbled and he took off at full speed through the Grove, kicking up the shallow pile of leaves as he went. He knew that she was close and he cursed himself for daydreaming, but he did so love the fall and he always found himself becoming enthralled by the delights that the season had to offer.

"Marco!" Molly called again.

"Polo!" He heard the voice of his best friend Denny holler back to her and he heard her laughter as she knew she was near. He heard other voices reply, but they were distant.

"C'mon Max!" Molly called, "Cheater, cheater compulsive eater!"

"Damn it!" Max cried and called back unwillingly, "Polo!"

"You're close dearest brother, I can smell your bubblegum!" Her voice was filled with the arrogance of an older sibling.

"Bite me!" He yelled and turned back on himself to try and put distance between them. He broke through into a clearing that was bathed in succulent October sunshine and again he was awed by the beauty of it all. The tree's branches were all free of leaves and he watched as two squirrels frolicked through them and then scampered up the trunk of a tree where they chased each other over the leafless branches and then out of sight. He smiled, he loved animals and one day hoped to work with them, be it as a vet or a zoo keeper.

A single magpie flew into the clearing and landed on a branch and stared at him.

"One for sorrow." Max said instinctively as if the phrase had been programmed into him and then gave it the quickest of salutes.

The bird seemed to glare at him with a look that did not appear friendly. It made Max shudder and he tried to shoo it away but it remained unaffected by the boy's jumping up and down and waving of his arms. Even some of his best ugly faces that he regularly pulled at his sister did nothing.

"Oh, bite the big one birdie!" He seethed and unleashed his middle finger that was still consumed by his mitten.

The magpie did nothing.

Max slipped off his mittens and they hung out of the sleeves of his jacket on orange string, before unleashing two middle finger salutes with a face full of grimacing teeth to go with the insult.

Still the magpie did not react.

"Marco!" Came the cry from his sister again, but this time her voice was fainter, he grinned smugly, he knew he had put distance between them.

"Polo!" He called.

"Polo!" called the others, that were so far way now that he hardly heard them.

"Polo!" He heard a voice call, the voice of his best friend Denny, his call was followed by a playful shriek that echoed through the Grove.

"She got you Denny!" Max grumbled, "But she's not getting me!" He snapped defiantly.

Max looked around and noticed a rocky structure sitting in the centre of the clearing, consumed by an old bramble. His scarf had fallen loose with all his running and he adjusted it, pulling it tighter under his chin before tucking it into his multicoloured gilet and securing the zip up as high as it would go before heading towards the bramble. He gazed at it wondering what treasures it concealed behind its thorns and berries. He grabbed at the ageing vines and yanked at them, a thorn piercing his thumb and drawing blood.

"Owie!" He hissed and looked at the droplet of blood that had emerged upon his throbbing digit. He should have maybe quit while he was ahead but he saw the stone structure of the well underneath its arable confines and curiosity got the better of him. He gripped the brambles again, making sure to grab them from a part of the vine where there were no thorns to pierce his skin and tugged. The bramble erupted from the soil with ease, its age telling and Max was able to haul it one side to unveil the well. The well itself was built up of rocks, almost as tall as he was. The dishevelled structure was crooked, obviously hand built and seemed to lean to one side slightly. The craggy rocks were caked in a layer of moss and roots burst out through the gaps, gasping for air, reaching to the light. Strangely the well was topped with several rotting boards, boards that had been nailed into place, as if to cover it up.

"Marco!" He heard Molly call but this time he ignored her, there were no other calls of Polo so he assumed that he was the only one left.

"Why would anyone board up a well?" He scoffed, his

face scrunched up with confusion.

"Marco!" He heard Molly shriek with impatience, but he was transfixed by the well.

"Max! Goddamn it! I said Marco!"

"Yeah, yeah...Polo!" He called unenthusiastically rubbing his hand across the boards, the weather had worn them severely and he managed to get a hand in-between two boards and with a good yank, he dislodged and removed one of them. He gazed into the darkness, the sun from above, sliced through the gap, unveiling the inner wall and a very inviting ledge, just wide enough for him to balance on and he would never get caught.

"Ha Ha!" Max laughed, "You won't get me this time Molly."

"Marco!" She called, her voice closer than it had ever been, she had made up the distance between them, so he needed to act quickly.

"POLO!" He called, and the well scooped up his words and abducted them pulling them down its shaft and into the darkness below. His words returned and echoed around the clearing, the sound was amplified and Max winced for he did not know whether that would help Molly or hamper her. Max pulled off another board and another and then climbed inside, hanging down until his sneakers squeaked on the ledge. He positioned himself on the damp ledge and clung on the inner wall as low as he could, to be shrouded by the shadows.

"Marco!" Came the cry again and this time she was very close.

"Shit it!" He whispered, he knew that he had to reply, but he was wary about the echo giving his position away.

"Marco, you douche bag, Marco!" Molly bellowed.

"POLO!"

Again the words echoed around the well and escaped into the clearing. He heard a screeching sound from below and he looked down into the darkness, but he saw nothing.

"Probably just rats." He told himself.

"Marco!" Came the call and she was oh so close now, she must have entered the clearing. He pulled himself up and peeped out over the lip of the well and saw Molly and Denny stepping through the foliage and into the clearing, their eyes were full of wonderment, seemingly amazed that they had never discovered this place before.

"Marco, Marco, Marco, Max, c'mon you big cheat." Molly called.

"We know you're around here somewhere Max." Denny added playfully.

"Judas!" Max growled, "I thought you were my friend Denny, but you've gone over to join the dark side!"

The sound of screeching came again from below and again he looked down into the long dark shaft, the sound seemed to be closer than before.

"Stupid Max, rats can't climb up walls... can they?"

Something chattered and scraped against the inner wall and Max suddenly felt very uncomfortable, he felt like he was being watched, but looking down he saw nothing.

"Max c'mon, you know the rules, you have to say it."

Denny tapped Molly her on the shoulder and smiled, pointing towards the well. She smiled back mischievously.

"I'll give you one last chance or I'm leaving and I'll go home and pull the head off your He-Man doll!" Molly hissed. Denny gasped as if she had just said something blasphemous. Those words refocused Max and took his mind of whatever creature was lurking at the bottom of the well.

"Bitch!" He growled under his breath, he knew that she knew where he was now, but he was so very stubborn that he still wanted to go down fighting.

"Here it comes numb nuts. M....ARCO!" She called, drawing out the word for comic effect.

"POLO!" He replied, again the sound travelled and Molly jumped up and down on the spot knowing now that she had him. She placed her finger on her lips and Denny nodded in agreement and the pair crept towards the well.

Max's calls had stirred whatever moved around in the darkness, annoying it with his high pitch cries, and this time the chattering and squealing was ever so close. He stared into the darkness and he saw two eyes shining in the sunlight.

"Holy shit!" He whispered frozen to the ledge with fear as a beak sliced through the shroud of shadows, he immediately lost control of his bladder and a dark wet stain appeared on the crotch of his beige corduroys.

"Marco!" Molly laughed, but Max did not reply as a claw burst through the darkness beneath and grabbed his foot, he gurgled a cry that seemed to lodge in his throat and make no sound

"Marco!" Molly sighed, only yards away from the well now, shaking her head. "You might as well say it Max, we know your in there."

"P-P-PO..." Max stuttered and then screamed a bloodcurdling scream as he lunged towards the top of the well, clambering to pull himself up and out of it's damp confines.
Denny and Molly stopped dead in their tracks and looked at each other and then at the well as Max appeared, his face pale with horror as he reached to his sister and his friend to help him.

"Mag...magp..." Max whined before his eyes grew wide and he was pulled back down the well, "...paaaaa!"
There was silence in the clearing and Molly and Denny crept towards the well and looked down into it, both of them hoping that Max was just fooling around and would jump out and scare them when they got close enough. But that did not happen, there was nothing but darkness and a pair of woollen mittens on an orange string hanging from a protruding root.

"M-Max?" Molly whimpered, her voice carrying down the well and immediately they heard a flurry of wings, it sounded like a hundred pairs of wings and deafening shrieks to accompany them. The pair fell backwards onto the floor of the clearing as hundreds of magpies erupted out of the well and into the air swirling around in a black cloud of feathers.

"RUN!" Screamed Denny and he grabbed Molly's arm and yanked her from the floor and the pair ran away through the Grove. The magpies circled the sky shrieking in victory and then slowly took their places on the branches of the trees, their beady black eyes watching over the well intently.

BLACKFOOT RIDGE, PRESENT DAY.

There wasn't much left of the institute in Blackfoot Ridge. There was only a weary shell of bricks and mortar, that had been heavily damaged by fire to indicate that anything ever stood upon the hill. The downpour had finally ceased and a man draped in a grey raincoat that was slick with rain, kicked his way through the rubble. His green eyes focused on what lay at his feet as he intensely scoured the debris, searching for something.

"There has to be something here."

Jimmy Johnson, Jr. had combed the grounds extensively searching for, well he did not know exactly what he was in search of.

"Anything!" He groaned, "Anything at all!"

He stooped down in the rubble and fished out a bronze plaque that read, THE M.O.N.S.T.E.R HOME and etched below it were the words, The Mental Observation of Non-human, Supernatural and the Tormented, Ethics and Research.

"What a fucking mouthful!" Scoffed Jimmy and turned the plaque over in his hands, before discarding it back into a bed of bricks and ash. He looked up to the sky and already more rain clouds were drifting across the dreary looking sky, seeming to be adamant that they would be settling above him.

"Fucking rain." He grumbled as he pushed his slick, dark hair back into place. "Seems to have been following me ever since I left Studd City."

He stood up and scowled at the clouds.

"Well, it will take more than a bit of rain to stop me in my search for what happened to you Pops. I'll find out what happened, you see if I don't." Jimmy became a little choked up and turned away from what was once an institute filled with the most unlikeliest of patients.

He wore smart tapered pants and his shoes were Italian and expensive, but now both had been ruined by mud. He didn't seem to care about his weathered damaged clothes, there wasn't much that he did care about these days apart from finding out what actually happened to his father.

His father and his partner had gone missing a few years ago, last seen at this very spot, investigating the murder of one of the institute's patients. The case had been closed by the local authorities and Jimmy's father was filed as deceased. It said in the report that his father and partner had both died in the blaze, but the bodies of either man were never retrieved.

Apparently the charred remains of 256 bodies, which included staff and patients were found, but there was no answer to who or what started the fire. Amongst the bodies identified was the head of the institute, Professor Evelyn Black, Jimmy managed to sneak a peek at the forensics file when he still worked for the VPD and it had said that her cause of death was a slit throat, which was later altered.

"It all smells too fishy if you ask me."

He walked across the gravelled driveway, moist stones crunching under his heavy steps, they were the heavy steps of someone who carried the weight of the world upon their shoulders. He leapt across a small stream that surrounded the hill, the remains of a broken bridge lay within it, but the stream did not care acting as though the bridge's remains didn't even exist, moving effortlessly around the shards of broken wood. His car was parked on the road, it was a worn Volkswagen Beetle in the tones of tired yellow and rust. He took the keys out of his pocket and swung them around his index finger, his eyes staring into space again as the cogs begin to turn in his head.

"I'll walk the road." He said to himself. "Yeah, walk the road to where Pop's car was found."

He stuffed the keys back into the deep pocket of his raincoat and started to walk down the middle of the road. He didn't have to worry about traffic, who would be out here anyway? He stopped on the spot and swivelled on his heels to look back at the remains of the institute and then at the road that ran past it to the West.

"The report said that fire services from Blackfoot and Maple Falls came via that road." He pondered for a while, clicking his tongue in that annoying way that he always did when he was thinking.

"They would never have seen the car, there wouldn't have had any need to come out this far."

He continued to walk along the road and then the heavens

opened once again. Jimmy was not even phased by it, he simply pulled up his collar and stuffed his hands into his pockets and carried on about his business.

He walked the long road as he tried to find a reason for such inaccuracies within the reports.

He seemed to walk for an hour in the rain uncaring of its relentless cold shards that pricked at his exposed flesh. Finally he reached a yellow cross that had been painted on the asphalt near the side of the road, indicating where the car had been discovered.

"So why did the file say the empty car was found by a Maple Falls firefighter? Out on the road, well away from the institute? And if Pops and his partner had died in the fire like the reports say, then how did their car get way out here?"

He stood on the yellow cross, trying to feel what happened, it was a technique that his father had instilled in him, to always go with his gut instincts.

He stood and pondered, all the while the rain attacked him from above in relentless sheets.

"'Junior, if it smells like shit, then it probably is!'" Jimmy smiled showing a handsome set of white pearls through a few days stubble. "Yep that was one of Pops favourite sayings. And he was right. This most definitely smells like shit to me. Smells like a goddamn cover up."

He looked at the gigantic redwoods that sandwiched the slender road, if only they had the ability to speak, what tales they would have to tell.

"The report said that the passenger's door was open

but that the vehicle was empty." He pondered for a moment, clicking his tongue again loudly. "That would mean that either someone opened it to get at them or whoever was in the passenger seat opened it in a hurry to give chase."

His eyes glanced over at the trees that would have been the passengers side and trudged onto the sodden grass that surrounded the trees, a welcome mat to the wilderness.

After all this time he would be a fool to think that there would be any evidence, like footprints or...

"Broken branches." He grumbled to himself, there were several branches of trees that had been snapped clean through.

"Something passed through here alright. Something big!"

He reached up to the broken branches that could not have been made by a human, they were too high and too wide.

"Maybe a moose or a grizzly?" He murmured, his tongue clicking rapidly as he thought.

But the shape of the broken branches was strange.

"A bear would have broken through the foliage much lower, on all fours...and even at full force would a moose cause such random damage?"

He pondered for a moment, surveying every inch in front of him.

"Very strange, it looks like someone drove a bulldozer through here."

Bravely he stepped into the gloom, the gargantuan trees acting as cover from the rain, although it was muted he could still hear it falling rapidly. He looked around at the wall of trunks that were spread out in front of him. He rustled around in the inside of his raincoat and found a damp box of Freebirds and popped out the last remaining cigarette.

"Now, I am not an idiot, even though it might look like it as I stand here talking to myself, another trait I can blame on Pops, 'Always talk it out, your ears won't lie like your mind will'."

That made him smile, whenever he used his father's sayings it always gave him a warm feeling inside.

I know that the probability of my Pops still being alive is incredibly slim. I have actually come to terms with this, I know deep down that he has gone. But what happened to him, now that is a different story, that is what I want to find out.

He dropped the empty packet into his pocket and probed all the possible places his lighter could be, finally he discovered it in his pants pocket. The lighter was pewter and engraved with the words *with love from Pops*, it was the only thing he had left to remember his father by and he cherished it. He flicked it into action and the flame danced for him like a greedy lap dancer. He lit the tip and then extinguished the flame before dropping the lighter and empty packet of Freebirds into one of his deep raincoat pockets.

"Probably against forestry regulations to have a lit cigarette in a wooden area, but screw it. I need this." He inhaled deeply and watched as the tip turned to ash. He exhaled, unleashing a thick plume that was immediately eaten up by the moisture in the air.

He walked on into the woods glancing at the trees for signs of anything that didn't quite belong, after a few moments suddenly there it was. The trunk of a large redwood winked at him, something metallic lodge in the bark twinkled in the gloom.

"Bingo was his name." He said and quickly made for the tree. He rubbed his finger over the remnants of a bullet that had been buried into the wood, the bark splintered around it from the impact and Jimmy looked at it with confusion furrowing his brow.

"Peculiar slug. Not police issue..." he clicked his tongue again and from the deep damp pocket of his raincoat he retrieved a Swiss army knife. He unclipped the small blade and used it to gouge the bullet fragment from the tree. He slid the Swiss army knife back in his pocket and held the nugget of metal in his hand.

"Silver?" He said and before he could ponder what bullets made of silver could mean his cellphone chimed annoyingly, with the high pitch din of a bad version of Stan Bush's 'Dare'.

"Yep!" He said casually as he answered the phone, he listened to the person on the other end for a time, cigarette hanging from the corner of his mouth as he examined the silver slug gripped between his thumb and index finger.

Well, whoever fired this slug missed.

"Yeah, I'm listening. Okay it sounds like something I can do. Yeah, I understand that others may say that but not me. I'll be there by this time tomorrow. Okay, bye."

He hung up the cellphone and let it fall into his pocket of

mysteries and exhaled again.

"I guess I'll have to put this investigation on hold Pops, duty calls."

He flicked the silver nugget in the air, caught it and placed it in the inside pocket of his raincoat, which was what he affectionately referred to as his evidence bag.

"Next stop, Hope Springs."

IV

The black Pontiac Grand Ville drove smoothly through Portland and into Hope Springs.

"They could have gotten us a better car than this hunk of junk." Groaned Agent Wren, her Liverpudlian drawl made the sentence sound aggressive.

"Standard issue when we're in the states." Said Valerie Kite who shrugged her shoulders and continued to drive.

Wren sighed like a petulant child and started meddling with the sun visor, flipping it up and down rapidly causing the light above the little mirror to burst into life in annoying flashes.

"Stop that!" Kite said sternly, her eyes not leaving the road.

Wren mimicked her superior, her face contorting comically as she did so.

"I saw that." Kite said, again her eyes remained on the road as she sat up straight and proper, her dark hair tied back in a smart bun and a black suit with the small badge pin on her lapel etched with the silhouette of a gliding bird of prey, a kite.

Wren slouched into the passenger seat and started to open and close the glove box.

"Stop it!" Kite intervened once again.

Once more the disinterested Wren sighed, arms folded across

her bosom, creasing her white blouse. She wore black pants, her jacket had been thrown onto the backseat where it sat in a creased ball.

"So how long before we get there?" Wren asked.

"Not long."

"Jeez, your a bundle of laughs aren't you?" Wren scoffed, running her fingers through her auburn hair that was styled in a sharp bob, scooping its length behind her ears.

"I have been known to let my hair down occasionally." Kite smirked, full pink lips standing out against her dark skin.

"Really?" Wren said in surprise, she adjusted herself in her seat ready to hear all the sordid details.

"Oh yeah, I'm known for being a bit of a wild child in my hometown."

"Alright! I knew you would be wild, it's always the quiet ones." Wren smiled with excitement. "What sort of things do you get up to?"

"Well..." Kite giggled coyly, "...I have been known to take part in the odd karaoke session."

"Karaoke?" Wren looked at her blankly, "Seriously?"

"Oh yeah, you should see me bang out some Diana Ross." Kite laughed.

"Wow, you're so wild." Wren mocked settling back into her seat and immediately began to breathe on the window, fogging up the glass and then taking her finger to draw what appeared to be the start of a penis.

"Will you just quit it!" Kite cried, finally losing her cool, so much so that they swerved into the other lane and almost hit an oncoming car, its horn lambasting them for their recklessness. Kite growled in her throat in frustration and she turned into the nearest lay-by and stopped the car, gripping the wheel and cursing under her breath.

"Shit, Valerie! What the hell has gotten into you?" Wren asked.

"What's gotten into me? Into me!" She growled.

Wren just stared at her, Kite's eyes were wild and burning back at her.

"Firstly you will not refer to me by my first name. Ever! You are Wren and I am Kite! Got it?"

Wren nodded slowly as she blushed with embarrassment.

"And please cut this shit out!"

"What shit?"

"Your childish behaviour! It's like I'm babysitting and not getting paid!"

"I just get bored."

"Well, you need to learn another way. Because this shit that you are doing is not working for me."

Kite sighed and rested her forehead on the wheel and slowly but surely she mellowed.

"Look, I get that we have to take you agents out with us and give you some experience in the great wide world, but this shit we do is the real deal and we can't afford to get loose, you understand?"

Wren nodded.

"If you want to keep your mind occupied, read through the case file again. Hell, they picked you to be an agent for some reason, so let's see what it is."

Wren smiled and nodded, she reached around to the backseat and retrieved her black leather satchel that contained the case file.

"Okay, good." Kite said, more to herself than to Agent Wren and with that she eased the car back onto the road and they were off on their way again.

Wren unlatched the satchel and slipped the case file from inside, it was wrapped in a manila folder that she placed on her lap. As she opened it up she was immediately greeted by the glowing face of a pretty girl in her early teens smiling back at her. Wren sighed with sadness as she took in the long blonde hair that had been tied up sweetly in two pigtails, her smile twinkling metallically by the two rows of braces that framed her misshapen pearls.

"Pretty girl." Kite said glancing over at the photo.

"Yeah." Sighed Wren, it only took one look at the photograph of this missing girl to straighten up her behaviour.

"We got a name?" Kite asked.

"Abigail Jones, known to all as Abi, thirteen years old, blonde hair, blue eyes, 126 pounds, 4 feet 11 inches..." Wren searched the file for more personal information on the child. "That's about it."

"It's enough to go on."

Wren nodded in agreement.

"Where was she last seen?"

"She has been missing for three weeks, went missing in Parliament Grove? What's a Parliament Grove?" Wren asked.

"I presume it's a forest of some kind." Kite shrugged.

"Says here that she was last seen by her best friend a… Lucy Knight."

"Okay were nearly where we need to be." Kite said as she passed the entrance to the town of Hope Springs.

"Erm, I think you missed the turning?"

"I like to do things a little differently, Wren." Kite smiled.

"Oh?"

"I like to investigate the area that the person went missing first before I go and chat to the parents or guardians. Just helps me get in the zone a bit bitter, you know?"

"Okay, sounds like a plan." Wren smiled.

They drove past an old wooden sign that had the words 'Parliament Grove' etched on it, the sign was severely weathered and almost stripped of the blue-green paint that once illuminated the Grove's existence.

They pulled off the road and Kite killed the engine.

"Grab your jacket then rookie and we'll go and have a look."

Kite burst out of the car with childish enthusiasm and Wren frantically struggled to slide the case file back into the satchel and then retrieve her heavily creased jacket. She slipped it on, her own lapel pin flickering gold, showing the shape of a tiny bird, a wren. The pair of them now wore matching attire looking the same, but so very different. The only item to differentiate the two outfits was the golden buckle that Kite wore on her belt, like the shield of a police detective. This shield glimmered in the light, the symbol of a hand clutching a wooden stake was visible, the seal of the Secret Hunters Horde. This was something that Agent Wren had yet to earn.

Wren straightened her jacket and tried to wipe the creases out of it as Kite watched on in amazement.

"What?" Wren said looking up at her.

"It's not going to make it look any better." Kite turned away and walked down the dirt track into the grove, "It still looks like shit."

"Oh thanks!" Wren mimicked her while her back was turned.

Both agent and hunter wore a handgun on their hips, Wren held her hand on its butt, where as Kite strolled with her hands nestled in the small of her back, relaxed and taking in the scenery.

"There's a lot of birds around here." Wren said, eyes wandering.

"Duh!" Kite scoffed rolling her eyes.

"No, look! There's a shitload of magpies in those trees."

"So there is." Kite agreed looking up at them as they walked, their beady eyes watching their every movement.

"A parliament!" Kite announced.

"Sorry?"

"A parliament of magpies! I guess that's why they call this place Parliament Grove."

"One for sorrow, two for joy..." Wren started but was interrupted by Kite.

"Say what now? Two for joy? What's that shit?"

"That's what we say in the UK. One for sorrow, Two for joy, Three for a girl, Four for a boy, Five for silver, Six for gold, Seven for a secret never to be told…"

"No shit?"

"No shit!"

"Well, you Brits got some crazy ideas, but that's a new one on me."

Kite then took it upon herself to recite the version that she had grown up with.

They came to a halt at a large trunked tree that was covered in missing children posters, the various colours of paper fluttering gently like the feathers of a tropical parrot.

"Would you look at that!" Kite said shaking her head, the fliers seemed to reach up around seven or eight feet of the trunk, some of them half destroyed by time and weather, but still defiant, refusing to leave the bark from the drawing pins and tacks that held them there.

"That's a hell of a lot of missing kids!" Said Wren.

"Yeah, some crazy dates on there too." Kite agreed, running her fingers over dates going back to the eighties.

They walked passed an old cottage, that was surrounded by cats, some of them walked across the broken tiles on the roof while the majority just relaxed in random places, one of them even hung out of the post box that was askew, adjacent to a broken wooden gate.

The post box read, KRATZ.

The ugly net curtain that hung in the window twitched at their arrival.

"Kite, level with me?"

"Sure."

They stopped and they continued to survey the area.

"We're not just here to investigate a missing child are we?"

"No, no we're not." Kite turned away from Wren and looked back up at the magpies that glared at her. "Those bastards just don't care do they." She shook her head and then shouted to them, "Hey, motherfuckers! It's rude to stare."

"So what are we actually looking for? SHH would not send us out here without information on this thing, whatever it is."

"No, they wouldn't." Kite agreed and carried on walking through the grove, Wren had to quicken her pace to keep up with her.

"So what is it we are dealing with here?"

"I'll fill you in, but I wouldn't get too excited about this one."

"Why?"

"I don't believe this one is for real."

"Oh!" Wren's face fell a little and her shoulders loosened.

"Sorry, to disappoint, but I'm scratching this one off as an urban legend. It's more than likely that the person responsible is that fat old broad gawping at us through her nets back there."

Wren looked over her shoulder just in time to see a rotund black woman sweep back behind the net.

"Think it could be her?" Wren pointed a thumb over her shoulder.

"Possibly!" Kite nodded, "Crazy old woman, kidnaps kids and then blames some supernatural Bird-Witch for it. Classic stuff."

"A bird witch?"

"Pretty much."

Kite walked off towards the dirt track that led deep into The Grove.

"A little bit of a coincidence that all those missing posters are stapled to a tree a hundred yards away from the Kratz residence."

"Should we not go and question her?"

"Let her stew." Kite said, "We'll get her on the way back."

They both walked off into The Grove and the door of the Kratz residence screeched open, an old croaky voice called for her cats. Ten cats stretched their limbs before tottering into the house. One cat remained half asleep hanging from the post box, a chubby ginger tabby that seemed to ignore her calls.

"Noris!" She cracked, "Now you get your fat ass in here now!"

Noris slunk out of the mailbox and slowly sauntered past her thick, hairy legs that were riddled with wormlike varicose veins.

"Shit's about to hit the fan, yes it is." She murmured to herself, "I'm not losing no more damn cats!" The door closed behind her and several bolts and chains were worked into place. She stood at the window, dirty nets quivering in her chubby digits as she waited.

There was the sudden sound of gunshots and then the magpies left their perches and swooped into the grey sky spiralling altogether before disappearing behind the cover of the trees. There was a loud shriek of victory and then silence.

Mrs Kratz sighed heavily and repositioned the curtain to hide all the horrors of the outside world.

Jimmy Johnson's dilapidated Volkswagen coughed and spluttered its way along the road into Hope Springs. Just as Jimmy had perceived, the rain clouds had continued to follow him. A black cloud hung over head as if it had a personal vendetta against him. The rain peppered his windscreen relentlessly, as the only active windshield wiper worked overtime to beat away the aggressive storm and clear a way for Jimmy to see the road.

"Come on Olive, old girl, hold it together."
The vehicle, which had lovingly been christened with the name Olive, a gone but not forgotten family member, responded by backfiring loudly, emitting a gust of thick black smoke from its exhaust pipe.

"Fucking rain, can't see a Goddamn thing." He growled, his eyes squinting to see the road in front of him through the veil of rain.

"Oh, shit!" He sighed as he whizzed past the turning to the town of Hope Springs, "Perhaps I can turn around up here somewhere."
The storm finally lifted and only a sheet of fine rain continued to fall, but at least it had lifted enough for Jimmy to see where he was actually going. The car had to climb a steep hill and it did not appreciate being pushed so hard by the driver.

"Come one, come on, Olive." Jimmy groaned through gritted teeth as he willed the car onward. It made it up the steep hill, but then the motor stalled and Jimmy was stranded on top of the hill, in the middle of the road.

"Great!" He howled, slapping the steering wheel viciously, "Just great! Thank you Olive!"

He tried the ignition, nothing, and again, nothing. He tried several more times, each time the key was turned with slightly more aggression.

"I hate my life." He cried and head butted the steering wheel which set off the horn, "At least the horn works."

He punched at the horn several times before sinking his head onto the wheel again, pretending to sob.

There was a tapping at the window and Jimmy was jolted from his juvenile outburst, he looked up to see a stern looking Chief of police scowling back at him through a curtain of rain.

"Everything okay in there?" The Chief asked, a thick moustache quivering which each word.

Jimmy wound down the window and even that would only go halfway before it jammed tight.

"Yeah, sorry, she won't start." Jimmy said and watched as the Chief stared at him suspiciously, rain dripping from his moustache and the lip of his blue-green campaign hat.

"You're holding up the traffic, Son." He said and Jimmy gazed into his rearview mirror and saw several cars piled up behind him.

"I'm really sorry, but she just won't go."

"Would you mind stepping out of the vehicle, Son?"

The Chief said stepping back from the door and adjusting his waterproof poncho. Jimmy thought he was reaching for his handcuffs.

"But I..."

"C'mon now, Son make it quick."

"Oh shit, I'm gonna get arrested and I haven't even made it into town yet." He said to himself as he stepped out into the drizzle, unable to throw on his raincoat, immediately his creased shirt became wet through from the unrelenting rain.

"Are you ready?" The Chief asked.

"What charges are you taking me in on Chief?" Jimmy asked, holding his wrists out to be cuffed.

"Goddamn it Son, I'm not going to arrest you!" He chuckled, his wet moustache quivered on his large face.

"You're not?"

"Of course not!"

"Then what are we doing?"

"We're going push this piece of shit off the road."

Jimmy smiled at him, he'd only just met this guy and already he liked him.

"You steer and I'll push." The Chief said and he was right to do the pushing too, he was a middle-aged man but had a broad chest and back and he towered over Jimmy, whose growth seemed to have stunted early and he'd been 5 feet 8 inches since college.

They managed to move the decrypted contraption off the road, pushing it up behind a black Pontiac Grand Ville that seemed to have been abandoned at the side of the road. In front of the stranded car was the Chief's 1994 Jeep Cherokee, painted in beige and blue-green. Hope Springs Police plastered on the side with its badge visible, a redwood tree with a magpie perched on top. The red and blue lights flashed wildly to show passing cars that he was there and to proceed with caution along the road. Jimmy grabbed his raincoat and slipped it on over his drenched shirt as the Chief signalled for the cars to pass, which they did, each one sounding their horns at The Chief who in turn waved or tipped his blue-green campaign hat to the ladies. Jimmy assumed that they were all locals that passed by so pleasantly.

"So what brings you to Hope Springs, Mister..." The Chief trailed off to let Jimmy introduce himself.

"Jimmy Johnson, Jr., pleased to meet you." He held his hand out and the Chief took it in his rough mitt, but gave it the gentlest of shakes.

"Damn Son, that's a mouthful." He chuckled.

"Yeah, I guess it is." Jimmy scoffed.

"The name's George Gable, but most people round these parts know me as 'Chief'!"

They shared an awkward moment neither knowing what to say next.

"At least the rain is stopping." Jimmy scoffed.

"Means I can take this stupid thing off." Chief Gable said as he removed his hat so that he can peel off the police issue poncho. He revealed a blue-green jacket that concealed a beige shirt and blue-green pants, striped on either leg with a slender beige stripe.

Jimmy couldn't miss the exceedingly large magnum that was stationed at his hip, a weapon that did not look police issue.

"You got a license for that cannon, Chief?" Jimmy laughed.

"Ha!" Chief Gable chuckled, patting the large firearm on its butt gently, "That's old Betsy. I'd rather have her at my side than the peashooters they carrying around with them these days. But yep, I have a license for it. You wanna see the paperwork city boy?"

"I belive ya." Jimmy laughed.

"So what brings you here, Jimmy?"

"I'm a private detective here to meet with a Ms. Rachel Jones about the disappearance of her daughter Abigail."

The Chief looked at him, with a look that gave nothing away.

"Is that a fact?" He finally answered.

"Yes, Sir!"

"The girl's been missing for over three weeks now!"

"Yeah, I was aware of that."

Chief Gable turned away and walked towards the Pontiac, Jimmy sensed that the atmosphere had taken a turn and that maybe The Chief was not happy with an outsider investigating this particular case.

"I understand you might feel as though I'm treading on your toes here. But nothing could be further from the truth, I would like to work with you on this case."

"You're not the only one." Gable scoffed.

"Sorry?"

"What do you make of this?" Gable said and he opened

the passenger door to the Pontiac and pointed to the satchel that sat on the seat.

"Take a look-see." The Chief sniffed with authority and placed his hands on his hips, waiting for Jimmy to discover what he had found a few minutes ago. Jimmy slid the case file out from the confines of the satchel and gazed upon the photograph.

"Is that the missing girl?"

"Yep." The Chief nodded, "That's Abigail Jones."

"But, who..." Jimmy started and then trailed off as he tried to configure his thoughts, tongue clicking again annoyingly "...what is this?"

"Exactly!" The Chief said, "A local informed me that this car has been stranded here all day, so I thought I'd mosey on out here and see what it was all about."

"Do you know whether Ms. Jones has been in touch with another investigative bureau?"

"Damned if I know." The Chief shrugged, "I guess that's something you'll have to ask her yourself."

Jimmy flicked through the file and made a mental note of all the information on the child, when it came to faces his mind was like a bear trap, photographic memory his father used to call it. So just one glance was all it took for the image to become embedded in his brain.

"I'll have to have that file, Jimmy." Chief Gable said with authority.

"Of course." Jimmy handed it back to The Chief and both of them appeared to be puzzled by the situation.

"The local also informed me that two ladies came by her way, said they looked important, both packing sidearms. Could well be the FEDS, but seems like an awful lot of trouble to take over a missing kid."

"Where were they last seen?"

"Out by Parliament Grove where the girl went missing, where they've all gone missing."

"All?"

"This is not the first missing child that we have had around here I'm afraid to say, happens too damn frequently for my liking."

"And you have no leads?"

"I've got leads alright! Most of them accusations or supernatural mumbo jumbo!"

"Supernatural?"

"Pah!" Gable waved the comment away, "Urban legends. This part of America is full of shit like that. Pay it no mind."

"So who is this local that seems to have seen everything?"

"She goes by the name 'Krazy' Kratz around here."

"Sounds like a reliable source."

"Oh, she's as nutty as a fruitcake, but nothing happens around The Grove without her seeing it."

"I shall have to pay her a visit." Jimmy said, clicking his tongue as he pondered this case that had suddenly become a lot more complex than he thought it would be.

"I'm going over to question her now if you want to tag

along?"

"I'll take a rain check." Jimmy said and just then the heavens opened again and down came the rain.

"You had to open your big mouth." Scoffed The Chief, "Get in the jeep and I'll take you to a little bed and breakfast that I know in town."

"What about 'Krazy' Kratz?"

"She'll keep. Grab your gear and hop in."

Jimmy retrieved his small travel bag from the backseat, he always traveled light. He jumped in next to Chief Gable who started up the engine and turned the jeep around, heading back towards the turning that Jimmy had missed earlier.

"Is she going to be okay there?" Jimmy asked as he watched his little beetle, Olive fade away in the rearview mirror.

"Don't worry I'll have Charlie the local mechanic take a look at her for ya."

"Sounds expensive." Jimmy scoffed.

The Chief laughed loudly.

"Now you're catching on."

A man stood in the rain and stared up at the window of Bertha's bed and breakfast. He watched quietly as Jimmy Johnson unpacked his small bag, retrieving his toiletries and stowing them safely in the small en-suite that led off the modest room. A bed, a chair and a bedside table was all that there was to offer, but Jimmy didn't mind as long as there was a bed, that is all he needed anyway.

He happened to gaze out of the window and noticed the gaunt man standing in the middle of the road, completely soaked through, staring up at him.

"What's this guy's problem?" Jimmy asked himself.

He thought that if he had been caught glaring at someone, he might have carried on about his business or in the very least turned away. But this guy seemed to have other ideas, he looked serious and if he had to stand there all night to make his point then it appeared that he would.

There was a knock on the door, opening immediately and completely defeating the object of knocking in the first place. In waddled the rotund frame of Bertha Colley, her chubby cheeks blemished with two red spots and her breathing was heavy, just walking up two flights of stairs had taken its toll on her.

"Oh my!" She gasped, sweat trickling down her face, two plush towels gripped tightly to her huge bosom, "What must you think of me Mr. Johnson."

"Please call me Jimmy." He said offering her the chair to rest herself for a moment.

"Oh no, I mustn't or I will not want to get back up."

"This is a big place for you to run yourself. Have you ever thought of downsizing."

"Oh no, I could never do that!" She shook her head from side to side vigorously, her tight permed hair wriggled on her head comically.

"Just seems like a lot for you to manage on your own, Ms. Colley."

"I guess you're right, but I love this place and I could never part with it now. It used to be a farmhouse you know."

"Oh really, I guess I can see that now you mention it." Jimmy had been drawn to the window again where the man still stood glaring up at him.

"Almost burnt down in the seventies, it did."

"Oh really?" Jimmy absently replied, still focussing on this strange individual outside.

"Killed their Mother and Father it has been said. Yep, killed them and then burnt the place down."

"Sorry? Who killed who?"

"The sons of the farmer and his wife that used to live here. Killed them the sons did and then torched the place."

"That's cheery!" Jimmy scoffed sarcastically.

"Oh, I'm probably scaring you poor lad." She smiled and handed him the towels, "My daddy got the place for a steal and fixed it up good and proper and it's been my only source of income ever since. Mind you, not much business doing these days, not many people passing through you see."

"Ms. Colley can I ask you a question?"

"Of course my dear."

"Who the hell is that?" He pointed out of the window directly at the strange man that stood in the rain watching him.

"Oh, that's just Denny you don't need to worry about him." She waddled over to the window and opened it wide and then squeezed her massive bosom through the gap and called to him.

"Away with you now, Denny! Go on now!"

Denny looked up at her and then at Jimmy one final time before walking away.

"Who is he?"

"Some say he's a drug addict, others say he's the one responsible for taking all the children away."

"Oh really?" Jimmy replied and then the clicking of the tongue started again as he added another name to his list that he would have see about for this peculiar case of the missing Abigail Jones.

"He's harmless though if you ask me." She said closing the window, "If he comes back, just close the curtains. That'll dampen his harder."

"Lovely!" Jimmy grimaced.

"It's getting dark now, you get yourself settled and I'll bring you up some hot cocoa and some freshly baked cookies."

Jimmy lay down on the bed, and grasped his hands together behind his head.

"I could get used to this." Jimmy smiled, but in the back of his mind the cogs were feverishly turning, names swirling of all the people he had to speak with, swirling before his mind's eye. More players were entering the game and Jimmy Johnson, Jr., had to find out just who was responsible.

VII

Ms. Jones placed the mug of black coffee into the cold hands of Jimmy Johnson, Jr., it was a pleasant sensation and it made him shiver with comfort.

"Thank you Ms. Jones."

"Please call me Rachel." She sniffed as she sat down adjacent to him.

"Of course, Rachel."

He took a sip of his coffee and then placed it on the low table by his knees. He had noticed that she had placed her cup of Earl Grey tea on there too, but he wondered if she actually intended to drink it for her mind seemed miles away. Her eyes were puffy from many tears that have been shed over the past few weeks and a piece of Jimmy's heart broke at the mere thought of what she was going through.

He gazed around the lounge of her colonial home, dozens of family photographs stared back him, most of them of her and her daughter Abigail, precious moments capturing all the usual occasions, Christmas, Easter, Fourth of July and many, many birthdays showing an evolutionary scale of Abigail's growth before his eyes.

He wondered whether they would share anymore photographs together again.

"Is it okay if I take some notes?" Jimmy asked,

reaching into the inside of his raincoat for his notepad and pen.

"Yes, of course." She sniffed and pulled her legs up onto the armchair, gripping a soft toy tightly to her chest, it was a large floppy sheepdog, it was frayed in places and had lost some of its stuffing over time from the love it had received.

"Is that one of Abi's toys?"

"Yes." She nodded and looked at it, a smile breaking the glum features that she had on display, "This is Angus." She lifted it up to her face and inhaled, "It smells of her." A tear rolled down her cheek and became lost in Angus' thick black fur.

"Does Abi like animals?"

"Oh yes, she loves animals." Rachel smiled again, a memory of a time spent at a petting zoo in Pepperville the first memory to greet her, "She's always been very kind to animals."

"That's nice!" Jimmy grinned and he could see that she was becoming a little more open, which would make the line of questioning go easier.

"What kind of things is Abi into?"

"Things?"

"Oh, you know, music, tv, hobbies, that kind of thing."

"Oh, she likes reading, she a bit of a bookworm, devours books she does."

"That's good, it's important for youngsters to read." Rachel nodded.

"She also likes art, always sketching and drawing she is."

"Oh really? Do you have any pieces to hand? I would

love to take a look at some of her work."

"Sure!" Rachel said and rose from her seat still clutching Angus tightly, she left the lounge passing through the wide hall into the dining room adjacent.

Jimmy gazed around the room again, apart from older members of the family, which he believed were grandparents or aunties and uncles, all the photographs were of Abigail alone or with Rachel. There were no photographs of a Father figure.

Rachel returned and handed Jimmy a large drawing pad.

"Yeah, she is fascinated with birds, always drawing birds. That particular pad is pretty much all birds."

Jimmy opened up the pad and fingered through the pages, glorious birds of the world exploded in radiant colours in front of his eyes, he passed macaws, herons, nuthatches and a curious looking black crane before stopping on a page which contained a sketchy charcoal piece of a lone magpie.

"She is very gifted." Jimmy smiled placing the pad on the coffee table.

"Oh she is." Rachel beamed with pride.

"How is school? Any trouble there?"

"Some troubles with a group of girls last year, but that's just girls of that age."

Jimmy nodded.

"But no bullying of any kind?" He asked scribbling notes quickly.

"Oh, no, nothing like that."

"Has Abi ever done anything like this before? Ran away I mean?"

"Oh, no, never!"

Jimmy nodded again and took a sip of his coffee, gearing himself up for the question he had dreaded asking.

"Is there a Mr. Jones on the scene?"

"No, my husband, that is my ex-husband left us several years ago."

"And how did Abi take that?"

Rachel sighed, it was obvious by her face that ugly memories were rearing their heads.

"It was a long time ago and she was too young to understand."

Jimmy nodded as he scribbled notes down on his pad that were barely legible.

"Why did he leave you?"

Tears welled up in Rachel's eyes.

"Was he aggressive towards you?" He probed.

Rachel could only nod as she dropped her head in sorrow.

"I am sorry if I have upset you Rachel, I just have to ask these questions. If he was still on the seen or had he come back to take Abi..."

"Oh, no he would never do that."

"He wouldn't?" Jimmy asked unconvinced.

"No, he left us for another man. He was leading a double life."

"Oh!" Jimmy reacted with shock, he had not been expecting that.

"His aggression was more out of frustration I believe, I caught him one night with a work colleague of his and I threw him out. He left and hasn't been back since. Moved to Puerto Rico. He still sends birthday and Christmas cards for Abi but that's about it."

"I see."

There was a moment of silence and Jimmy took in another large gulp of coffee while Rachel continued to inhale the odour of her daughter's toy, Angus.

"What was she wearing the last time you saw her?"

"She was wearing lilac corduroy pants, a thick red woollen jumper and a bright orange padded vest."

"Quite the ensemble!"

Rachel actually laughed, the sound of it was music to Jimmy's ears and he smiled back at her.

"Yeah, she really likes bright colours."

He paused for a moment as Rachel seemed to drift off, no doubt remembering her dear sweet daughter draped in all colours of the spectrum. When her eyes returned to Johnson's he continued with his questioning.

"Who was the last person to see her, do you know?" Jimmy asked.

"Her friend, Lucy."

"Do you have a surname?"

"Knight. She lives over on Applebee Plains."

"Right, I may need to talk to her."

"I can tell you what Lucy told me."

"Okay." Jimmy replied, reaching down for another shot of his coffee as Rachel spoke.

"They were walking home from school and Abi was

supposed to meet me at Elmer's."

"Elmer's?"

"A diner in town, I work there you see, just part time waitressing, nothing that is going to set the world on fire. But it pays the bills you know?"

"And she usually met you there?"

"On Friday's yes, I always work a shorter shift on Friday's. She would meet me for a milkshake before walking home. It's those precious moments you don't get back." She sobbed.

Jimmy let her cry, what else could he do, she buried her face into Angus' soft torso and let out her emotions. Jimmy took the opportunity to finish off his coffee and waited for her to regroup.

"I'm sorry about that Mister Johnson."

"It's perfectly understandable, just take your time."

"Lucy said that Abi wanted to take a shortcut through Parliament Grove, but Lucy's dad won't let her go in there."

"But you allow Abi too?"

"I don't like her going that route and I have told her about staying on the road, but you know kinds of that age?"

Jimmy did not, he had no children of his own, didn't have a wife or girlfriend, hell, he didn't even have a love life.

"Rebellious." Jimmy smiled.

"Yeah, I guess they are. Tell them not to do something and they just have to do it."

Jimmy chuckled and waited for her to wipe her eyes and continue.

"So, Lucy carried on the long way around and Abi went through the Grove and that was the last anyone saw of her, of my poor baby." She began to cry and again buried her face into Angus.

Jimmy rose from his seat and lifted his raincoat that seemed so heavy with all that was consumed within its deep pockets.

She looked up to see him readying himself to leave.

"You will find her won't you, Mister Johnson? Please say you will."

He smiled.

"I'm not leaving Hope Springs until I find her, Rachel."

In his head he wanted to add whether she was dead or alive, but obviously such words could devastate her.

She smiled back at him and started to rise herself.

"No, need to get up, I can see myself out. You drink your tea now, it's getting cold. I will be in touch when I have more information."

"Thank you." She sniffed and reached down to retrieve her oversized teacup and he watched her sip at it.

"Oh just one more question, if I may?" Jimmy said.

"Of course."

"Have you been in touch with anyone else about Abi's disappearance apart from Chief Gable and I?"

Her brow contorted as she tried to search for an answer that made sense for this particular question.

"I don't know what you mean?"

"Did you contact any federal agents about investigating the matter?"

"Erm, no!" She shook her head and looked at him blankly.

"Just a routine question."

Jimmy smiled and said his goodbyes, leaving the Jones household hoping that when he returned he would have some good news for Ms. Jones.

He leaned up against the front door as soon as it was closed and sighed heavily, these type of investigations were the absolute worst.

VIII

"Come on Andy, this is the place." Sherry called as she laid out her blanket in the clearing next to an old well.

Andy trudged through the foliage moments later, seemingly unimpressed by it all.

"I hate nature." He shrugged, "I mean really what's the point of all this." He poked around the clearing at the trees that surrounded them and shook his head. "I don't get it."

Magpies began landing on the branches and Andy gazed up at them and shrugged again with disinterest.

"Oh stop being a grouch and come and sit with me." She rummaged in the wicker picnic hamper that she had placed next to her and smiled at him mischievously, her skirt rose above her knees as she moved, enticing him with her long slender thighs.

"I have something very special for you." She winked and arched her back and he watched on as the shape of her pert breasts creased the tight sweater she wore that was striped in the Hope Springs High school colours of blue-green and white.

"Yeah?" Andy asked, and removed his letterman jacket and discarded it to the floor before kicking of his sneakers too.

"What are you doing?" She asked, a confused look on her face.

He collapsed next to her and began breathing heavily and

nuzzling into her neck.

"So what is this special treat you have for me then?" He pawed at her breast and she rolled her eyes and brushed away his advances.

"Close your eyes you naughty boy." She giggled as she rummaged around in the picnic hamper.

"Oh yeah! I'm a naughty boy, alright." He groaned, eyes closed tightly as he bit at his bottom lip with anticipation.

"Now hold out your hands." She said.

Andy chuckled to himself and did what was asked of him and in his hands she placed a large submarine sandwich.

"Ta da!" She exclaimed as he opened his eyes.

"It's a sub." He said with very little enthusiasm as he sat there staring at it.

"It's your favourite, its got three different types of meats in it."

He just stared at the sub and then back at her, when realisation sunk in that he was on an actual picnic, he sighed heavily. His warped mind had led him to believe that today was going to be the day that the pair finally took the next step in their relationship.

"Look, it's got chicken," Sherry said excitedly, lifting the top layer of bread to show him what treats lay in store for him, "Beef and ham! All your favourites!"

She beamed at him with excitement and he grunted at her before taking a bite out of the sub and munching on it while Sherry, retrieved a small tub that concealed a variety of sushi within.

His eyebrows rose from the taste of the sub, it was a hell of a good sandwich, but damn it he felt as though he had been brought here on false pretences and he had had enough. He threw the sub down onto the blanket.

"Something the matter?" Sherry asked as she drizzled soy sauce from a small decanter onto her sushi.

"You bet your ass there is!" Andy grunted.
Sherry stared at him clueless.

"How long have we been going steady now?" He snapped.

"Six weeks, four days, sixteen hours, forty-three minutes and about ten seconds!" She beamed and kissed him on the end of his swollen nose that had been broken at least three or four times during his time as linebacker for the Hope Springs Magpies.

"Well, damn it Sherry I want a little bit more!"

"What do you mean?"

"You know!" Andy winked at her and moved his eyebrows up and down vigorously as if doing a bad Groucho Marx impression.

"Oh!" She exclaimed, "You mean sex?"

"Yeah I mean sex! But every time I get near you, you brush me off."

Sherry slowly placed her tub of sushi on the ground and then pounced on him, kissing him eagerly and he responded the same.

"Oh Sherry!" He groaned and he lay her down and ripped of his shirt and then started to eagerly unbuckle his jeans when there was a flurry of wings above him and it made him halt proceedings. He gazed above at the mass of magpies watching him and all of a sudden he had an eerie sensation.

"I don't like those birds glaring at me." He grumbled, trying not to make eye contact with any of them, "I feel as though they are mocking me."

They cackled and cawed as if they had heard his words and now he sat back down seemingly unable to perform.

"Don't worry about some silly birds." She said and she shuffled over to him and kissed his bare chest. "They are only magpies."

"Magpies! But aren't they supposed to be bad luck? I mean our teams named after them so... Hey! No wonder we never win!"

"Don't be silly." She rolled her eyes, "They're not bad luck if you know the right words."

"What words?"

"Well, if one brings sorrow all you do is salute it," which she did "and say 'Good morning, Mr. Magpie, how are Mrs. Magpie and all the other little magpies?' And just like that you've broken the curse."

She continued to kiss him and caress his muscular physique, but Andy was lost in thought.

"Good morning, Mr. Magpie, how are Mrs. Magpie and all the other little magpies?" He said and saluted.

"That's it!" She said lying on her back and pulling him on top of her, "Forget the damn magpies now."

"But Sherry, that rhyme is all very well and good if

there is one magpie but what do you say when there are hundreds."

They both looked around and sure enough the trees were amassed with an army of magpies all screeching loudly at the petting pair.

Their shrieks were so high pitched that Sherry clasped her hands over her ears.

"Make it stop! Make it stop!" She squealed.

Andy rose to his feet to address the on looking magpies that cawed wildly and he bellowed at them all to be quiet. It must have worked because all of a sudden there was silence and the magpies sat motionless, but their eyes remained fixated on the pair.

"Oh, my hero!" Sherry swooned.

Andy posed with his hands on his hips proudly, like some half naked super hero.

"It was nothing." He declared, "Now let's get back to business."

Magpa's attack was so swift that Andy did not even have time to react and it was with such velocity that her claws cut clean through flesh, muscle and bone. The cut was made with such precision that he did not realise anything was wrong until his head slid from his shoulders. His hands even moved in a gesture as if to finish his speech, before his headless body collapsed next to a bemused Sherry. She let out a scream when she saw Andy's dumfounded expression frozen on his face, looking up at her from the picnic blanket. She scrambled to her feet and ran across the clearing, but something large swooped over her head and suddenly she had been hoisted into the air, claws gripping her shoulders and tearing at her sweater. She screamed in terror as she was whisked through the air and then sent hurtling towards a dead tree where she was skewered on a long protruding branch where she remained suspended as her entrails were pushed out from inside her and fell to the floor of the clearing in a hot steaming pile of viscera. Sherry coughed and spluttered blood as dozens of magpies swooped down to feed on her as she died. She started to weep and then she saw a creature that burst from the treetops, The Magpa came for her with a harpies war cry that silenced her for evermore.

IX

Chief Gable had made good on his promise that Charlie Mendoza would fix up his battered old Volkswagen Beetle, he had even joked with him about possibly trading it for a different model. When Jimmy had asked what sort of model he should trade it with Charlie laughed and said Heidi Klum.

Jimmy made it up the steep hill this time with no trouble and headed toward the entrance to Parliament Grove. The yellow Beetle scuttled past the Kratz place, a dozen or so cats roamed around the front yard. When he reached the tree that was consumed by a mass of missing children flyers he brought the car to a sudden halt. He exited the car and flipped the collar of his raincoat, although the rain had finally ceased, there was a bitter wind that blew through, attacking the nape of his neck.
He lit a cigarette from a fresh box of Freebirds that he had purchased from the vending machine at Charlie's garage.
Slowly Jimmy walked towards the tree of flyers.

"I don't believe it." He gasped as he gazed upon the dates on the posters.

"There must be at least a hundred missing people advertised here." He shook his head and focused his attentions on the latest flyer to have been pinned up and it was obviously that of Abigail Jones. Several questions went through his head.

Where is Abigail Jones?
Why were those federal agents investigating this case?
Where are the federal agents now?
Who is Denny?

"And why do I feel like I'm being watched?" He said out loud and he turned slowly to see those grimy net curtains of the Kratz residence quivering as 'Krazy' Kratz made herself scarce. He flicked the cigarette onto the dirt path and extinguished any smouldering with the sole of his shoe. As Jimmy walked into The Grove, he heard Mrs Kratz calling in her many cats.

As he reached a clearing he smelt the unmistakable smell of blood, rich and metallic in the back of his throat and nostrils.

"What a stench!" He scoffed and then realised that the blood may well belong to Abi. Just thinking about such things made him sick to his very stomach. He approached a well made of misshapen rocks, but there was nothing of any interest for him there.

"Perhaps she has fallen down the well?" He said to himself and he called down into its dark vast shaft. The echoing of his voice the only reply.

He continued to survey the clearing, he found no traces of blood or bodily function that could create such an unpleasant aroma. He gazed up into the trees that were consumed by what appeared to be hundreds of black leaves, Jimmy had never seen such a tree before and squinted at it for the longest time. At the foot of the tree he saw something catch his eye, it flickered when it caught the dying light of sunset and he hurried over to it. He crouched down and retrieved it, a small lapel pin, golden, with some kind of bird of prey etched onto it.

"That's one for the 'Evidence Bag'." He said as he examined it closer before slipping it into his inside pocket of his coat.

He noticed that the bark of the tree had broken away in places and several chunks had been taken out of the bark.

"A flurry of bullets could have done this..."

Then there were what appeared to be scratch marks along the inside of the branches above his head, as if someone had been dragged up into the tree. Jimmy clicked his tongue as he pondered this particular tree that rose above him menacingly, leaves of black in the dusky evening.

He began to climb.

"I haven't done this since I was a kid." He grimaced as he found it most difficult to scale the tree, but getting closer he could see that they were in fact scratch marks, even a subtle fleck of nail polish could be spotted if one looked close enough or had the trained eye and knew what to look for.

He heard a noise from above him just as that crisp breeze swept through the clearing, it ruffled those black leaves above him, it was then he realised they were not black leaves but feathers, the feathers of a hundred magpies all staring at him. He stared back at them and did not like the way that their black eyes seemed to burn holes in him. He slowly started to descend but noticed that they followed his every move. He became frantic and he lost his footing and fell at least ten feet onto his back. He grimaced at the sudden impact and shook the shock to his system away, looking up to the descending mass of black feathered harpies. It was then that he spotted something as he gazed up into that tree, it may have been a slight concussion or a trick of the falling sun, that made it appear to Jimmy that there was one gigantic magpie sitting perched at the top of the tree. Before he could refocus and gaze upon what was actually there he set off through The Grove heading back to his car.

As he moved through the trees quickly he could see several magpies flying over head.

"They're tracking me!" Jimmy gasped and he tried to change direction, but whichever way he turned to try and outmanoeuvre them was in vain for they stuck with him all the way until he could see his beloved Olive.

"That's it!" He exclaimed, "I need a drink."

X

Rhonda Kratz watched on through her lounge window as the man in the raincoat came bursting through the trees, bounding onto the dirt path, slipping and then colliding with the floor. His knees took the impact, but he had no time to worry about such menial matters, as he rose quickly to his feet again and headed towards his car. Mrs. Kratz could see the sweat gathering on the fleeing man's brow and knew just what had happened.

"Lucky boy!" She sniffed, stroking a tortoiseshell cat that had jumped up on the windowsill, in search of some affection. She stroked the cat along its spine, its tail poker straight with the enjoyment of the caress.

"Yep, Cassie that's one lucky boy right there."
The man moved with such speed past the flyer tree that the posters of missing children flapped violently, as if they were looking to fly away after him. All the while the man kept peering over his shoulder as if he were being followed, being chased.

"There ain't many that get away from her." Mrs Kratz scoffed, her tone was nonchalant and matter of fact, it was the life she had known for the last forty years or so, living this close to Parliament Grove, she had become accustomed to the peculiar goings on within its dark clutches. More cats joined

Cassie, all wanting Rhonda's attention. Cassie hissed at the oncoming killjoys that looked to spoil her moment with her master.

"Now stop that Cassie!" Rhonda cried, pushing the cat out of the way, she dropped from the windowsill and strutted away to the kitchen, if she couldn't have some affection without being disturbed perhaps she could find some food instead.

Mrs. Kratz's old eyes flitted from side to side behind thick lenses that resembled the bases of glass soda bottles. She watched him rummage in the pocket of his raincoat of his pocket in search of his car keys and then back to the dirt path on which he had just came.

"Here they come." She said, no part of her voice seemed to will the man on in his mission to escape, it was if Mrs. Kratz and her cats were enjoying the suspense of it all.

He dropped the keys to the asphalt and cursed his luck.

"Of course he dropped his keys." She almost chuckled, the cats sounding off in unison as if echoing her words.

The magpies came in a thick black cloud, dangerously close together, one would wonder how they could fly so close together, but they did. They moved as one like the flowing of waves on the ocean, a wave that was rising into the darkening sky ready to descend upon the flustered man.

"He's done for if he doesn't get a move on." She said, unwrapping a boiled sweet that she had found in the pocket of her apron and stuffed it into her mouth slowly, sucking on it loudly as if this was some sort of half time entertainment for her.

There was a hideous shriek that sent the cats fleeing from the window in search of refuge, but Rhonda Kratz remained, she knew that she was quite safe where she was and watched on as something large joined that wave of black high above the tops of the trees, hovering ready to strike like the poisoned tail of a scorpion.

The man jammed the key into the lock, turned it quickly and dove inside the Volkswagen Beetle, slamming the door shut behind him. He glared up at the dark cloud that hung above the car for a while, hundreds of eyes twinkling at him with menace. He thrust the key into the ignition, crunched the gearshift into reverse and hurtled backwards onto the road, tyres screeching as they span around before straightening up and heading back towards Hope Springs.

Mrs. Kratz continued to suck loudly on her sweet as she witnessed the man leave in a plume of thick smoke before turning back to the collection of magpies that had already started to disband until only a few strays remained at the entrance as if to keep a look out for any others that would be foolish enough to set foot in Parliament Grove.

"Show's over!" Mrs. Kratz sniffed and shuffled over to her recliner where she sank down into it unceremoniously, lifting the television remote and using it to bring her set to life, *Wheel of Fortune's* theme tune blasted from the sets old speakers and the black and white cat that lay half asleep on the set grumbled with complaint.

"Oh, quit your whining Pepe!" She lambasted launching a slipper at him, causing him to wail and then jump down from the set. Several other cats gathered around her looking for a space on her lap.

"Lucky boy that one," She said through brisk sucks, "Yes, sir, a lucky, lucky boy indeed."

XI

Jimmy Johnson. Jr., slammed on the breaks and came to a quivering halt on the carpark of the only local bar in town, Buddy's. His breaths were heavy and his skin clammy with sweat.

"What in God's name was that?"

His voice cracked and he almost choked on the words as they passed through his quivering lips. He prised his fingers from the steering wheel, leaving behind the tacky remnants of where his hands had gripped it ever so tightly.

"Shit me." He whispered as he started to relax a little and his breathing pattern returned to some kind of normality. The neon sign screamed in pink flashes the word 'BEER' over and over again before his eyes.

"That's what I need." He stuttered, "Or maybe something a little stiffer."

He placed his forehead on the steering wheel, and controlled his breathing until it returned to a pattern that felt normal. He looked down at his muddy shoes and his muddy knees and almost laughed.

"Jesus wept," He chuckled sitting back up and leaning back in the driver's seat, "I think I shit myself back there."

There was a slamming sound on the driver's seat window and Jimmy cried out in anguish as the man who had been watching him last night appeared at his window, palms of both hands pressed against the glass, a strange, wide-eyed expression on the pocked and scarred face of Denny Lamont.

"FUCK!" Jimmy seethed and stared at this bizarre individual glaring at him.

"What the hell do you think you're doing?" Jimmy growled, but he dared not open the window or door to confront this unpredictable fellow. Jimmy locked the door, keeping his eyes on Denny, who refused to interrupt his stare with even so much as a blink. His eyeballs were bloodshot and several bags hung under them, his features were gaunt and his flesh was heavily marked with scars and scabs.

This guy must be into fucking everything going.

Then Denny finally spoke.

"You saw her didn't you?" His breathes were very heavy, almost congested as if he struggled to speak.

"What?" Jimmy replied, confused, "Saw who?"

"You saw her damn it!" Denny cried, fire burning in his eyes.

"Look fella, I don't know what you're talking about."

"LIAR!" Denny screamed and slammed the palms of his hands against the window, the glass shook wildly in its frame and Jimmy was adamant that it would shatter into a thousands pieces and this lunatic junkie would throttle him.

"Get the hell outta here man!" Jimmy roared back, hand rummaging blindly in his raincoat in search of his Swiss army knife if the need to protect himself arose.

"Tell me, tell me!" Denny shrieked, eyes filling with

tears as his fingertips squeaked unpleasantly on the glass, "Tell me, damn you!"

"Tell you what?" Jimmy cried, "I don't know what you mean?"

Denny just screamed at the top of his voice and then his face was up as close to the glass as it could get and his rapid breaths caused the window to fog, but he did not blink and the two remained in a frozen stare, locked horns like two warring rams. Jimmy flicked the large blade from the Swiss army knife and held it tightly his quivering grasp, still concealed in his pocket.

"You saw her I know it." Denny whispered, "I know, I know." He nodded and then started to smile, his mouth almost empty of any teeth, those that remained were sharp and rotting. Jimmy slowly slid the knife from his pocket, readying himself.

"I don't..." Jimmy tried again to let Denny know that he did not understand, but Denny interrupted him.

"The magpies!" Denny smiled.

Jimmy's eyes widened and he relinquished his grip on the knife which fell to the floor of the car, sliding lost underneath the seat.

"What?"

"Mag...pa!" His hissed at him, saliva spraying the window.

"Magpa?" Jimmy frowned, "I...I don't know what I saw."

Denny's brows rose up to his receding hair line that was peppered with tufts of white.

"I knew you saw her, I knew..."

"HEY!" Came a bellowing voice and the pair turned to see Chief Gable standing in the entrance of the bar.

Denny looked terrified but turned to Jimmy and whispered, to him.

"Find me and I will tell you everything. Find me!"

"DENNY!" Chief Gable called again, "Get the hell outta here! Go on now, GET!"

Denny ran away out of sight and The Chief approached the window.

"You okay, Son?"

"Fuck me, he's extreme." Jimmy sighed.

"He sure is, goddamn junkie." The Chief grimaced, watching Denny run away down the street, "We could do without his kind around here that's for sure."

Jimmy opened the door and stepped out.

"I'm sure he's harmless, Chief."

"Don't you believe it!" The Chief sniffed, his moustache ruffling, "You would never believe some of the things I have found that pest doing over the years. Goddamn menace he is!"

Jimmy slammed the door behind him and breathed a long and weary sigh as Chief Gable looked him up and down, his clammy pale face, the leaves stuck to his hair and raincoat and his knees splattered with dirt.

"What the hell happened to you?" He scoffed.

"Don't ask, Chief."

"Well, whatever it is you look like you could do with a good, cold stiff one!"

"Only if you're buying, Chief."

"Pah!" Chief Gable laughed, slapping him on the back and leading him into the bar, "On my salary, you must be joking."

The pair stumbled into the dimly lit bar, Chief Gable slapping him on the back and laughing loudly. Jimmy tried to mimic his enthusiasm, but he was still a little shook up from his ordeal in Parliament Grove. All the locals who sat at booths and tables greeted the police chief with welcoming gestures and smiling faces, there was no getting away from the fact that Chief Gable was a helluva guy and everyone loved him.

"This is it Son," Gable announced, grasping Jimmy tightly by his shoulder and waving his large paw across the bar, "this is the hub of Hope Springs."

The locals gazed at the stranger and gave curious smiles, some already reeling from the effects of too much alcohol, swayed from side to side in their seats as they raised their glasses.

Jimmy awkwardly smiled back, raising his hand in an embarrassed wave.

"Buddy Race?" Gable bellowed and a large balding rotund man appeared at the bar, beaming pleasantly.

"Who's making all this racket?" Buddy called, "Have I got to call the authorities?"

"Buddy!" Gable chuckled, "Look after my friend here," He said slapping Jimmy on the back and almost thrusting him towards the bar, "get him whatever he wants, it's on me."

"Goddamn Chief! What is he royalty or something?"

Buddy chuckled, the fat rolls that hung over his throat wobbled like jelly, "Ain't often you go splashing the cash."

"Shut your pie hole and pour him a drink." Chief said before leaning into Jimmy and informing him that he had just got to go and see someone. Jimmy dropped onto the barstool and almost collapsed on the bar, it took all he had to keep himself propped up. He watched as Chief adjusted his belt, sucked in his gut and brushed at his moustache with the back of his hand and strolled across the bar.

"Ah, he's gone to visit Widow Lockwood." Buddy sniffed appearing at the bar adjacent to Jimmy.

"Who?"

"Gloria Lockwood." Buddy replied, "Local widow, husband died about nine months back and all the town's bachelor's have been vying for her attention ever since. None more so than The Chief."

The pair watched as The Chief approached an attractive middle-aged blonde smiling at him through bright red lipstick. He removed his hat and swiped his hair back as he joined her at her table in the corner of the bar.

"The sly old dog." Buddy laughed and then sniffed loudly as if to get Jimmy's attention, "So what can I get ya stranger?"

"I'll take a Bobby's Light." Jimmy said horsely, his throat had become tight and dry.

"Sure you don't want something a bit stronger?" Buddy asked, looking Jimmy up and down.

"Huh?"

"Well, you look like shit, thought you could do with a stiff one."

"Yeah, okay, hit me with a shot of Moondog."

"That's more like it!" Buddy announced, as he decanted some Moondog whiskey into a shot glass and placed it on the tacky bar, "That'll put some hair on your chest, you see if it don't!"

"Thanks." Jimmy replied, the words came out but his mind seemed miles away.

He could not fathom what he had seen in those trees, those eyes so humanlike, a shiver tinkered down the bones of his spine like a pianist's fingers and he grabbed the glass and drank it down fast. The whiskey scorched his throat and he grimaced openly, before gasping loudly as if he were a dragon about to unleash a ball of fire from the pit of his stomach.

Buddy stood laughing at him.

"Told ya! You can feel the hairs growing already can't ya?"

"Something like that." Jimmy croaked and Buddy laughed again, "You can have that on the house, I'll get you a Bobby's, seems more your style."

Buddy slid the cold beer across the bar and Jimmy wrapped his hand around the cold glass, he scooped it up and took a long swig before slamming the half empty glass back on the bar and wiping white, bubbly froth from his upper lip.

"That cooled you down a little?"

Jimmy nodded and looked around the bar, he gazed at the window and saw Denny's face and hands pressed up against the glass, staring at him again. As the two made eye contact, Jimmy groaned and Denny entered the bar cautiously making a beeline for Jimmy at the bar.

"HEY!" Buddy growled, "Denny, get your ass outta here! I don't want none of your shit!"

Denny froze on the spot and gazed around at the sneering faces that greeted him unpleasantly, as if everyone had trodden in the same piece of dog shit and the stench had caught in their nose and throat.

"Go on now, GET!" Buddy roared.

Denny saw Chief Gable wearing a very annoyed look on his face having his moment with Gloria Lockwood interrupted. He swallowed heavily and left the bar quickly.

"Buddy, can I ask you something?" Said Jimmy.

"Shoot."

"Who in God's name is that? He's been stalking my ass since I got here."

"Pay him no mind."

"Yeah, people keep telling me that, but I would rather know a little background on the guy. I mean am I gonna get my throat slit or butt raped in my sleep? Just want to know what sort of loon I'm dealing with." He took a swig of beer.

"He's the local junkie, I mean he's pretty harmless."

"Oh yeah, he looks it." Scoffed Jimmy in response.

"Your fresh meat around here, I figure he's just trying to get his hooks into you so he can sell you some coke or heroin or whatever it is that these shit heels are taking these days."

"He spoke to me outside, asked me if I had seen her?

What did he mean by that?"

Buddy looked away and sniffed, slapping a damp cloth on the bar and wiping it vigorously, making sure not to make eye contact with Jimmy.

"I don't what he meant by that." Buddy snapped and before Jimmy could continue his questioning, Buddy moved on down the bar to talk with some of his regulars who were propped up against the bar watching boxing on a small television that hung in the corner of the bar. The screen flickered erratically as it displayed 'Left Hook' Lewis Johnson holding aloft his newly won heavyweight championship.

Jimmy pondered the peculiar behaviour and sipped at his beer. Chief Gable slumped himself next to Jimmy, which was accompanied with a hefty slap on the back that made Jimmy swallow his beer and then explode in a riotous coughing spree.

"Sorry about that Son." The Chief laughed.

"It's okay." Spluttered Jimmy, "Let me get you a drink."

"Oh no, I won't hear of it." The Chief smiled, and then gestured to Buddy with a wavering finger, "The usual."

Buddy nodded and disappeared underneath the bar, returning with an old bottle of Hackenschmidt whiskey. He placed the half empty bottle on the bar and slid a whiskey glass up against it, the glass on glass sang as they collided and Buddy smiled leaving the pair to see to his other customers.

"This is the good stuff son." The Chief smiled, unscrewing the lid from the bottle and pouring a generous amount of the golden whiskey into the glass.

"Expensive?" Jimmy asked.

"Very," He chuckled, "Twenty five years old this particular bottle is, great age, great age." He said boastfully, his tonguing licking at the excess that had settled on the bristles of his moustache, as if to waste a drop of this vintage would be a crime.

"I love the way it warms the pipes." Chief Gable chuckled.

"Rather you than me," Jimmy laughed, "I don't think my palette is as refined as yours."

"Oh poppycock!" The Chief, cried rising from his stool and reaching over the bar to retrieve another whiskey glass that he unceremoniously slammed down in front of Jimmy as he was finishing up his beer.

"Oh Chief, I really don't think..."

"Nonsense!" He said pouring Jimmy a generous amount.

"But, it would be wasted on me I'm sure."

"Get it down your hole!"

They raised their glasses and they toasted to...

"Gloria Lockwood's cleavage." Chief Gable sniggered and the pair laughed, before the sound was lost by the striking of glass on glass.

"Now, Jimmy, you tell me about yourself."

"How long have you got?" Jimmy scoffed.

"All night." The Chief smiled.

"Well, I'm from New York originally, Brooklyn to be exact."

"I thought I detected the accent."

"Yeah, Pops always said, you never really lose it."

Jimmy beamed and The Chief smiled feeling the warmth radiate off him as he spoke about his Father.

"Pops moved us all to Vancouver where he was supposed to be winding it down and heading into retirement, but once a cop always a cop, couldn't stand working at a desk and he was soon out working the top cases again. I followed suit and joined the VPD too, I guess you could say it runs in the family."

"But you're not a cop now?"

"No, these days I'm a private detective, working out of Studd City."

"How come you made the switch?"

"I couldn't bring myself to work for them after how they handled my Pops'... death."

"I'm sorry to hear that Son." Gable shook his head and sighed, "My dad was a right bruiser. Tough love was the aim of the game in our household. But he instilled all the fundamentals I needed, guess I owe what I am to him."

"To Fathers!" Jimmy smiled and the pair toasted again.

"So what happened to your daddy? Did he die on the job?"

"Yes and no."

"I don't understand."

"They said that he passed in a fire, but his body was never found."

"That's hard to take."

"It was the fire at the institute in Blackfoot Ridge, you

may have heard of it?"

"Oh, I heard of it all right, nasty business that!"

"I won't go into too much detail, but I managed to peruse some case files and the reports had blatantly been altered. Even some of the causes of deaths were changed and well, the whole thing just doesn't sit right with me, I can feel it in my gut that something is not right and that's why I left the VPD. I'm currently investigating what exactly happened."

"Well, Son, in my experience you should always go with your gut, makes a whole lot more sense than your brain half the time."

Jimmy's eyes widened, the words echoing those of his father.

"Agreed." Jimmy said and took a deep swig of the whiskey, it helped to wash away any emotion that was welling up inside him.

"I gotta ask you some questions though Chief, about this place, about Parliament Grove."

"Yep, I thought you might."

"I've been down there and I…"

"You've seen something right?"

"Yes."

There was silence between the two, someone slipped a quarter into the jukebox and *Yes, Anastasia* by *Tori Amos* filled the bar.

"I wish I could say you will find that little girl, I really do."

"I sense a but." Jimmy smirked.

"You won't." The Chief snapped, "You won't find head

nor tail of Abigail Jones."

"How do you know I won't? I may have different techniques and..."

"PAH!" Gable interrupted, "You won't find her, just like all the others."

"How has this been going on for so long?" Jimmy asked, shaking his head in disbelief, "How is that none of these missing people have never been found?"

"Goddamn it, I've done all I can!" Gable snapped, "I always do all I can, not without the feeling that I've already lost though."

"I meant no disrespect Chief," Jimmy sighed, "it must be very frustrating."

"Frustrating isn't the fucking word for it!" He downed the whiskey and immediately poured himself another. "You don't know how hard it is Son. To give all you've got and find nothing! To have no information to even close the case. To tell their parents that you don't know where their child is, that you have nothing to go on. You don't know how much of a lousy human being that makes you feel and what a complete waste of space it makes you look. It's gut wrenching to watch their heart break in front of you and witness all hope leave them through those tears that they shed."

Chief Gable's old eyes started to well up, thinking of all those cases that remained open on his desk and having nothing to go on to close each one.

"You just don't know." He added.

"No..." Jimmy began, but was interrupted, when The

Chief turned to him and stared at him.

"But you will."

"Sorry?"

"You'll feel all those inadequacies and all her pain when you tell Rachel Jones that you can't find her daughter. You'll feel it all right, it will stay with you like a weight around your neck. I've got that many weights around my neck its a wonder I don't drown every time I take a bath."

"And there's never any leads? Never any suspects?"

"Oh, if you ask the locals they'll point their fingers here and there, telling you exactly who was responsible for it all. But that's just speculation."

"Denny Lamont and Mrs. Kratz I take it?"

The Chief nodded.

"No evidence, no motive…" Jimmy started.

"No nothing!" The Chief scoffed, "There isn't anything on either of them, and if you ask me neither are responsible for the disappearances anyhow."

"What else is there? Is there a pattern to the disappearances? Is it seasonal?"

The Chief shakes his head.

"Like those disappearances up in Maple Falls, that's seasonal." Jimmy pondered, tongue clicking as he thought. "Only happens in the winter time they say…"

"No, it's nothing like that. Never has no reason or rhyme. It can be quiet for years and years and then something happens and whammy! It all begins again."

There was silence again and Gable topped up their glasses.

"You haven't told me what you saw out there."

"No," Jimmy whispered, "No, I haven't."

"And why not?"

"Because... because..." Jimmy could not find the words.

"I'd think you were crazy wouldn't I?"

Jimmy nodded.

"Yeah, I hear that a lot." Gable nodded.

"So there is something in Parliament Grove, hidden in those... magpies."

"Could be."

"But you don't believe in that kind of mumbo jumbo?"

"Exactly. I can't put any of that in a case file or tell the missing child's parents that some Bird-Witch took their baby."

"A Bird-Witch!" Jimmy murmured, his memory trying to piece together the fragments of the evening's events together to create this Bird-Witch in his mind. Was that what he had seen?

"If you ask Rhonda Kratz or Denny Lamont about it, that's exactly what they will tell you. I've heard the same story from them for the past thirty years. Their story never changes."

"But you don't believe them?"

"How can I?" He laughed, "That would make me a laughing stock around here if I started siding with the fruitcakes."

"Have you ever seen anything?"

There was a pause as if Chief Gable was giving the answer way too much thought.

"No." He finally answered, "Can't say that I have."

They downed their whiskeys, Jimmy could already feel the effects on his head as everything in the bar seemed to sway. As he stood his knees trembled beneath him. Not being big drinker himself, he would most definitely regret this in the morning.

"I'm gonna call it a night." Jimmy announced, "I appreciate the drinks."

"Don't mention it Son."

"I guess I'll see you tomorrow."

"No doubt."

"Good night, Chief." Jimmy said and Chief Gable replied with a nod as he stared into the bottom of his glass, swirling the dregs of his whiskey around and around as if he were a fortune teller searching for answers. Jimmy turned to leave, legs wobbling as he staggered from side to side.

"Jimmy?" Chief said and it stopped him in his tracks.

"Yes, Chief."

"I do hope you find her."

"Me too, Chief, me too."

Jimmy staggered out of the bar and into the night, the air was fresh and the clouds that gathered around the moon meant one thing, rain.

He waddled over to his car and rummaged for the keys in his pocket and then as he looked at his car and saw three of them form before his eyes, he thought it best to walk home tonight.

"A fine night for a walk." He splutter drunkenly, "Night, night Love."

But as he approached the car to give it a pat on the hood he noticed a piece of paper held tightly between his windshield and wiper.

"What's this?" He scoffed, eyes trying to focus on the messy penmanship that said 'Call me' and a cell number scribbled underneath.

"Maybe it's from Widow Lockwood." He tittered, stuffing it into his pocket before walking in the direction of Bertha's Bed and Breakfast.

"She must have seen my tight tushy across the bar," he laughed, "The Chief would have my guts for garters!"
He staggered across the road flicking his collar up and sinking his hands into the deep pockets of his raincoat as the heavens opened up and rain again descended upon Jimmy Johnson. Jr,.

XII

Lucy Knight screamed at her father in defiance as she stomped heavily upstairs to her room. Her father appeared at the foot of the stairs, frustration etched on his face, but with worry in his dark eyes.

"I won't allow you to do anything so stupid, Lucy!" He cried, his hand gripping the ball cap of the newel post, squeezing it tightly, choosing to take his aggression out on the smooth mahogany and not his daughter.

"You just don't want to help!" Lucy sniffed, tears streaming down the plump ripeness of her ebony cheeks.

"That's just not true and you know it!" Her father called up the stairs.

Lucy span around on the spot, two dark jewels glistening with moisture, her face glowing in anger.

"Mom would have helped." She hissed.

Her father closed his eyes tightly for a moment, taking in the hurtful words, steadying himself on the newel post as those words constricted around his heart.

"How could you say that?" He murmured, fighting back the emotions caused by her words.

Lucy knew how to get to him, she would hate herself later for it, she missed her mother so much and she knew that her father worshipped the ground she had walked on. She knew how hard it was for him too, but she also knew that her words would make an impact and have the desired effect.

"But, it's true, Dad." She whimpered, "She would have been the first one out there to search for Abi."

"But..."

"And, she would let me search too. Abi's my best friend Dad!"

"I know..."

"You can't expect me to sit here and do nothing. Just pretend that it hasn't happened!" She wiped the streaming tears from her eyes and seemed to focus, "She's been missing for over three weeks now!"

"I know, Lucy."

"Three weeks! I dread to think what's happened to her..." her father's eyes met hers as she spoke and she could read his thoughts on the matter, Lucy gasped and her voice sounded strained, "you think she's dead, don't you?"

He looked away, his head hanging, not able to make eye contact with her.

"How could you think that?" She said, her bottom lip trembling.

"It's been over three weeks, Lucy. There's just no way..."

"Oh my God! I don't believe you!" She screamed and bounded across the corridor towards her bedroom. Her father ran up the stairs to try and catch her before she could shut him out of the conversation.

"I'm just trying to be realistic, Lucy."

"Well, I still believe she's out there even if you don't!" She screamed turning around to meet him at her open door, posters of movie stars like *Bret Lennox* and musical acts like *Vanda and the Hell Sings* and *Darla Kincaid* all stared back at the spectacle taking place in the doorway, a silent audience.

"I am going to prove it, with or without your help!" She growled.

"Oh no you're not!" He roared back, no longer would he treat her with kid gloves, his words caused her to silence her tongue, she had not heard her father raise his voice like that in years. Lucy knew he was serious.

"Y-Yes I am!" She shouted defiantly.

"NO!" He roared, "I'm not having you go out there. I won't allow the same thing to happen to you."

"What will happen to me, Dad?" She asked with a sprinkling of sarcasm as children of that age often do, believing that the horrors of the world could never effect them.

"It's not safe out there." Was all he said calming a little, trying to be more nurturing with his tone.

"Why?"

"When there are people like Denny Lamont out there, who knows what can happen!" He growled, still believing that Denny Lamont was responsible for his wife's death, when she died in a car crash several years ago. He still blamed him and for all the missing children too, in Donald Knight's eyes everything that was wrong with Hope Springs was because this menace had not been dealt with properly.

"Oh give me a break with the Denny Lamont hate

would ya!" She scoffed.

"Don't take that tone with me, Lucy! You don't know what he's capable of... You don't know any of what goes on in the real world!"

"I know more than you think I know Dad! I'm thirteen, not five! You can't keep me wrapped up in cotton wool for the rest of my life you know."

"I'm just trying to protect you."

"I know and it has to stop! It's getting old now!"
She moved into her room and picked up her bright pink parka that lay on the bed, a duvet that still screamed that she was but a child, as did the amount of soft toys piled up by the headboard.
No matter what she thought or said, she was still only a child.

"I'm going out there right now and..."

"No!" He cried, "Are you crazy, it's pitch black out there! No, I won't allow it. Maybe tomorrow we can both go take a look, yeah?" He smiled at her trying to win her round, trying so hard to get her to concede.

"No, I'm going right now." And she attempted to barge past him.

"Lucy!" He growled and grabbed her arm.

"Let go of me!"

"I can't let you go out there."

"You're hurting me Dad, stop." She whimpered and he pulled her into her room and let go of her arm.

"I'm sorry I did that, truly I am, but you just won't listen to sense." His eyelids were swollen with tears now, he could not believe that he had hurt his little girl, she stood there looking up at him rubbing at her arm, her young face consumed with shock.

"I'm sorry." He blurted and tried to console her, but she flinched away from him and sat on the bed.

"Just leave me alone."

"But, Lucy I…"

"I just want to find my friend and you just don't understand."

"But…"

"Just get out." She whispered.

"What did you say?" He gazed on at her in shock.

"GET OUT!" She yelled and rose from her bed and pushed him out through the door.

"Lucy! Don't you slam that…"

SLAM!

"…door!"

The doorframe almost splintered from the velocity of the door being slammed and then the sound of the key grinding as it locked into place.

Donald sighed and leant up against the door, sobbing silently so that she could not hear his sorrow.

Lucy pulled herself together, determination carved into her face, she wiped the tears from her eyes and the mucus from her nostrils.

"No more!" She said to herself, "No more tears, Lucy."

She pulled on her coat and sunk her feet into two yellow

Wellington boots that looked pristine and never used.

"I'm coming for you, Abi."

She pulled out a woolly bobble hat from her parka pocket and yanked it over her thick head of dark curls. She checked her cell phone, her finger print causing the screen to burst into life and displaying a photograph of Abi and herself, hugging and pulling silly faces. She tucked it into her pocket and slunk silently to her bedroom door, placing an ear to it. Her father had moved away down the landing now, she could hear his footsteps and the stairs squeaking spasmodically as he made his way downstairs.

She unlocked and opened the door as quietly as she could and crept to the top of the stairs, peering over the bannister into the large hallway of the colonial home. She heard the television erupt with an overenthusiastic sports presenter hyping this weekend's upcoming big fight which would see world heavyweight boxing champion 'Golden Gloves' Morgan Sterling take on the undefeated fan favourite, 'Left Hook' Lewis Johnson. The sound of a bottle top leaving its confines of a glass beer bottle was unmistakable, she smiled to herself, knowing that he would be there for the next few hours and probably even drift off to sleep in front of the boob tube. She thought about making her way down the stairs and escaping out the back door through the kitchen, but she realised that would be to risky and if she were caught, it would no doubt cause another argument.

Instead she scampered into the family bathroom and slid open the window, very cautiously she climbed out onto the ledge and then shimmied down the drainpipe. She managed this with ease, young and nimble, but shimmying down drainpipes was nothing new to Lucy. This wasn't the first time she had snuck out of the house, she had done it a number of times, usually to go and meet Abi, while she had been grounded for some reason or another. She reached the soft soil of the flowerbeds that surrounded the house, beds that at this time of year were barren of life.

But now she found herself alone in the darkness, friendless, something she hoped to change. She retrieved her bicycle from the rear porch and carried it down the porch steps, trying not to make a noise. Seated upon her pink mountain bike she peddled away from the house, not looking back, even once, she was determined to find her friend if it was the last thing she did.

XIII

Lucy's small headlight threw out a weak beam that flickered through the darkness, doing little to guide her way, but this was a journey she had made hundreds of times and pitch black or bright as a summer's day made no difference to her, she could make it to Kratz Korner (as the local children called it) in her sleep.

The heavens opened and she skidded to a halt, pulled her hood up as headlights of cars illuminated her for several seconds before moving past quickly. She continued on her way peddling along the main road out of Hope Springs towards Parliament Grove.

A single light illuminated the Kratz cottage that sat in relative silence, only the muffled sound of the theme tune to *Cheers* could be heard. Lucy skidded to a halt by the flyer tree and leant the bicycle up against it. The rain sliced through the night and attacked the freshly tacked posters of Abigail Jones, raindrops causing the ink to run eerily, deforming her face, her smile drooping into a scream.

Lucy made her way down the dirt pathway that led into Parliament Grove, the rain immediately churning the dirt underfoot, squelching as she headed deeper into the sea of trees.

She moved swiftly under the cover of the trees, which actually covered her a little from the torrential rain. Above her in the darkness she could hear rustling, she gazed up but saw nothing but darkness, her heart rate quickened and for the first time that evening she felt scared. The damp, the dark, the cold all seemed to grip her and injected her quivering muscles with an overdose of fear. She heard crunching of leaves, breaking of branches, the cawing of birds and the scratching of something sharp on the bark of the surrounding trees.

"Maybe this was a mistake?" She swallowed, eyes flitting around in the darkness.

She contemplated turning around and going home, but then guilt pricked at her conscience. She couldn't turn back, she owed it to her friend, she owed it to Abi to go through with this, she had to find her. She rummaged in her pocket and retrieved her cell phone, she flicked the flashlight function into life and immediately The Grove was illuminated in an eerie teal glow. She could see now that it was just magpies that were sheltering from the rain in the treetops, there were an awful lot of them she thought, bunched together seemingly to keep each other warm. Realising that these strange noises were being made by birds, her fear subsided and she breathed a sigh of relief, moving on through The Grove towards a clearing she knew, one she had visited with Abi and their other friends several times when they had been playing truant from school. Her father thought that she was a perfect little princess, but even the good children bent the rules from time to time.

"I'm not afraid." She murmured and then had an idea, "I shall go live! My girls will keep me company."

She switched onto her social media account, the one that her father didn't know that she had and started up a live feed, unfortunately this function made the flashlight defunct.

"Shit, I'd forgotten about that." She groaned into the screen as she waited for people to join her live video.

It had now become considerably darker with the loss of the flashlight, however the screen light did give off a subtle glow that would help guide her way through the darkness.

She could feel her breaths rising and falling rapidly, a quiver in her voice as she trudged through the wet foliage, fear was rearing its ugly head again and then a smile caressed her face as several hearts exploded on her cellphone screen. The relief she felt must have been obvious by those watching her live video as questions started to cover the screen. Her friends asking where she was and what she was doing.

"Okay, guys I'm live here in Parliament Grove!"

Shocked face emoji's erupted on the screen in droves as her viewer numbers grew and comments came thick and fast asking what she thought she was doing and that she must be crazy.

"I know, I know, I'm nuts right?" She chuckled as raindrops bounced off the phone screen, her battery now rapidly deteriorating due to the use of the live video.

"But look I have to do this!" She groans, "I have too!"

Actually talking on the live feed and knowing that her friends were watching, made her feel okay. It was enough to make the fear subside. She was talking and had a purpose which was all that was needed for her to forget how wet and cold she was and about those creepy birds that seemed to watch her every move, shuffling along the branches in a mass of black feathers mimicking her every move.

"I know that this is totally crazy!" She laughed as she mirrored her viewers sentiments, but then her face fell serious.

"But I have to do this guys." She took a deep breath and beat away tears with her eye lashes.

"Abigail Jones went missing three weeks ago." She said taking a moment for her words to sink in and to gage the feeling of her audience. Sure enough emoji's burst onto the screen again, huge red hearts throbbed and exploded, along with sad faced emoji's with a single tear rolling from cartoonish eyes.

"Three weeks is a long time to be missing. The police have found nothing, not a trace of my very best friend. How haven't they found anything? It's disgusting! Someone isn't doing their job right if you ask me!" She growled, continuing to trudge through the woods blindly towards the clearing where a crooked well stood in its centre.

"She went missing in The Grove and hasn't been seen or heard of since. Someone must know something, but nobody's talking. Grown ups shield us from the outside world way too much. Of course we all know the ghost stories of Parliament Grove, but I'm not buying no Bird-Witch myth. There's no Magpa, its all complete bullshit to keep us out of here. We are children, but we're not stupid. They need to start treating us with respect and telling us the truth."

Her screen froze and the dreaded buffering wheel reared its

ugly head, it was then she noticed her battery had ticked down considerably and she was almost running on empty.

"Oh shit, my battery!" She groaned as the feed came back with shocked face emoji's warning her about something, comments asking her what was behind her and then the feed died, leaving only one percent of battery left.

She looked around her but in the dim light she saw nothing, she flicked on the flashlight again and twirled it around in the air, the energy seeping rapidly from its once bright beam.

It caught the reflection of a hundred black eyes shining in the darkness.

There was a strange sound coming from behind her and a breeze swirled around her as if something large had flown down and landed behind her, kicking up leaves from the ground and swirling them around her. She turned slowly as her flashlight died, leaving only the subtlest glow of the phone screen that depicted the photograph of her and her missing friend. The insufficient lighting picked out something standing hunched over her a short distance away. Feathers flickered wildly consuming her, clawed feet gripped the moist soil and a chattering sound caused her cold muscles to shudder uncontrollably. The glimmer of a slick black beak caught her eye and she focused on two eyes that looked human, rolling to display marbled whites as the beak opened wide and a shriek from the creature froze her where she stood as her battery died and there was only darkness.

XIV

Jimmy's cellphone chimed annoyingly as his morning alarm filled the room with its random din. The handset vibrated so widely as it skittered across the bedside table that it collided with his half empty mug of cold cocoa causing the ceramic to sing loudly. It continued to sing and quiver towards the edge of the bedside table, past a dirty ashtray, a half empty packet of Freedbird's and a pewter cigarette lighter. Jimmy stirred underneath the thick comforter that was decorated with summer flowers, a groan escaped from the confines of the duvet and a hand escaped from a dark crevice, searching the bedside table, clambering across the surface like a blind spider as he searched for the blurting handset. The cellphone worked its way to the edge as if it was about to fling itself off like some suicidal lemming, but finally Jimmy's hand fell upon it and blindly tapped around on the screen until somehow he found the right spot ending the alarm. Jimmy sighed with relief and then groaned, it was the groaning of a man who had had too much to drink.

"Oh God my head!" He growled and he emerged from the comforter, his hair in disarray and his eyes thick with sleep. His throat felt like he had swallowed cotton wool and he reached again towards the bedside table where he found the mug and swigged from it, immediately wishing he hadn't and let out a loud retching sound. Cold, leftover cocoa that has been sitting all night was not the cure for cottonmouth and hangovers.

"You never called me," Came a voice which caused Jimmy to bolt upright in the bed, rattling the headboard against the wall with reckless abandon.

"JESUS!" Jimmy gasped as he saw Denny sitting on a chair in the corner of the room watching him patiently.

"What the..." was all that Jimmy could manage, as thoughts started to spiral in his head about what could have happened while he had been passed out in a room with this looney toon.

"I said, you never called me."

"I...I..."

"I left you my number and you never called."

Denny sat poker straight in the chair, his raincoat draped over his knees. His hair was damp with no real style to it, but it was in-need of a shampoo and a cut that was for sure.

He stared at Jimmy, who was still trying to come to terms what was going on, rising from sleep and finding a stranger in your room was unsettling to say the least.

"I said you never called, Mr. Johnson!" Denny said with a touch of annoyance in his tone, he folded his arms around his meagre torso, his physique made up of more bone than flesh as if he was suffering seriously from malnutrition. His bare arms were riddled with various scars and scabs, some quite fresh, others very old, but all of them screamed self harm and needle marks.

Jimmy found that the sight of his deformed flesh very alarming and even though he tried, he could not tear his gaze away, so much so that he was staring at the wounds, without even trying to answer Denny's questions.

"Mr. Johnson!" Denny snapped and it was enough to focus Jimmy.

"Denny..." Jimmy said, finally making eye contact.

"Oh, so you know my name?" Denny smirked.

"I...I got very drunk with Chief Gable last night and I..."

"That's about all that old walrus is good for, getting drunk!" Denny scoffed, "He should be out there finding those missing kids, instead of propping up bars and chasing widows."

"I'm sure he is doing all he can." Jimmy fired back, feeling like he had to protect The Chief's good name.

"I'm sure he has!" Denny smiled sarcastically, "If ignoring the words of reliable sources and eyewitnesses is 'doing all he can!', then he's doing a stellar job."

"Eyewitness?"

"Ms. Kratz."

"Oh, but..."

"You think she's a nutty old broad, don't ya?" Said Denny, again interrupting Jimmy before he had a chance to finish his sentence. "Just because you've been told things, doesn't make it gospel. You haven't even spoken to her yourself yet, so you shouldn't judge until you have questioned her yourself, isn't that what a good detective does?"

Jimmy could hear his father's voice reverberating around his head, saying the same thing.

Denny was right.

A good detective should not listen to hearsay, he should always explore every avenue and make his or her own mind up when they have all the facts.

"No, I haven't." Jimmy shook his head, "She was my next port of call."

"Good!" Denny smiled, "Straight from the horses mouth."

"Wait, how did you know that I haven't questioned her yet."

Denny smiled.

"I've been keeping an eye on you that's why. Been watching your every move since you arrived."

That sent a shiver down Jimmy's spine and he instinctively pulled his bed clothes towards his chest.

"That's comforting!" Jimmy said trying to smile and hide the fact that this guy made his skin crawl.

"Isn't it just."

"And I take it you are the reliable source?"

"Indeed!" Denny smiled proudly, "Maybe we could talk now and I will tell you everything you need to know and why the authorities won't find the children. They don't know where to look."

"Well, I don't think I'm dressed appropriately for such a discussion." He said releasing the bedclothes and showing a bare torso.

"Maybe after breakfast?" Denny said rising from the chair, leaving behind a wet imprint in the cushion.

"Wait, what did you mean by 'they don't know where to look'? What do you know Denny?"

"Everything!" He sighed, heading for the door, "That's the problem, I know everything."

"Wait!" Jimmy cried, scrambling from the sheets in his underwear and grabbing his pants, frantically pulling them on.

"We can talk now! I need to know..."

There was a knock at the door and Bertha burst in, shrieking at the sight of Denny standing in front of her wringing his wet raincoat in his hands, a puddle forming on the exposed floorboards.

"Denny Lamont!" She growled, "What in tarnation's are you doing in here?"

"I'm just leaving, Bertha." He said and walked past her, slipping on his raincoat.

She gazed at Jimmy sliding into his pants and blushed.

"Oh, lord have mercy!" She whispered, crossing her chest.

"It's not what it looks like, Ms. Colley!" Jimmy cried, understanding how sordid the scene would look to her.

She wore a mask of disgust as if she could vomit at any time.

"Call me when you want to know the facts, Mr. Johnson." Denny said as he left.

"Get outta here, Denny!" Bertha cried, whipping at him with her dishtowel, "Get now, get!"

Jimmy approached her, sliding on his crumpled shirt and trying to button it.

"Ms. Colley, it's really not what it looked, like." He

pleaded with her to believe him, "I woke up and there he was. I don't even know how long he had been here for."

She smiled, her eyes announced to the world that she believed him.

"It's not the first time it's happened." She sighed.

"It's not?" He gasped, buttoning his shirt blindly and making a complete mess of it.

"I always thought it was a drug thing when he came in here, dealing whatever it is he takes. I've thrown many a paying customer out on their ear for their dealings with Denny Lamont."

"Maybe you made a mistake." Jimmy grimaced, not wanting to come across as condescending, "I think he just wanted someone to listen to him."

She frowned at him, her cogs turning with this information as if she had only ever thought there could be one reason he was here.

"I don't even think he's a drug addict if I'm honest with you." Jimmy said trying to tuck his shirt in his pants, buttons all out of sink.

"Poppycock!" She smiled, "Get that shirt off and let me run the iron over it for you."

"Oh, thank you kindly, Ms. Colley!"

He pulled it off over his head and handed it to her, she took it and left the room, calling back over her shoulder.

"Now, come down to the kitchen and I'll make you some pancakes."

Jimmy stood half dressed in the middle of the room, rubbing at his temples, thinking what a crazy start to a day this was.

XV

Jimmy enthusiastically tucked into a thick stack of pancakes, that were sodden by a thick smothering of maple syrup. He ate eagerly, syrup dripping down his chin as he sat in his pants and a white vest. He devoured the pancakes greedily, making this particular scene look like one taken from a wildlife programme, life on a farm perhaps and this was the section on pigs. Jimmy had found that he was always very hungry after a night of heavy drinking, although he didn't tend to take part in these sessions very often, a hefty breakfast was always the best cure for a hangover.

"How're you liking those pancakes, Mr. Johnson?" Bertha asked from the other side of the kitchen.

She stood behind an ironing board as she skimmed the hot plate across the sleeve of Jimmy's cream shirt. He turned nodding eagerly, his mouth so full with chewed up pancake and syrup that it was impossible to answer her. She smiled as she became engulfed in a cloud of hot steam.

"No better way to start the day than a big stack o' pancakes!" She chuckled, her heavy bosom and stomach quivering behind her floral pinafore. She slapped her stomach with her free hand and announced proudly, "I'm a testament to that."

Jimmy smiled awkwardly at her.

"We are what we eat." She said, "Food is there to enjoy. I'm not living like no nun, no Sir. No diets for me, I like my food. Enjoy it I say! Now eat up those pancakes you lightweight."

He chewed up and swallowed what was in his mouth and he could finally speak.

"Too true, Ms. Colley."

"I've told you to call me Bertha."

"Only if you call me Jimmy?"

"Deal!" She laughed and the pair smiled at each other.

Jimmy thought he could stay here forever and Bertha loved having someone to look after, whether she was getting paid for it or not. She had a mother's instinct, but sadly had never had children, so in many ways those that stopped with her during their time in Hope Springs were her children and boy did she spoil them.

Jimmy looked around the farmhouse style kitchen, it was very homely and for the first time in forever he saw luscious sunlight breaking through the kitchen window, the back door was even open to let in the warm breeze.

"Rapid change in the weather today." Jimmy said.

"They call it an Indian Summer I believe, makes a change around here." She sniffed, "Make the most of it, probably rain again tomorrow."

He smiled and nodded, believing that she was probably right.

As Bertha finished up ironing his shirt Jimmy found himself gazing out through the open back door, a square of bright green grass lay before him and a magpie landed on it, which caused an immediate flicker of anxiety to scuttle across chest. It stared at him and squawking aggressively before pecking around in the earth in search of worms.

"There are an awful lot of magpies around here." He said absently, still staring at the bird that was going about its business of breakfast.

"There sure are." She replied, shuffling over towards him, holding aloft a freshly pressed shirt in her hands.

"Seems strange to see one alone, after seeing so many." He laughed, but Bertha didn't answer, she just stood behind him watching the magpie.

"One for Sorrow!" Jimmy added.

"They're never alone, Jimmy." She murmured, "You be careful of those creatures, they never bring anything but misery with them."

Jimmy turned to her, but she continued to gaze at the magpie, almost as if she had been caught in a trance. He gazed into her eyes and it was fear that he saw, fear held her gaze, not the fascination of one of God's creatures in its natural habitat, but fear.

"Nope, they're never alone." She said again as another magpie joined the search for breakfast, "I've watched them you know."

She spoke as if her mind were miles away, the tone in her voice was no longer jolly, it was more of a whisper now as she continued.

"Military precision."

"Sorry?"

"Those magpies, they act with military precision. Never alone, never scavenging like you'd think, but hunting."

"Hunting?"

"Hunting the weak, that's what they do! They prey on the weak and feeble, bully them into submission. Safety in numbers like they were some street gang in the big city."

Jimmy had never heard this as a trait of magpie behaviour before, but in fairness he had never really been around them to study their antics. There weren't too many magpies around in Studd City.

"Maybe they're after your family jewels, Bertha." He joked, "Better make sure your jewellery box is locked up good and tight."

"That's a misconception, Jimmy!"

"What is?"

"That they are attracted to shiny things."

"It is?"

"Yes, Sir!" She sniffed, tightening her grip on his shirt, creasing it all over again, "It's power and control that these harpies crave, not trinkets. Don't get me wrong, I wouldn't put it past these little bastards to take you for everything that you've got, but they would sooner peck your eyes out and eat your brain than steal your cufflinks."

"I never knew they were so malice."

"Malice is the word." She suddenly snapped out of her musing and looked at the shirt, "Oh, would you look at that! Going to have to run the iron over it again now."

"Don't worry, it's fine." Jimmy insisted standing and

reaching for it.

"No, no! I won't hear of it!" She said as she waddled back towards the ironing board.

"You really don't have to do that."

"No, I insist." She said spitting on the iron's plate and watching it fizz on the incredible heat.

"So, how come you know so much about magpies?" Jimmy asked.

"There's a lot I know about Hope Springs, Jimmy."

"Really? Do tell."

"If I did, it would curl your toes and you'd probably soil your pants."

Jimmy was about to probe further when the magpies exploded into the air with a righteous cry and Chief Gable appeared in the doorway.

"Morning Chief!" Bertha called cheerily, "Can I get you some pancakes?"

"No time, Bertha." Chief snapped, his brow was thick with sweat and his eyes overflowing with worry.

"What's wrong, Chief?" Jimmy asked.

"We've got ourselves another missing girl." He choked.

"Oh, God help us!" Bertha gasped and crossed her chest.

"Who?" Jimmy probed.

"Lucy Knight."

"Isn't she the best friend of..." Jimmy started but The Chief finished his sentence for him.

"Abigail Jones!" He nodded, "We're putting together a

search party, thought you might want to be involved."

"Of course!" Jimmy said grabbing his shirt from the ironing board and quickly slipping it on. Instinctively he grabbed his raincoat that was draped over the back of his chair.

"You won't need that!" Berth cried, "It's glorious out there."

"You never know!" Jimmy said as the pair left abruptly, before calling back over his shoulder. "Thanks for breakfast, Bertha."

She stood there holding the fizzing iron in her hand and sighed a heavy sigh, her face drooping with sorrow.

"Lord have mercy on that child." She whispered as the magpies returned to the grass and stared at her eerily. "Don't let that bitch have her."

XVI

Droves of Hope Springs residents shuffled through the sodden undergrowth, rain and wind accosting them, causing them to cower from its unrelenting attack of bitterness. Raincoats draped around the dozens of hooded figures that hunched over in feeble attempts to shield themselves from the elements, as they search for the latest child to go missing in Parliament Grove.

The troop had discovered Lucy's bicycle idly lent up against the Flyer Tree and that was enough to send Donald Knight into a fit of hysterics, but it was also enough to stoke the fires within him and he had bounded onwards to lead the search. He was way ahead of the others, frantically calling his daughter's name as his tears became lost with the raindrops that cascaded down his face.

Two figures moved slower than all the others, both wearing the hooded waterproof poncho's of the Hope Springs Police Department. They took their time to investigate every broken branch and ever trodden leaf, meticulously examining their surroundings for any sign of the missing child. One of the figures crouched on the dirt path that was now a stream of muddy water, his fine leather shoes completely submerged and ruined, this type of footwear was never meant be worn in such conditions. He ran his fingers over what appeared to be the remains of half a footprint, the tread of a wellington boot sole perhaps.

"Got part of a track here, Chief." Jimmy called, he had to raise his voice to be heard over the torrential rain that refused to stop. The other shrouded figure turned to reveal Chief Gable and he approached quickly, crouching down to meet him.

"What have you got Jimmy?"

"Looks like a partial print from a child's wellington boot, wouldn't you say?"

"Could well be." Gable sniffed, his moustache quivering from side to side to flick away the drops of rain that had settled upon it.

"At least we know were on the right track." Jimmy smiled.

"I think we all know where it will lead us." Gable sighed, "But you never know." He rose slowly, his knees crunching, he greeted this discomfort with a grimace and a groan.

"You okay, Chief?" Jimmy asked rising with speed without the obstruction of nagging joints.

"Just my arthritis Son," He groaned, "it has a love hate relationship with this weather. My knees hate this weather and the weather loves making them suffer."

"Is it raining?" Jimmy smirked, "I hadn't noticed."

"Cute, kid, real cute." Chief Gable smirked.

They both gazed around the woods, a spectrum of drenched raincoats floated past as far as the eye could see, like different coloured spectres haunting the vicinity.

"Why do you waste your time Chief?" Jimmy asked.

"What do you mean?"

"With the search, if you know we will end up at that clearing."

"I have to do it by the book. I owe the parents that much."

Their gaze drifted over to Donald Knight trudging off ahead, his voice hoarse from calling his daughter's name and gargling on his own tears.

"I have to give them hope." Gable sighed, "Even..." He stopped and got a little choked, before trying again and failing, "...even if..."

"There isn't any." Jimmy finished his sentence for him.

The Chief nodded, solemnly before wiping the rain away from his face with a sodden handkerchief.

"C'mon, let them search, we will head to the clearing."

As they walked towards the centre of Parliament Grove, Jimmy plucked up the courage to ask The Chief a question, one that might end their friendship there and then. His words could be cast aside and he could be seen as yet another Hope Springs fruitcake.

"I think this Bird-Witch is real."

Gable glanced at him with wary eyes and continued to trudge through the mud and foliage.

"Did you hear me Chief?"

"Yeah, I heard ya."

"And?"

"And what?"

"You think I'm nuts, don't you?"

"Just like everybody else in this neck of the woods. It's nothing new to me."

"I don't mean it's real in a physical sense. I've not completely lost it. I don't for one second believe there is a feathered hag roaming the woods in search of children's flesh."

"I'm glad to hear it." Gable chuckled, but there was very little humour in the sound.

"But..."

"I hate that word." Gable scoffed, "There's always a but!"

"But!" Jimmy grinned, "Could there be someone parading around The Grove, disguised as this creature, giving the illusion of the Bird-Witch's existence."

"It's possible." Gable replied, "But there's never been any evidence that could point us in that direction."

"Denny Lamont and Rhonda Kratz?"

"Yeah," Chief sighed, "apart from the usual suspects."

"So they could be telling you the truth."

"I'd rather not think like that." Chief Gable snapped and quickened his pace as if to put distance between himself and Jimmy's words.

"Why not?" Jimmy called after him, but The Chief did not reply.

Jimmy hurried after him, "Why not?" He called again and grabbed at the Chief's poncho. Gable swivelled on the spot and for the first time Jimmy saw anger in The Chief's face.

"GOD DAMN YOU!" Gable growled, "Damn you and your fucking questions!"

"All I wanted was an answer."

"That's just what we all want, Jimmy! Answers!"

"Then why don't you believe their words? It could have..."

"Saved some lives? Is that what you were going to say?"

"Yeah!" Jimmy nodded.

"Well, that is exactly why I can't bring myself to believe their words, for if I did it would mean that I've failed. Failed as a police Chief, failed in my duty, failed as a man!" His eyes welled with tears as he turned away from Jimmy and looked up to the grey sky, allowing the rain to pelt his face. It was unclear to Jimmy whether the Chief of Hope Springs Police Department was actually crying at that moment, if he was the rain helped mask it.

"You're not a failure, Chief."

"No, I don't think I am." He sniffed, "But if I was to believe their words then I damn well would be one. I would have failed this whole community. If I believe their words there would be no coming back for me."

The pair stood in the rain alone, all the other members of the search party had spread out to the far corners of Parliament Grove, only the distant rumbling of Donald Knight's voice could be heard.

"Chief..."

Jimmy tried to talk but he was cut off.

"We're here!" Gable snapped.

The pair stood on the edge of the clearing and gazed around at their dank surroundings. The surrounding trees were filled with the dark wings of a horde of magpies, beady black eyes glistening in the damp atmosphere.

Just being there again made Jimmy feel queasy, an uneasy feeling that gripped his guts and churned them into mush, pleading with him to relieve himself of such a burden. There was no way he was going to vomit in front of The Chief.

They moved forward and silently inspected the area, with every step they found themselves closer to the well.

"I've lost count how many people have gone missing in this town since I've been Chief of police." Gable started, "In the matter of four weeks, Abigail Jones, Lucy Knight, possibly two federal agents, even though I've heard nothing back from my connections at the FBI and CIA, they don't appear to be missing any agents or have any recollection of sending any out this way." Gable pondered this for a moment, before continuing again. "And just last night I heard that two high school seniors have now gone missing. It's unknown whether they are connected to Parliament Grove or have simply ran away together."

"What's that?" Jimmy interrupted pointing to a broken wicker basket and a shredded piece of material.

"Looks like the remains of a picnic." The Chief said kneeling down next to Jimmy to investigate further.

Jimmy used a stick to dig through the remains of mud covered piece of material and two large letters were unveiled.

"H and S." Jimmy said thinking out loud.

"Hope Springs High." The Chief added, as Jimmy dug the stick under it and pulled out a dirty, sodden letterman jacket.

"Looks like those seniors are connected, Chief."

The Chief just sighed and rose, turning away from the scene, mumbled curses seeping out from underneath his thick moustache. He gazed up at the mass of darkness in the trees, and scowled at a hundred twinkling eyes judging him.

"Stop it!" He growled, "STOP FUCKING JUDGING ME!" He cried and scooped up a rock from the mud and hurled it into the Parliament of Magpies. The rock seemed to be absorbed by the birds because they did not move as if they were acting as a shield, protecting something within. They cackled back at him, mocking him.

"Bastards!" He seethed as he turned to see Jimmy leaning over the well.

"Be careful there Jimmy!" The Chief cried, grabbing him by the poncho and pulling him away, as he did some of the rocks came loose and fell into its maw.

"A little boy fell down there some years back. Magpies pecked his bones clean."

"Jesus!" Jimmy gasped, almost vomiting from the visual that the Chief had put in his mind and the fact that he may have been joining those falling rocks if it hadn't have been for him.

"Have you checked the well?" Jimmy said, his eyes wide as if he had just discovered the answer to everything.

"Of course we have!" Gable scoffed, his words were

joined by a rolling off his eyeballs.

"Oh!" Jimmy sighed dejected, "I just thought maybe, whoever is taking these kids…well, that's where they might be."

"First place I checked." The Chief smiled, and patted him on the shoulder, Jimmy liked that, the old Chief was back and it reminded him of his father.

"So which unlucky so and so had the misfortune of going down there?" Jimmy asked.

"Oh, nobody's been down there, God no!"

"Oh?"

"The well is far to unstable for that, I'm not sure it would take the weight and I can't risk the health and safety of my team."

"But what about the remains of boy that the magpies devoured?"

"This was back in the eighties." The Chief chuckled, "Way before I took the helm. All I was doing back then was routine questioning, I wasn't important enough to be given such an important task."

"Oh I see."

"It was Deputy Windwood who volunteered or who had drawn the short straw. Health and safety wasn't an issue back then, not like it is today. No, the powers that be deem it safer to use the marvels of today's technology."

"But you have checked the well?"

"Yeah, we've used lights, drones and cameras, you name it. But, there's nothing down there apart from an old bird nest. Goddamn magpies no doubt."

Jimmy leaned over again, removing his cell phone from his pocket, bringing the flashlight function to life and shining it down into the shaft.

"Here let me help." The Chief said and he slid his flashlight out from the loop that hung from his belt and shone it down into the well. The two beams of light duelled for a moment and then become one, helping to illuminate the bottom of the well.

Jimmy sighed, "I really thought…"

"I know, Son, I know."

They waited for a few moments just staring into the well as if any moment Lucy Knight or Abigail Jones would appear and the mystery would be solved and they could all go home safe and sound, the whole ordeal over.

"C'mon," The Chief said extinguishing his light, "we've done all we can out here this morning, let's head back to the rendezvous and regroup."

The Chief walked away from the clearing, leaving Jimmy to gaze from the well to the mass of glaring magpies again, before he started to follow the Chief.

Gable spoke loudly into his radio calling off the search for the day. There was a crackling sound as a broken voice erupted from the radio in response, agreeing with the Chief's sentiments that the weather was too much to contend with.

"I know Donald doesn't want to leave and I understand that!" Growled Chief Gable into the radio, "But, we've got to regroup and get some refreshments."

There was another broken response, informing the Chief that it wasn't going to be easy.

"Goddamn it Darryl, just get him to Elmer's!" He snapped.

Jimmy trod on an uneven mound of mud, almost turning his ankle and as he fell forward he instantly put his hands down to break his fall, he recoiled immediately with pain as something sharp sank into the palm of his hand.

"What the..." He hissed and looked at his muddy palm, a small hole seeped with blood. He looked past his hand to see who the culprit was and saw something shining brightly. He reached down and retrieved it, turning it in his hand. It was a badge pin, almost identical to the one he had found the last time he had ventured to the clearing in Parliament Grove. Only this one did not have a bird of prey etched on it but a small bird, like a robin or a wren. He wiped away the mud from it to look at it more closely, clicking his tongue against the backs of his teeth before retrieving the other pin from his pocket, he gazed at them both, intrigue flickering in his eyes until the Chief called him bringing an end to his musing.

Jimmy slid both pins into his inside pocket.

"Everything all right, Jimmy? You okay down there?"

"Yeah, I'm just coming!" He called and pulled himself out of the mud and joined Chief Gable.

As Jimmy caught up with the Chief he could hear him growling at his Deputy on the other side of his radio.

"Goddamn it Darryl! That's all I need right now!"

Jimmy could see that he looked troubled.

"Goddamn it!" Gable groaned again, attaching his radio

back into place on his belt.

"What is it Chief?"

"Crazy Kratz! That's who! The office just informed me that she has insisted on seeing me and it's urgent."

"What's it about?"

"Apparently a missing cat!" Gable rubbed at his temples.

"A missing cat?" Jimmy chuckled.

"Don't Jimmy." Gable started to chuckle too.

"What are you? The Chief of Police or a veterinarian!" They both started to chuckle as they made their way back towards the way they had come.

"Look, you have a hell of a lot of shit going on right now." Said Jimmy.

"Well, that's the understatement of the year."

"Let me take some of the burden off your shoulders."

"What do you mean?"

"Let me pay Ms. Kratz a visit."

"I don't know..."

"You said it yourself it's about a missing cat! She only wants someone to listen to her. I can do that. Plus it will give me a chance to ask her some questions of my own."

"Okay, knock yourself out."

"Give me a lift back to town though so I can grab a change of clothes then I'll drive up in Olive."

"You've got a deal, Son!" Gable smiled, "Oh, a word of warning."

"Oh, now there's a warning?" Jimmy laughed.

"Don't eat the cookies."

XVII

The rain continued to fall as Jimmy Johnson, Jr., sat upon Rhonda Kratz's tired old sofa, surrounded by cats, all of them vying for his attentions as he awkwardly held a cup and saucer filled to the brim with hot tea. He sat poker straight, his body rigid and terrified of moving in case he spilled it. Each movement of a cats tail sent him on edge as if they were competing with each other to knock the crockery from his grasp.

"And you're working together with Chief Gable on these missing children cases?" Called Rhonda Kratz from the kitchen.

"Yeah, pretty much." He called back, pushing away cats with his elbows.

"Pretty much?" She queried, "What is that supposed to mean?"

"Well, I was contacted by Rachel Jones about finding her daughter, Abigail, and well, there have been a few more disappearances occur since."

"Won't be the last either." She sniffed matter of factly as she entered from the kitchen with a plate of freshly baked chocolate chip cookies. She placed them on the table in front of Jimmy and fell into her recliner.

Jimmy found himself staring at the cookies, they looked

perfectly baked, with big chunks of chocolate protruding out from them. They looked very appetising indeed, but Chief Gable's words of warning whispered to him. He turned to Ms. Kratz and smiled.

"While I am here I wanted to ask you about the disappearance."

"Ha, which one?" She laughed, then her brow furrowing as if she was agitated by something, "Are you not going to try a cookie, Mr. Johnson?"

"Oh! I erm..." He gulped, his face blushing with embarrassment, "I didn't like to take one without asking."

"Nonsense!" She scoffed, "That's what they're there for!"

"They look delightful." He smiled, slowly taking one from the plate and holding it in one hand while balancing the overflowing cup and saucer in the other. She stared at him and he realised that if he didn't have a bite of one of these cookies he would not hear the end of it.

"Go on! It won't poison you." Ms. Kratz said as he slowly brought the cookie up to his lips and took a nibble. His eyebrows climbed up his forehead in astonishment at how good they tasted and promptly took another bite, chewing it eagerly.

"Oh, Ms. Kratz, this is a wonderful cookie!" He exclaimed.

"Of course!" She snapped, almost offended by there being any doubt, "I'm not in the habit of serving shit to my guests you know!"

Jimmy gulped down the cookie and balanced it on his saucer

while he took a sip of tea to help wash down any crumbs of that had clung to the back of his throat.

"Now, I though you'd come about my cat?"

"I have, but I hear that you are the eyes and the ears of Hope Springs and I wanted to pick your brain."

"Ha!" She laughed loudly, slapping her large thigh, that sounded like a gunshot, causing most of the cats to disperse, apart from Tigger who curled up on his lap and Bonnie who plonked her huge bulk on the headrest of the sofa, its thick white tail flicking at his face annoyingly.

"I bet that's not all they say about me." She sneered, "Eyes and ears is a new one though."

"I've heard nothing but good things." Jimmy lied, grinning widely, falsely.

"Oooh, if you continue on this route Mr. Johnson, you will have my eye out with that growing nose of yours."
He stared at her, the stupid grin remained on his face. He took another bite of the cookie, just so he didn't have to meet her gaze.

"I don't care what they have to say about me anyhow!" She announced proudly, "I know what I see out here. I know what goes on. Even if everyone else around here refuses to see the truth."

"And what is the truth, Ms. Kratz?"

"The truth being that the Magpa comes for them, that's the truth."

"The Magpa!" He smirked.

"Yep!" She said, leaning forward and grabbing a cookie,

stuffing it into her mouth and devouring it instantly, "I thought they would have at least filled you in with tales of the old witch."

"A Bird-Witch, has been mentioned, but not a name."

"Well, it... I guess, SHE is more like it, but yep, Magpa is her name, on account of all the magpies that surround her."

"The magpies?"

"Don't tell me you haven't seen them either? For a private detective you don't seem very observant."

"No, I have seen the magpies. So they would be Magpa's..."

"Disciples I reckon. Worship her they do. In their best interests to I guess."

"How's that?"

"Well, they get the leftovers don't they."

That sent a shiver down Jimmy's spine and he bit into the cookie, enjoying the flavour so much that he finished the remaining piece gripped between his thumb and index fingers.

"Have you seen this Magpa?"

"Of course I have! Well, not up close and personal you'll understand, but yep, I've seen her all right." She snapped, "She's in there you know, in The Grove, probably watching us right now."

Jimmy swallowed nervously and turned to the window, but he couldn't see through the dirty nets that hung in the way.

"Yep, she's probably very interested in you, Mr. Johnson."

"Really?" He stuttered, the crockery shaking in his grip

as he lifted into take another sip.

"Oh yes, no doubt, fresh meat aren't ya." She cackled, "Besides she is always curious about those that get away."

"Get away?"

"You don't have to try and fool me, Mr. Johnson. I saw you just last night, when you'd gone to investigate The Grove."

"You did?"

"White as a sheet you were."

He stared at her lost for words.

"That's it!" She chuckled, "That's exactly how you looked last night. I guess I am the eyes and ears around here."

"Yeah, I guess you are."

"Have another cookie!" She offered, leaning back into her recliner. Jimmy did as he was told and found himself tucking into another cookie.

"You saw her then didn't you?" She asked, "Up close, like, what did she look like?"

"I..." He thought for moment, should he lie and say he didn't see anything? But where would that get him? What was the point of lying about it when they both know that this creature was real! He thought how best to describe what he had witnessed and he couldn't.

"...I saw her but I couldn't even try to explain what she was."

"Sounds about right."

He took another bite of cookie and an odd smell caressed his nostrils, but he thought nothing of it because there were a lot of strange smells floating around in Ms. Kratz's lounge.

"What can we do? How can we stop it?" Jimmy asked.

"Damned if I know, Mr. Johnson." She shook her head, "It goes quiet from time to time and just when you're lulled into a false sense of security, it starts happening all over again. Unfortunately I don't have any more answers for you."

The sound of magpies cawing outside interrupted their conversation and they both instinctively looked towards the window.

"It'll continue I guess until someone finds out where she nests."

"Nests?" Jimmy whispered to himself, the usual clicking of his tongue replaced by the sound of cookie being crunched.

"Yeah, like all those old Dracula movies. They always got him in his coffin when he was sleeping. I guess if you wanna kill this thing you've gotta find the nest."

The realisation of where Magpa's nest might be, dawned on him and his face brightened.

"Unless that happens Hope Springs will continue loosing its children and its cats!"

"Ms. Kratz you're a genius."

"Well!" She blushed, "I wouldn't be saying that."

Jimmy smiled and he eagerly chewed the last of his cookie, grimacing a little as a tough bit of chocolate that he had to bitten down seemed difficult to devour.

"Oh dear!" She sighed leaning forward and gazing at the plate of cookies.

"Something the matter?"

"It appears that one of my little beauties as gone and done their business on the cookies."

Jimmy's face soured as he swallowed the last piece he would ever eat in the Kratz residence. Immediately it felt like it wanted to return but Jimmy denied it and instead gazed at the cookies. Sure enough with closer inspection there were some suspicious looking droplets scattered on the tops of several cookies. He took another sip of tea as other cats rejoined him on the sofa as if to pen him in.

"Oh, it won't hurt you none." She laughed, waving away the ordeal with swipe of her hand.

"Cats!" Jimmy sneered.

"Oh yes, now we can get down to the reason you are here!"

"Oh yeah, your missing cat!" Jimmy grimaced, eyeballing the surrounding needy felines hoping that the culprit would give themselves away and he could empty the remains of his cup on its head.

"Missing?" She scoffed, "No, my cat ain't missing."

"Sorry?" Jimmy said confusion etched on his face, "But I was told this was about a missing cat."

"No not missing! I have the cat right here. I just want to know what you're going to do about it."

"About what?"

Ms. Kratz leaned over the side of her recliner and Jimmy could hear her rustling around in what sounded like a plastic bag.

"This!" She suddenly announced unveiling the dead torso of her ginger tomcat Norris. She stood holding it aloft by its furry tail, most of the fur and flesh had be torn away leaving behind the jangling collection of bloodstained bones.

"I'm gonna be sick!" Jimmy announced leaping from his seat, letting go of the cup and saucer and dropping the remains all over himself as he backed away towards the front door.

"Well?" Ms. Kratz called, holding out the dead cat towards him and shaking it vigorously, "I want to know what you're gonna do about this?"

"I...I..." Jimmy stuttered as he found the front door and burst through out into the rain, but he didn't care, he was used to the rain now and he ran down the crooked pathway and leapt over the broken gate at its end. Jimmy ran towards his dishevelled Volkswagen and climbed inside slamming the door behind him as he tried to control his breathing. He tried not to laugh, he tried not to cry, he tried not to vomit after all the absurdity of it all.

"Nutty as a fruit cake!" He announced as he reversed away from the cottage and turning into the dirt road by the flyer tree and that's when the car's engine stalled.

"Oh, you have to be kidding me!" He groaned, frantically turning the key again and again, "Not here Olive! Not know!"

The engine coughed and gave up.

"Too much rain must have messed with the engine." He sighed.

A Magpie landed on the hood of the car. Its dark eyes twinkled at Jimmy through the windshield, staring straight at him. It was soon joined by another and another and more and more until the hood of his car was consumed by them. He struggled to see just how many of them there had gathered, there was no way of knowing. The dark feathers made it appear quite dark in the car, blocking out the light.

"Get out the way fuckers, I haven't got time for this." Jimmy seethed and banged on the windshield with his fist, they cawed in defiance, the sound of their voices was horrendous. His hollering and thumping did not faze the magpies, they didn't move a muscle. He tried again, but nothing, he beat the glass rapidly, creating a tedious, dull cacophony. Still it had no affect on them and then one of them started pecking at the windshield, rapidly, relentlessly and then the others joined in.

The sound was atrocious and it made Jimmy want to jam his fingers into his earholes just to stop it. The glass started to crack and the end of beaks started to protrude through the windshield. He tried to open the driver's side door and was met by a dozen magpies throwing themselves up against the glass in a frenzy, so slammed it shut. He scrambled over to the passenger seat and was about to try to open it but the same thing happened again forcing him to fall back in-between the two front seats. He opened the glovebox and removed a Smith & Wesson Model 36 revolver, it had belonged to his father, a gift for him when he graduated from the police academy.

He held it tightly in his grip, pointing it at the windshield and then at the side windows. The pecking and cracking of glass continued, it was maddening, until suddenly it stopped and there was nothing but the sound of rain falling constantly on the roof. Jimmy's breaths were heavy for a time until he felt more relaxed, but as he adjusted to move towards the door again he heard something land on the roof, something big.

Heavy foot falls caused indentations on the weak metal of the roof and something scratched at it, a hideous sound like tapered fingers on a chalkboard. The gun quivered in his clammy hands and he froze, he had never been so scared in all his life, even with everything he had ever had to deal with during his time in the police, nothing had made him feel like this. The scratching sounded as if whatever was on the roof was trying to carve open and entrance to the dilapidated vehicle and it made Jimmy's blood run cold. Even if he wanted to pull the trigger, he didn't think he could, he couldn't move and his index figure was so moist that it continued to slip from the trigger.

Suddenly the sound stopped and again there was only the rhythm of the rain drops to accompany the jittery thump of his heart.

Again he tried to move, but as he did whatever was sat perched on the roof burst into life and this time it seemed that it wasn't messing around. It hammered the roof the melody of a woodpecker paired with the fury of a jackhammer as something dented the roof above him. Jimmy instinctively slouched down away from these dents that were appearing in the roof and then what happened next made him vomit in his throat, as a huge black beak erupted through the metal, inches from his appalled face. Again and again this gigantic beak burst through the roof, carving through metal and tearing through the thin layer of upholstery that acted as a useless barrier between him and the attacker.

The attack seemed to spur the magpies on and they began pecking vigorously at the windshield once again and throwing themselves against the windows. Jimmy peered through one of the holes as something crooked and feathered passed by above him through a shroud of rain.

"Oh sweet Jesus!" Jimmy murmured as an eye met his gaze, the eye looked almost human, shining at him like a newly pressed coin.

"Magpa..." He whispered, there were no more words that he could utter, words had become lost in a shallow pool of vomit in the back of his throat.

Magpa's beak again hurtled down upon the roof and creating massive holes and then came sharp talons, trying to claw their way in and pull apart the twisted metal to get to Jimmy. Three claws worked away at the flimsy metal of the roof and finally Jimmy had been pushed into a place of panic that he could never return from and he screamed unloading the revolver everywhere at once. He unleashed the power of his Smith & Wesson, driving one bullet through the roof, impossible to know whether it did any damage to the Magpa. A second bullet hurtled through the windshield, shattering it and causing the magpies to disperse. Another tore through the roof and he heard the Magpa shriek, but he continued to release bullets, another through the roof and another through the passenger side window. The magpies all left and flew back to the safety of the trees.

Magpa shrieked again as Jimmy shuffled backwards towards the driver's door and lent on the car horn, as he did so it let out an audacious cry that caused the Magpa to shriek again wildly, it was then that he realised that the creature was not calling out in pain, but out of discomfort. Jimmy jammed his hand down on the horn again and her howling of agony was like joyful music to his ears.

He scrambled backwards and managed to open the door, almost diving out of the vehicle and spilling out onto the gravel and dirt. He clasped the revolver tightly in his hands and pointed it to the roof of the car as he made it to his feet, backing off down towards the main road into Hope Springs. The rain lashed down on him as he pointed the revolver at the dark figure on the roof. The creature was draped in its tattered feathers and then it stopped shrieking to rise up onto its grotesque clawed feet, human in status but severely crooked. Two wide wings where arms should be, spread and flapped as a claw reached out from her torso, skin like leather, pimpled with the flesh of a bird. He gazed at the Bird-Witch with wide eyes and an open jaw, but had no words for what stood before him.

A large beak hung down from her face, and beneath it he heard the chattering of teeth, then there were those eyes, those human looking eyes.

Jimmy screamed and pressed the trigger of the revolver relentlessly, but it was spent. As soon as Magpa new there was nothing left from the little man's contraption to hurt her tender ears, she adjusted herself and spread her wings wide shrieking at him viciously.

He screamed again and threw the gun at her before turning around and hightailing it back towards town. As he hurtled down the road, his damp shoes slapping on the asphalt and the tails of his raincoat flapping behind him he made sure of one thing and that was not to look back, not even once, because if he saw that she was in pursuit it would drain all the hope out of him that he had left.

"I fucking hate the rain!" He growled as he ran down the wet road back towards Hope Springs.

XVIII

Elmer's Diner was alive with commotion as droves of soaking wet members of the search party ploughed inside. Tired and dejected the Hope Springs locals stood around in sodden raincoats and ponchos, dirty puddles forming at their feet on the red and white checkerboard linoleum. The owner of the diner, Elmer Bass was an ageing man who was heavily scarred from the rigours of the Gulf war. Shrapnel in his hip had ended his military career early and he came home to Hope Springs where he opened up his own diner, but that was thirty years ago. He limped over to the door as quickly as he could and ushered people inside, offering them shelter from the torrential rain that lashed down outside. As they piled in, Elmer watched on as a river rolled down Main Street.

"Holy Moses!" He cried, "It's shitting it down out there! C'mon, now every one make room."

He looked on solemnly at the tired, wet faces of those that had taken part in the search, not one of those faces didn't look dejected.

"Please help yourself to hot drinks and pastries." He called to the new arrivals, hoping that it would help lift their morale.

Although this was by far the fullest that Elmer's Diner had ever been, he would not be making any money from those within.

Elmer had volunteered up his establishment to the needs of the community and it was free coffee's, tea's and pastries for all those involved in the search.

Rachel Jones stood behind a table of refreshments clad in her red waitress uniform and white apron, busily she poured hot drinks for the new arrivals. She smiled at them, a thankful smile to those that had been searching, they smiled back, but could not bring themselves to make eye contact with her as they had been through this same routine only a few weeks prior and they new that she was still trying to come to terms with a life without her own child.

Donald Knight, rocked back and forth on a chair surrounded by his close friends, a blanket wrapped around his shoulders, a polystyrene cup clasped in his hands, attempting to warm the ice cold tips of his fingers. He was inconsolable, his heart crushed, unbelieving that they had yet to discover any information on his missing daughter.

Chief Gable was the last to enter the diner and as soon as he did, all eyes were on him. He truly despised this part of the job, everybody always looked to him when there was difficult decisions to make. He got it, he knew that he was the senior authoritative figure in the town and it was up to him to guide them through hard times. It was difficult, sometimes very difficult, he understood that it came with the territory, but sometimes it was hard to be the candle in the darkness, when you were almost burnt down to the wick.

He removed his campaign hat, a layer of water flicked from it and splattered the floor, he removed his handkerchief and wiped away moisture from his face and his thick grey moustache.

His Deputy acknowledged his arrival with a tired smile, bright white ivories shining pleasantly as he quickly made his way to greet him with a steaming coffee in hand.

"Chief," said Deputy Whittaker as he approached, his dark skin glistening from the moisture of the rain, eyes dropped with fatigue, "I got you a coffee."

Gable waved it away.

"No thanks, Darryl." He said, "I have business to attend to before I do anything else."

"Oh, okay." Whittaker replied and looked at the hot steaming cup in his hand.

"You have it Darryl, you've earned it." Gable smiled.

"Thanks Chief." Whittaker sighed with relief, he was glad that he did not have to be so hard skinned as his Chief and sipped away at the cup heartily.

"Might have to keep an eye on Donald, Chief." Whittaker added leaning in closely and whispering the words in his Chief's shell-like.

"Oh yeah?"

"He was hysterical when we told him we were done with the search. Practically had to drag him outta The Grove."

Gable nodded and then Deputy Whittaker backed away to join the gathering of Hope Springs faithful's, as they waited with bated breath.

Had she been found? Was there any news or information on her whereabouts?

"Ladies and gentlemen, I would like to personally thank you all for your hard work and dedication during today's search."

"Did you find her, Chief?" Donald sniffed, "Tell me you found her please!"

Donald was coming to the end of his tether and needed to know one way or the other, if his daughter was dead, he needed closure.

"After a thorough search..." Chief Gable started, but was interrupted by some wisecrack.

"That means no!"

Gable eyeballed the one responsible and tried again.

"After a thorough search of the area that we believe Lucy went missing, we have unfortunately found no traces."

"Told ya!" Seethed the same voice.

Gable clenched his teeth together, he knew that it was always dangerous when getting so many people together in one room at one time, for it could lead to mutinous actions, usually one voice stirs the pot and things get blown out of proportion.

"We understand that this is not what any of you wish to hear, it's not what Donald wants to hear either. But, the weather has played a huge factor here, tracks have been covered up by rain and mud, but this is by no means the end of the search."

"Your damn right it's not!" Donald screamed and leapt from his chair, shaking with adrenaline, "I want to go back out there! I want to find my baby girl!"

"I know, Donald, I know." Gable sighed approaching

him, trying to calm him down, "But we have done all we can for one day. We will go out again tomorrow, I promise."
Gable placed a caring hand on Donald's quivering shoulder, but Donald brushed it aside.

"NO!" He shrieked hysterically, "I demand we go back out there now!"

"But..." Gable attempted but was cut off by Donald.

"I'm tired of listening to you! The rain has lifted now, I'm going back out there and you can't stop me. Donald raged as he brushed off his friends who were holding him back, his blanket fell from his shoulders and he launched his cup of coffee up against the wall. The thick black liquid, stained the white and red tiled wall and dripped down to meet the floor.

"Sit down, Donald." Gable asked quietly, but Donald approached him and shoved him, Gable hardly moved, he was much larger than Donald, but it looked like he didn't seem to care.

"I will not sit down!" Donald growled and prodded the Chief in his wide chest, "You have let us down again, Chief!" He spat with derision.
Gable's fingers clenched and he stared into Donald's crazed eyes that were burning with fury.

"Sit down, Donald." Gable tried again.

"NO!" He screamed and unleashed a slap that connected with the Chief's face. There were several gasps in the crowd and nobody seemed to move, frozen in a moment of surrealism, unbelieving of what had just taken place. Some of them watched on probably wanting to see the pair go at it, so they could film it with their camera phones and watch it go viral on social media.

"I'm sick to my back teeth of listening to your bullshit, Chief!" Donald spat, "We all are!" And with that he gestured to those surrounding the pair with arms out wide and spinning around on the moist linoleum. It was if Donald spoke for all of them, he did not of course.

"You continue to let us down again and again!" Donald continued his tirade, "You have continued to let Hope Springs down! How many children have gone missing under your watch?"

"Don't..." Chief murmured, his cheek stung, his pride was wounded and his muscles were tightening with every word that slithered from Donald's angry tongue. Chief Gable was a powder keg and Donald Knight had lit the fuse.

"You don't know do you?" Donald laughed hysterically, tears rolling down his cheeks, "You don't even know! This has been going on for way too long, we want answers! Answers that you can't seem to give us. WHERE THE FUCK ARE OUR KIDS!"

Rachel began to cry, the scabs of her own worry were still fresh. She had tried to stay strong and put a brave face on in front of the Hope Springs community, but the pain came flooding out of her. Elmer was quick to wrap a caring arm around her to console her.

"That's enough now, Donald!" Elmer cried.

Donald shoot him an ugly look, snarling back at him, but Elmer was not deterred by snarls and looks, he'd seen it all, a lifetime ago on the hot desert sands of Iraq and Kuwait.

"We've all suffered, Donald." Elmer added, "Some of us still are suffering." He gestured to Rachel, who he held in his arms.

This did not seem to deter Donald Knight who continued with his rant.

"I'm suffering too, Goddamn it! And who the hell is helping me?" He pushed Chief again and it was the straw that broke the camel's back.

"SIT DOWN!" Gable roared and he grabbed Donald and drove him back into his chair with such force that the chair skidded across the wet linoleum, and then came to a halt, with Donald staring up at Gable with moist eyes like saucers and a look of shock etched into his face.

"I'll let you have that free shot, Donald, because I know how much you are hurting right now. But don't test me, because you will not get another one."

Donald's eyes lowered and he looked at his feet, like a school child being reprimanded by the head teacher.

"Your words are born from anger and frustration, I know that. But words can hurt, especially when they're laced with such poison. How dare you stand there and say that you have had no one to help you, how dare you!" Chief Gable growled and then took a moment to calm down.

When he started to talk again his tone was softer.

"These people that stand in this room now, all of these people, the community of Hope Springs have been here for you! All fucking day, in the rain, trudging through mud and shit looking for your daughter, Donald. That is how much they care, that's how much we all care! We are ALL here for you and we will ALL continue to be here for you and anyone else in the community that needs us."

"I'm sorry." Donald snivelled, his eyes meeting those around the room who were tired and drenched through, and feeling useless by his words.

"Elmer is right!" Gable continued, "We have all suffered. When Hope Springs loses one of its own, we all feel it. It breaks my heart to stand here and tell you that I don't know the whereabouts of all those that we have lost. I am only human and I have tried my utmost to find them, truly I have. But there has never been any evidence left for me to find. No trails to follow, nothing to go on."

The heads of the crowd dropped and stared at the wet squares of red and white, tears in their own eyes, mirroring those of the Chief.

Donald lifted his head as if to say something and Gable cut him off, knowing that he was going to push blame onto the one that the finger was always pointed at.

"I know that some of you have a notion that a member of the community is responsible for all of this, but I assure you I have explored this particular avenue every time and I have found no evidence that the person you point your finger at is responsible. There is not one shred of evidence that connects him with any of the disappearances."

"I still believe it's him!" Growled Donald and a few from the crowd even echoed his sentiments.

"And you are entitled to that opinion." Chief nodded, "All of you are! But speaking as a man of the law there is nothing to indicate that Denny Lamont has anything to do with any of it. And now as a man, not a police chief, but a member of this community it is time that we leave the guy alone."

There was derision in the crowd, some agreed and some didn't.

"I can't make you all conform to my opinion and I would never ask that of any of you. That is your freedom of speech and choice as an American citizen and you can believe whatever you wish. But if you think that there is someone in this town that can give you more in the role as Chief of police then I will remove this badge and step down." Gable removed his badge that he had worn for the more than thirty years with pride on his broad chest and held it up for all to see, the fluorescent lighting catching the round badge made of nickel and brass and it flickered, immediately catching everyone's gaze.

His words were met with nothing but silence, until Elmer spoke.

"Nobody wants to see that, George."

"Good!" Gable said with relief in his voice and he returned the badge to where it rightfully belonged.

"Everybody is tired, I suggest we have a goodnight's rest and start again tomorrow. This time we come at it from a different angle, we'll search the Bittern estate and work our way into Parliament Grove."

Everyone looked tired and forlorn and Gable addressed them again.

"All those that have helped today, we thank you for your time and of course a huge thank you to Elmer and Rachel for the refreshments."

"Anytime!" Elmer smiled, "I will offer up the same for the search party tomorrow."

"We can't ask you to do that, Elmer." Gable pleaded.

"No, I insist! It's the least I can do." He sighed, "I wish I could be out there with you all, but this damn hip!"

"We understand Elmer. Thank you again."

"Thank you." Donald said meekly, seeming to turn back to his true nature and feeling a little embarrassed about his words and actions.

"Remember, it is not compulsory for any of you to help search, but we really do appreciate the help."

The door swung open and Jimmy appeared out of breath and soaked to the skin, his raincoat so wet that it no longer appeared grey but looked almost black. His hair was stuck to his face and he stumbled in steadying himself on the back of a chair, trying to catch his breath.

"Jesus, Jimmy!" Chief gasped, "What the hell happened to you?"

All eyes watched him as he leaned over the chair, almost dry heaving. Rachel brought him a glass of water.

"Here you go Mr. Johnson, looks like you could do with it."

He nodded, and panted a reply that may have been a 'thank you' but the words could not be heard. He downed the water in one go and slammed the empty glass on a nearby table.

"Well, Jimmy, what in God's name is going on here?" Gable asked again.

"Do you have news of my Lucy?" Donald said rising.

"Or my Abigail?" Rachel gasped, echoing Donald's sentiments.

"Magpa!" Was the only word that left his lips.

The room gasped as if he had farted in church during a funeral.

"What are you saying, Jimmy?" The Chief growled, he was annoyed that he had finally got the people back on side and now Jimmy had thrown a curveball which would disrupt them again.

"You people…" He panted, "You're all blind!"

They looked at him angrily, they did not take kindly to being offended by an outsider.

"You are no doubt here discussing where your children are? What has happened to them? Why there is no evidence, blah, blah, blah!"

He stared around at them and staggered into the middle of the room next to Chief Gable.

"The Magpa took your children!" He cried, "And you may think I've gone bat-shit-crazy! But I've just escaped the fucking bitch from turning me into a human pin cushion!" He cried and everyone gazed at him as if he were insane.

"I think that's enough excitement for one day." Gable said, "Let's make it an early start tomorrow, if you're joining in the search we will meet here at 7am."

And with the Chief's words the crowd started to disperse and leave the diner as if Jimmy did not exist and his words were not spoken.

"WHAT IS WRONG WITH YOU PEOPLE?"

Jimmy screamed and that got everyone's attention and they stopped where they were and gazed at him again.

"Why won't you people listen to me? I'm telling you the truth here!"

"C'mon now, Jimmy lets get you back to Bertha's." Gable said, "You've been out in the rain for too long."

Some of the congregation laughed and that rilled Jimmy up further.

"Don't laugh at me!" He seethed and pushed Gable away, "My car is parked up by the Kratz cottage, who in the way is fucking nuts!"

Nobody stopped him to tell him he was wrong on that score.

"I have been attacked in my car by this Magpa and now my car looks like a piece of Swiss fucking cheese!"

"It didn't look great to begin with to be honest." Said the mechanic Charlie Mendoza, his words caused a trickle of laughter to seep through the crowd.

"Oh, very funny!" Jimmy sneered sarcastically, "This Magpa, this Bird-Witch! She has your children in her nest."

Laugher again and shakes of their heads met his words, some had seen enough and left altogether.

"And where is this nest?" Gable chuckled.

Jimmy glared at the Chief, he was very offended that a man that he had grown close to over the last couple of days could treat his words as if they were that of a court jester.

"I believe it's the well, in the clearing of The Grove."

"I told you, Jimmy, we've checked the well on numerous occasions, there's nothing down there."

"But, you haven't been down there!" Jimmy argued, "I'm going to go down there and investigate it properly!" He said and scampered over to Rachel, "I'm going to go down there and find your daughter!" He smiled and then looked to Donald and said the same thing.

"You're just as nuts as Denny Lamont!" Donald spat. Jimmy stared at him and started to rummage in his inside pocket, for a moment Gable thought he was reaching for a gun and reluctantly grasped the handle of Old Betsy, he released his grip when he saw that all he held in his hands were two lapel pins.

"Mr. Knight, do these belong to Lucy?" Jimmy asked and held them out to him. Donald looked at them and shook his head, then Jimmy asked the same question to Rachel, she also replied with a shake of her head.

"I found these at the clearing."

"Wait a minute, Jimmy!" Gable cried, "You've been taking evidence from a crime scene?"

"I believe that these belonged to two federal agents that went missing a few days ago in Parliament Grove." Jimmy continued ignoring Chief Gable, "These pins were all that were left of them."

"What?" Donald gasped, "Others have gone missing?" The crowd started to grumble and turn their attention to Chief Gable.

"Why didn't you tell us, Chief?" Rachel added.

Chief Gable looked dumbfounded, he was obviously trying to keep a lid on things as to not cause panic and now it was too late.

"We also found a Hope Springs letterman jacket and the remains of a wicker picnic basket, that we believe belonged to a couple of high school students that have also been reported missing this week." Jimmy dropped another bombshell and Gable closed his eyes and listened to the crowd erupt around him.

"WHAT?" Came the unanimous cry from the crowd, who suddenly became hostile and moved in around Jimmy and the Chief, like hungry sharks sensing blood in the water.

"What have you done, Jimmy?" Murmured Chief Gable with annoyance.

"They have to know the truth, Chief." Jimmy replied.

"And what is the truth, Jimmy?" Gable said grabbing him by his shoulders roughly and shaking him angrily.

"Magpa is real!" Jimmy seethed, "Why won't you believe me?"

Chief Gable stared into Jimmy's eyes and he saw that he was telling the truth, he released his grip on him and before he could say anything the crowd were consumed him. All of them asking him questions at the same time, questions he didn't have the answers for.

"You've left me in a right pickle here, Jimmy." He grimaced.

"It had to be said, Chief. I'm going down that well and I'm going to finish this!"

"No, Jimmy!" Chief Gable growled and he made a grab for him again, to stop him from going, but the mob of concerned Hope Springs citizens pushed in between them and Jimmy was able to put space between him and the Chief.

Suddenly there was a bang on the window and a drenched Denny stood pressed up against the glass staring at those within.

"Denny!" Jimmy whispered.

"IT'S HIM!" Donald Knight cried and pointed at Denny, spittle rolling down his chin as he growled furiously.

The mob echoed his words and a shrieked accordingly, baying for blood.

"Denny Lamont! I told you, he's responsible for all of this!" Donald ranted, his words riling the room up into a frenzy, "We need to rid ourselves of this menace once and for all!"

Denny's eyes grew wide and he fled, leaving behind two hand prints on the rain splattered windows.

"No, Denny is not to blame!" Jimmy cried, "If anyone is to blame, it's you!" He bellowed and all the eyes of the room became wide with in disbelief.

"All of you have turned a blind eye to the truth for far too long. You have become immersed in your own denial and looked to slander and abuse those that tell the truth!"

"Who do you think you are?" Donald Knight crowed, "Some big city outsider coming here and telling us our business!"

The crowd rallied behind Donald with angry cheers.

"We all know that Denny Lamont is responsible for this

and I'm going to make sure he pays!" Seethed Donald Knight, raising his fists as if to rally a mob of those that agreed with him.

"Oh no you're not!" Growled Chief Gable moving in front of Donald who had looked to make for the door, "We do this by the book!"

Chief Gable's Deputy and several officers moved through the crowd to act as buffers against the forceful mob that were quickly surrounding their senior officer.

"By the book?" Donald snapped, "I've got news for you Chief, whatever is written in your book isn't working! You have failed us too many times and it's time we took matters into our own hands."

Jimmy made for the door but turned around on the spot, the wet, rubber soles of his shoes squeaking loudly as he did. The sound was of such a pitch that he gained everyone's attention and they stared at him.

"It's Hope Springs as a community that have failed these missing children, no one else. Call her what you want, be it myth or urban legend, Bird-Witch or Magpa! She is real and this nightmare won't end until she has been stopped."

Jimmy left the diner and into the gloom of the late afternoon, there was no rain now, but Jimmy didn't seem to notice anymore, he was used to that raincloud following him wherever he went. He gazed at the piece of paper that had been left on his windshield by Denny Lamont just a few days prior. He looked at the torn piece of paper that had started to be consumed with moisture, causing the letters and numbers that were scribbled upon it to warp. He slipped his cell phone from one of his deep raincoat pockets and quickly tapped in the number before it was lost forever. It rang and rang and then finally Denny Lamont answered.

"Let's talk." Jimmy said and walked away down Main Street leaving the heated scene of the diner behind.

There was a gunshot fired from within the diner and Chief Gable stood holding aloft Old Betsy, its nuzzle pointed upwards, a hole carved into the ceiling.
The mob shrieked in unison and instinctively collapsed to the wet tilled floor cowering.

"Jesus wept, George!" Elmer grumbled, "Look at my ceiling!"

"I'll pay for that to be fixed, Elmer."
They gazed up at him as he slid Old Betsy back into her holster.

"I'm issuing a town-wide curfew."
There was a quiet rumbling through the crowd, not one of dispute but one of dismay.

"Return to your homes now." Chief Gable said calmly.
Donald Knight rose from the floor of the diner and scowled at him, tears streaming down his cheeks, tears that he no longer knew he was shedding.

"ANYONE!" Gable sneered, staring right into Donald's eyes, "Found out of their homes this evening without a good reason will be arrested."
There was gasp from the crowd and as they all picked themselves up from the ground, they whispered what all this

meant for the town.

"I will not have mutiny on my watch." Gable said before leaving the diner and glancing up and down the street in search of Jimmy Johnson, Jr.

"Goddamn it, Jimmy!" He sighed.

XIX

Jimmy stood outside the dilapidated trailer home that that was situated a short distance from the tree-laden boundary of Parliament Grove. The structure was topped by the dead, wet leaves of many an autumn past. To say that this residence was unwelcoming was a huge understatement.

"It looks to me like Denny Lamont hasn't helped his relationship with the people of Hope Springs, when he lives in the squaller of such a monstrosity!" Jimmy murmured under his breath, "It doesn't scream 'welcome' now does it?"

The trailer would have once beamed proudly in a subtle tone of cream and striped elegantly with a thick band of cobalt, that was obvious by some of the paint that still remained. But now it sat in decline like it had suffered from leprosy, festering in its own filth of rust and mould.

"And I thought my car was bad." He scoffed and walked up the crooked pathway that led to the trailer. Either side of him waist length grass had grown out of control, uncut, unloved. Inside the long slender shards of green lay hidden all manner of junk, from a shopping cart, beer kegs, a reel of rope, car tyres and piles of damp and useless blanks of wood.

Jimmy opened up the screen door, a door that was almost devoid of the actual mesh screen panels, the top one barely hanging on swaying with the movement of the door.

It screeched with annoyance, the sound like a wailing cat who has had its tail trodden on.

Jimmy paused for a moment and clicked his tongue erratically, wondering whether he was doing the right thing, by visiting Denny Lamont in his natural habitat. What if he entered to find the dead bodies of all those missing children hanging from the ceiling? He waved the thought away as absurd, but still swelled hard, not really believing that.

Finally he knocked on the door and heard nothing stir from inside, there seemed to be no sign of life in or about the trailer. He stared at the door and noticed, the deep marks carved into the wood frame, as though one of Rhona Kratz's cats had been using it as a scratch post.

Or as if someone or something had tried to gain access.

His first thought should have been rational, that it were the townsfolk that had left the marks behind, trying to get their hands on Denny for the atrocities they believe he had committed. But instead he found his mind settling on the truth, he knew exactly what had made those marks and scratches and then realised why the homeowner wasn't rushing to come forward and open the door.

Jimmy knocked again, actually pounded on it with a balled up fist, there was no time for niceties and formalities, the Hope Springs community had been wasting their time with that for decades and it had gotten them nowhere.

"Denny!" He called, "Denny Lamont!"

He heard movement from inside and the sound of shuffling drawing near, somewhere a light burst into life and bathed the dirty windows in a glow the colour of honey. The net that hung in the nearest window twitched and he heard the sound of shuffling again and then it stopped behind the door, he could hear the thick congested breathing of Denny Lamont on the other side.

Jimmy thought that Denny may have a serious chest infection, or maybe something even worse, if his breathing could be heard through a door, then that must be a red flag. But Jimmy gazed around at the surroundings and at the squaller that he was living in and realised that you were bound to pick up some health issues living like this.

"Who is it?" Came the voice from behind the door.

Jimmy realised that Denny must not have seen who it was when her peered through those dingy nets that hung in the window.

"It's Jimmy Johnson."

Suddenly there was a frenzy of noise from the other side of the door, the scraping of metal and opening of locks, before the door opened quickly and there was Denny, dangerously thin, dressed in only a vest and his underpants, but wearing a wide, craggy smile on his face.

"I knew you'd come!" He announced and then suddenly reached out and grabbed Jimmy by the collars of his raincoat and hoisted him over the threshold and into the trailer. Denny took a quick fleeting look outside and then quickly closed the door and started to slide in the many bolts back into place. Jimmy looked on in astonishment as at least four bolts, a chain and two hasps secured with two hefty padlocks.

"Better to be safe than sure, right?" Jimmy chuckled nervously.

Denny turned and gazed wide eyed at him, the flesh that hung under his eyes was red and raw, it was easy to believe that these were the eyes of a drug addict, but to Jimmy they were the eyes of a severe insomniac with a trouble mind.

"I'm so glad you've come." Denny said, those tender eyes filling with moisture.

"Hey, c'mon now, there's no need to get upset." Jimmy said, his face contorting with pity.

Denny wiped away the flow of tears that seemed to come far too easy, as if all he ever did was cry, and for all Jimmy knew that's all he did when he was trapped in here alone with no family, no friends, no nothing.

Jimmy approached Denny and placed a cold hand on the scarred flesh of Denny Lamont's shoulder, he instinctively flinched away from his touch, it had been a very long time since he had made physical contact with anyone. His eyes widened with shock as droplets of tears hung from his lashes illuminating the pain and fear within.

"It's okay, Denny." Jimmy said calmly, "I believe you, I believe you."

Denny smiled again, his gaunt cheeks tattooed with two matching lines of woe. Jimmy had not seen Denny's flesh up close and exposed like this and he found himself staring at his wounds and scars. Flashes and welts of raised flesh consumed his arms, his skin was like the texture and look of a tree trunk. He did not mean to stare but he found himself mesmerised by them.

"It's not true what they say you know." Denny said, his words reclaiming Jimmy from his trancelike state.

"Oh, I'm sorry, I didn't mean to stare." Jimmy glowed with embarrassment.

"It's okay." Denny chuckled, "Everybody does."
Jimmy smiled awkwardly and nodded in response.

"But it isn't true," Denny continued, "I want you to know that."

"What isn't true?" Jimmy asked.

"That I'm a drug addict or dealer or whatever it is they call me. And I assure you that these are not the wounds of someone that self harms."
Jimmy looked at those scars again and then at Denny's face, he seemed not to believe him. Working as a Police detective in the past he had obviously come across all sorts and even if he didn't think that Denny Lamont was an addict, he wore the marks of someone who battled against their own mind.

"You think I'm in denial, don't you?" Denny chuckled, wiping his eyes.
Jimmy found that he couldn't lie, his face would have given it away if he tried to, so he did what he thought was best and told the truth.

"Yes. Yes I do."

"I admire your brazen honesty," He laughed, "But, let us take a seat and I will tell you how I came by these scars."
Denny gestured to the seating area that was made up of two recliners and an ancient looking coffee table that was covered

in the deep embedded rings of many a coffee cup. Jimmy looked on in awe at the seating area that was layered with empty packets and crunched up soda cans.

"C'mon," Denny said patting him on the back, "take a seat and I'll get us some drinks."

"I will if I can find one." Jimmy said under his breath as Denny moved into the kitchen area, piles of unwashed pots and pans, glasses and cups teetered on top of each other like some horrific game of Jenga.

Jimmy shuffled through the debris, it was like he was a child kicking through the fresh fallen leaves of Autumn. He reached a recliner and brushed off the empty packets and sat down, wrapping his raincoat around him as if it would protect him from the grime.

"How long have you lived here, Denny?" Jimmy called, trying to make small talk and take his mind off the muck he sat in.

"Oh, all my life." He said opening the refrigerator and rummaging around inside, "My folks croaked it when I was a babe in arms, so I was brought up by my nana."

"I'm sorry to hear that." Jimmy sighed, knowing too well how much grief the loss of a parent can effect one's psyche.

"I don't even remember them anymore to be honest." Denny said emerging from the refrigerator holding two cans of Koko Pop soda, "I was very young. Nana did a great job of rearing me from this shit-hole, I had a great childhood, I can't complain. But she's been gone a fair few years now, bless her."

Jimmy had been surveying the trailer while Denny had been

filling him in on his past and his eyes halted at the shotgun that lent up against the adjacent recliner. The recliner was pointed at the window, the glass wore fractures, reaching across the pane like veins that snaking through flesh. Tape had been applied to hold the pieces in place. Jimmy realised that Denny didn't even have a television set.

"Tropical Punch or Lemon-Lime?" Denny asked and he was in front of him, which startled Jimmy.

"Sorry?"

"Soda." Denny said, "You want Tropical Punch or Lemon-Lime?"

"Oh!" Jimmy smiled, "I'll take Tropical Punch."

Denny handed the can over and collapsed into his recliner, spinning it gently away from the window to face Denny, the shotgun moved with the chair, dangerously close to toppling over and for a moment Jimmy had visions of the gun falling and going off, finishing up with a hole in his face. He shuddered but again his face said a thousand words.

"Oh don't worry about the gun." Denny chuckled, grabbing it by the barrel and placing it on the coffee table.

"Why have you got that Denny?"

"I think you know why, Jimmy." Denny scoffed, leaning back in his chair and yanking open the ring pull from his soda can, the sound of the compressed air whistled and he took a swig, yet more sugar to assault his rotting teeth.

Jimmy said nothing, but he opened his can of soda and sipped at the fruity fizz with some discomfort, he had never been one for carbonated drinks, he'd always been an iced tea man.

"So tell me about it Denny."

"You wanna know the whole thing?"

"You got anything else better to do with your afternoon?" Jimmy laughed.

"Not really." Denny sniffed, "Only plans I had was staring at this window for the rest of the evening, try and fall asleep and hope I don't get my throat ripped out."

The coolness of how Denny delivered his words made Jimmy shiver, it was the tone of a man that had nothing left to lose. But in the silence between conversation he could hear Denny's breathing, heavy and worrying. Perhaps he knew deep down that he didn't have anything to lose.

"At this point I know that you've seen her," Denny said, "You wouldn't be here if you hadn't."

Jimmy nodded.

"You escaped from her?"

"Yeah."

Denny's eyebrows rose up his forehead.

"Lucky boy." He smiled, "Many aren't so lucky."

"Indeed."

"She's been here a long, long time, first rearing her head in the eighties."

"How long are we talking?"

"1600's I believe."

"Get out of here!" Jimmy scoffed, but Denny's face remained serious.

"Around the late 1600's, I should say."

"Wait, you're serious?" Jimmy gasped.

"My research shows that it was during the witch hunts."

"Witch hunts?"

"Witch-hunting was rife in these parts during that time period, anything happen that people couldn't explain and it was down to witchcraft. Anybody die of illness or murder and it was a witch's fault. Basically witches were to blame for everything from bad weather to the plague."

Jimmy settled into his chair and sipped away at his soda, as he listened to Denny's words and watched as he frantically (and unknowingly) picked and scratched at the fresh wounds on his arms.

"Hope Springs was run by the Bittern family back then, a family that was well to do, they had power and money, a dangerous combination at that time. Tobias Bittern was the head of the family back then and became the self appointed judge of Hope Springs."

"What did he do as 'Judge'?"

"Whatever the fuck he wanted." Laughed Denny, "He made ALL the decisions in the town, whether it was for the good or bad of the community, it didn't matter as long as it was good for Judge Bittern, that was all he cared about."

Denny stopped for a moment to wet his whistle and swill the lemon-lime fizz around his drying maw before continuing again.

"In 1692 the winter had been very cruel and the community struggled to grow anything substantial in the frozen grounds. They were forced to slay livestock to have something to eat and many died through lack of food. There was an uprising from the people of Hope Springs, a mutiny if you will, challenging Bittern's rule. They held him responsible."

"Let me guess, Bittern's solution to the problem was witches?"

"Bingo was his name." Denny said taking another swig of soda, "Bittern informed his people that their town was infested with witches, who were sent from hell to punish those that dwelled within Hope Springs. He told them that it was because they were sinners and the only way to free themselves from this curse was by slaying these said witches."

"Hence the witch-hunts." Jimmy added.

Denny nodded.

"Judge Bittern managed to manipulate the people who were once against him to join with him and rid the town of this unholiness that plagued them and he formed a Witch Finders Council, where they tracked down witches and executed them publicly."

"And did he ever find any witches?"

"There were many 'witches' discovered and executed, usually hung or drowned, but Judge Bittern favoured getting up close and personal and liked to finish them off with his stone mallet."

"The bastard! Innocent women killed for one man to keep his position! That disgusts me."

"And so it should." Denny grinned, "He didn't go searching for them all at once though, he would make an example of a woman he claimed was a witch and then life would return to normal. He grew fat on the best foods and the best wine, the Bittern family did not want for nothing, but the people of Hope Springs were living day by day trying too scrape together enough food just to stay alive. And when there were droughts or animals dying from disease or rotting crops, he went out looking for another witch."

"And he always found one?"

"Of course he did." Denny smiled, "I found a list of names in the public library of women that were executed for the crimes of witchcraft. Emily O'Shea, Janice Hodge, Rebecca Wainwright. These were just some of the names of those tried for witchcraft under Judge Bittern's rule. And then came Nancy Cartwright."

Jimmy and Denny's eyes met and Jimmy knew exactly who he was talking about.

"Magpa?" Jimmy asked.

Denny nodded.

"What became of Tobias Bittern?" Jimmy added.

"He grew older and fatter and died of influenza."

"Are the Bittern's still around today?"

"Only one remains, an old recluse called Monty, lives at Bittern House at the far end of The Grove. The family have nothing now but that house and he never leaves it, he might actually be dead for all anyone knows."

"So for the Bittern family witch hunting is over."

"I doubt Monty Bittern could even walk, but obviously, none of the women that I mentioned, who were executed were actually witches. They were used by Bittern to keep his position. But, Nancy Cartwright, well, she was a different kettle of fish altogether."

"You mean she WAS actually a witch?" Jimmy asked with astonishment.

Denny nodded his reply and the pair took another swig of their drinks. Jimmy seemed to take longer over this menial task, noticeably mulling over Denny's story so far.

"Now, I have found evidence of O'shea, Wainwright and Hodge's demise because their remains were found and many years later buried in the Hope Springs cemetery. If you want I can take you to see their graves."

"But, what about Nancy Cartwright?"

Denny shook his head.

"Her remains were never discovered."

"So how do you know she was even one of these witches? Or even tried by Bittern?"

"Because of legend!" Denny said, finishing off his soda and crunching up the can and discarding it to the floor of the trailer with all the other garbage, "She was always mentioned along with these other women. Story has it that Bittern and his Witch Finders burnt the Cartwright family home to the ground, killing her husband and child in the process."

"But Nancy didn't perish in the fire?"

"No, apparently she escaped and made for The Grove, where she sort out a place to hide."

"The well!" Jimmy exclaimed.

Denny nodded, his breathing raspy like a broken car radiator.

"So they threw her down the well and what sealed her

in?"

Denny nodded again.

"But what happened down there?"

"I have no idea, Jimmy, but it was truth that she was a witch of some kind." Denny shook his head and left his seat to greet the badly repaired window pane with a brooding look. "No, I don't know what transpired in the depths of that well, but I know too well what came from it that day... that day I lost my best friend."

Jimmy waited while Denny took a moment, this was a trait that he didn't get from his father, his father was sometimes brash and could be aggressive with his negotiations. Jimmy thought that his process was better for getting results, if you waited long enough, they usually told you the truth, if you bombarded them with threats and raised voices they remained tightlipped.

"We were playing Marco Polo," Denny began, his tone was sullen and there was no excitement in his voice like when he talked about the Witch Finders on the 1600's, because he did not know the victims, he did not live it. To him it was just a story, a story that involved others.

It wasn't real.

"I used to love playing that game." Jimmy smiled, reminiscing of a time spent during those warm summer days with his father playing in their inflatable pool in their backyard, "Pops always cheated, was always peeking and then splashing me in the face with the water." Jimmy smiled.

"Yeah, we didn't play in water though. No public pools round here you see. Our variation of the game was like hide and seek." Denny replied, but it was an absentminded reply, he was miles away, back in 1987, reliving the events of that day again, like he did every night in his dreams.

"There was a bunch of us enjoying a game that day. Max and I got separated, but that was nothing new, he always liked going off and exploring."

A smile caressed his lips and he wrapped his scarred arms around his meagre frame, as if trying to embrace the memory of his friend and keep it close and never let go of it.

"Max's older sister, Molly was playing with us that day. She was cool, I had a bit of a crush on her if truth be told." Denny sniggered, it was a childish sound, but it was a pleasant one.

"She happened to be 'IT' and boy was she good at the game. She always found us, no matter where we hid. Well, on that day she had already found me and I followed her as she closed in on Max, his voice came from the clearing in the centre of The Grove. We very rarely played there because of the birds..."

"The magpies?" Jimmy asked.

"Yeah," Denny nodded, "fucking, nasty things!"

Denny stroked at the raised wounds on his arms, a layer of gooseflesh attacking him, visibly making him shudder.

"Well, yeah, we didn't play much there because of them, but on this day I was with Molly Chambers so I had to be tough." He laughed, "I couldn't show her I was afraid of some silly birds. So she zoned in on Max's whereabouts, it was obvious where he was hiding because his voice was distorted like he was in a tunnel."

"Or a well?"

"Yeah, or a well!" Denny scoffed and turned around to face him, "Max had removed the old boards that roofed the well, we had seen that the well had been sealed years ago, but never really took any notice."

Denny turned back to the window and sighed a heavy, congested sigh of unhappiness.

"If he'd have just left those boards where they were..."

"Someone else would have removed them sooner or later."

"True." Denny replied, "Just don't know why it had to be my best friend."

Tears rolled down his cheeks as he turned to face Jimmy again.

"Something took him down that well." He whispered, "Max's eyes were so bright, flashing with fear, I'd never seen his eyes like that before, he was terrified. Then he tried to speak. I think he was trying to say magpie, but as he was forcefully pulled down the shaft he called out and it sounded like Magpa!"

"And obviously you told the authorities."

"Oh, yeah, ran back home and had to talk with Deputy Windwood, Gable was there too but he was just an officer back then. He didn't even have a moustache back then." Denny laughed and sat back down in the recliner, his chest falling rapidly, his voice had become croaky.

"Here!" Jimmy said handing him the rest of his soda, Denny smiled and took it taking a hearty sip.

"Yeah, they sent out search parties and whatever, same thing they do now when somebody goes missing. They searched the well, I say searched," he scoffed, "Deputy Windwood had gone down there and retrieved Max's body but didn't find anything down there, but I guess they weren't looking for anything now were they. Just a kid that had fallen down a well."

"And I guess they didn't believe what happened?"

"Of course not, thought we were just dumb kids and they treated us like that through the whole ordeal. I think Gable thinks that the loss of my friend sent me crazy and I guess his theory is partially right."

"What happened then?"

"Children started to go missing, it fucked this town up royally, I can tell ya."

"Understandable."

"I guess so," Denny agreed with a nod of his head, "so Molly and I went out there while the bitch was sleeping and managed to seal the well up, not without taking some damage from those blasted magpies."

Denny softly rubbed at his exposed scars, his mind was miles away and he didn't even know he was doing it.

"The scars?" Jimmy asked, "The magpies were the cause of the scars?"

Denny nodded.

"Every time I've had to seal that damn well up, those fuckers have taken chunks out of me. Every time! For years and years, One for sorrow my ass! A fucking hundred for absolute misery more like it!"

"Jesus!" Jimmy murmured, "So they act like Magpa's guards?"

"More like a fucking army!" Denny laughed, "I'm living proof that magpies are without a doubt the biggest pieces of shit in the animal kingdom."

"What happened to Molly?"

"After we managed to seal Magpa in the well, Molly and her family left Hope Springs. Her folks just couldn't deal with the loss and I guess everywhere they went here they were reminded of Max. Molly knew what really happened so she just wanted to get the hell out of this place and I can't say I blame her."

"Where is she now?"

"I believed they moved to Studd City and although we kept in contact for a while, we soon lost touch when I lost my job at Charlie Mendoza's garage and had no money for such luxuries as broadband and telephones."

"You worked with Charlie? So are you a mechanic?"

"Kind of." Denny's face contorted with embarrassment, for anyone to say he was competent at anything made him cringe, "I know the basics, but this was back in my late teens and I haven't worked since!"

"Why not?"

"C'mon!" Denny laughed shaking his head in disbelief at Jimmy's naivety, "You really don't know?"

"Well…"

"The people of Hope Springs wouldn't piss on me if I was on fire. As far as they are concerned, I'm the one responsible for all of this."

"So why stay?" Jimmy asked, "Why not fly the coop like Molly did."

"If I left, who is going to act as gatekeeper to that bitch? Ms. Kratz? She's the only one that believes and a fat lot of good she would be!"

"Maybe she could feed Magpa some of her special cookies, might kill her off for good."

They both laughed and then a moment of silence consumed them.

"It definitely hasn't been easy." Denny sighed and his breaths were distorted, "Now and then some clown would dislodge the planks and let her loose and set her free and I had to go through the whole ordeal again."

"Happened a lot then?"

"During the late nineties and early noughties, it seemed to be older kids, or college goers. They come to get high and drink beer. Some even discovered the legend of Hope Springs on the internet, the information is there if you wish to find it. So that brought a lot of witch hunters and wannabe ghostbusters to The Grove and boy they wished they hadn't."

Denny's eyes flitted to the gun on the coffee table and he patted it gently.

"I managed to scare most of them off and reseal it once again, but in all honesty, I can't keep doing this, I'm...I'm suffering..."

"Your chest?"

Denny looked away and nodded.

"Have you been to get checked out?"

"No point." He shook his head in despair, "Too far gone now. That's why we have to end it once and for all!"

"We?" Jimmy gulped, but nodded, knowing Denny couldn't do this alone.

"Together we can stop her. We have to!"

"I know..."

"But?" Denny smirked.

Jimmy nodded.

"I mean I have some ideas, but we are pretty low on fire power aren't we? Is a single shotgun going to be enough? Will it even hurt her?"

"Who knows!" Shrugged Denny rising from his seat and shuffling over to a chest that sat in the corner of the trailer, he opened the lid, while summoning Jimmy to join him. Jimmy did and his eyes grew wide.

"Holy cow!" Jimmy exclaimed, gazing into the chest in astonishment, "I think we'll be alright." Jimmy grinned.

Denny lifted out a handful of flares from a huge collection of guns and ammunition.

"What you are looking at is thirty years of collecting, scavenging, lucky finds and I'm not proud but yep, stealing too."

"So what's the plan?"

"You used to be a cop right?"

"Yeah."

"Then I'll follow your lead, Detective."

XXX

Dusk had consumed Hope Springs and it bathed Parliament Grove in a fantastic shroud of reds and pinks, an indication to all in these parts that tomorrow's weather would be fine. The trees would indeed be thankful of this Shepard's delight, their tired branches hung limply, still dripping profusely after the week's horrendous rainfall. Magpie's had gathered near the entrance to The Grove, eagerly watching the moist posters on the Flyer Tree as they flapped in the breeze. They peered at the faces of the youthful children, all missing in action, their black eyes twinkling with arrogance like a serial killer returning to the scene of their latest crime. Also returning to the location were the unlikely duo of Jimmy Johnson, Jr. and Denny Lamont, they stooped low using Ms. Kratz dishevelled fence as cover, concealing themselves from those beady black eyes.

The net curtains of the Kratz residence twitched, but that was no surprise, they always quivered with agitation, concealing the paranoid eyes within. Ms. Kratz had obviously seen them crouching there, but she would be damned if she was going to draw attention to them, that would no doubt draw attention to her too. Rhonda Kratz was satisfied with staying out of the way and watching this all play out, there was no way she was about to get involved in their antics.

Denny and Jimmy crouched, each of them had a plethora of items within their grasp. Denny had a revolver tucked into the waistband of his jeans, a hunting knife hung from his belt and held his trusted shotgun in his hands. Jimmy was without his trademark raincoat and instead wore a thick red woollen jumper. A tatty rucksack bulged with unidentified objects, a hefty line of rope coiled around his torso and in his hand he held an old service revolver that was flecked with rust. He had worried whether the revolver would actually fire at all, until Denny proved that it was indeed in working order when he blew a hole in the trailer.

"Are you ready?" Denny asked, his breaths seemed even heavier in the cool air of the early evening. Jimmy deduced that it was the excitement of what they were about to do that had quickened his heart rate and sent a surge of adrenaline through his body, he knew this was the cause because he was feeling exactly the same.

"I don't think you can ever be ready for something like this." Jimmy smiled.

"I guess you're right." Denny chuckled.

They turned their attentions to the old, broken down Volkswagen Beetle that sat prone and riddled with holes near the entrance to The Grove.

"Poor old Olive." Jimmy sighed, "Look at the state she's in."

"Look on the bright side."

"There's a bright side?"

"Think how cool she'll be in the summer." Denny

grinned.

"Cute!" Jimmy scoffed.

Their humorous interlude managed to lighten the mode for a moment and remove the tension, but it didn't last long and they needed to act quickly before they lost their nerve.

"You know what to do?" Jimmy.

"Of course! Should be a piece of cake to kick start the engine."

"Are you sure?"

"Charlie Mendoza showed me a thing or two before he canned my ass. It's about time I put it to some use."

"Well, at least the keys are still in the ignition so you won't have to hot wire her?"

"Then I guess it's time to do this thing." Jimmy exhaled, his breathing quivering on par with Denny's.

"I'll lead the magpies away through The Grove as far as I can, it should bring the bitch out."

"Then I'm on my own." Jimmy gulped.

"We can swap if you'd like? If you'd like matching scars." Denny laughed.

"No thanks." Jimmy grimaced, "Lets stick to the plan."

"Okay." Denny smiled and held his hand out to shake Jimmy's, "Good luck and thank you."

"Thank you for what?"

"For believing me." Denny grinned and then finally he scampered across the asphalt and hid behind the back of the vehicle, luckily for them that model of car had the engine concealed in its rear. Denny opened up the hood and started tinkering around with the engine, this kind of mechanical tinkering always flew straight over Jimmy's head it was all beyond him.

Jimmy retrieved a squashed packet of Freebirds and his lighter, the items trembled in his fingers, fear and anxiety surging through his body, competing with each other to see which could break his will first. He lit up the cigarette and slid it in between two dry lips, he inhaled, already the action seemed to have a calming effect on the angst that consumed him.

"Good God I needed that!" He exhaled as he watched Denny tickling Olive's innards.

He had been craving lady nicotine all afternoon but he couldn't bring himself to light up in Denny's company, it was obvious that his new companion was suffering silently from some sort of chest disease. Severe Asthma, Bronchiectasis or possible even Cancer. Jimmy was not about to add to the poor man's ailments, so he would smoke alone and effect his own health instead.

"I should give up." He sighed and looked at the cigarette hanging between his fingertips, tip rapidly turning to ash and falling like tiny specks of snow to the ground.

He turned his attentions back to Denny and whatever it was he had to do to fix the old wreck, it hadn't taken long and he was soon signalling to Jimmy that he was good to go.

"It's go time." He whispered and took one final drag of his cigarette before he discarded it to the floor, it dropped into a bed of forgotten leaves, that once danced on braces full of life and colour, now lay damp and trodden into the ground.

Jimmy nodded back and Denny crept around the car and slipped into the drivers seat as quietly as he could. He started up the ignition it took several attempts for it to kick start and for a moment Jimmy had the sickening feeling that it wasn't going to work, but suddenly Olive burst into life and he could see his own relief mirrored on Denny's face.

The engine gagged and spluttered, sounding as if it was about to regurgitate the mass amount of rainwater that it had consumed after remaining dormant for the day in such atrocious weather conditions. The activity was indeed enough to garner the attention of the magpies.

Jimmy watched on as one by one magpies descended from the high up branches of the trees for a closer look.

"One for sorrow, two for joy, three for a girl, four for a boy..." He chanted, the rhyme that he had been brought up with, "...five for silver, six for gold, seven for a secret never to be told."

He watched on as Denny heaved the stiffened joint of the gear leaver into position, the ugly crunching sound seemed sickening to his ears, like the grinding of bone on bone.

"Eight's a wish and nine's a kiss," He continued as the curious raptors edged closer, "ten a surprise you should not miss."

The car shuddered and slowly rolled forward toward the opening of Parliament Grove, the tyres slipping with reluctance as it moved onto the dirt and gravel.

"Eleven for health, twelve for wealth..." Jimmy paused as Denny and the mangled piece of machinery juddered into

the cover of the trees. "...thirteen beware it's the devil himself!"
There were soon too many magpies to count and Jimmy pondered.

"I wonder if there are anymore words to this rhyme? What could the words mean for a horde of these malevolent bastards?"

They left their perches in unison, flanking the car at a safe distance with military precession.

"Whatever the words, it wouldn't mean anything good." He murmured and with that the magpies followed the bait, he crept forward and into The Grove. The net curtains of Kratz cottage quivered, stopping long enough for Rhonda Kratz to cross her heart and pray for the best.

XXI

It had been a very long day for the Chief of Hope Springs police, George Gable as he traipsed into Buddy's bar. The door swinging behind him as though he were some strange wanderer entering a saloon in some old western. The eyes of those drinking met him and acknowledged his arrival. Gable wondered what they were thinking. Did they blame him like he blamed himself? He paid no mind to what they were or were not thinking, he could do nothing about that.

"C'mon now boys and girls, there's a curfew in operation. Get yourselves home." He said, his tone was friendly but commanding.

The patrons quickly finished up their drinks and left.

As he walked towards his usual stool at the bar it was easy to tell that he had things on his mind, something that Buddy Race picked up on immediately.

"Well, George, you know how to clear a room." Buddy chuckled, "Must have a lot on your mind."

"Is it that obvious?" Gable sighed as he slumped onto the stool and slapped his hat on the bar.

"It sure is!" He laughed, "If you walk in here and you don't notice Gloria Lockwood wearing the lowest cut blouse you've ever seen. Then you have shit on your mind alright!"

"Shit!" Gable groaned and looked around the bar for a

glimpse of his favourite widow.

"Too late Romeo, Juliet already left."

"Oh!" Gable sighed and stared into the long mirror that ran behind the mass amount of bottles held tightly in their racks and pouring dispensers behind the bar.

"Are you going to order something Chief?" Buddy asked playfully as he cleaned a glass with his cloth, "I mean it's the least you can do after scaring off all my customers."

"Of course." Gable glared at the array of bottles ready to decant whatever poison he chose. Volkov Vodka, Queen Sherry, Moondog Whiskey all looked inviting but Gable's eyes met Buddy's and they smiled at each other.

"I'll have the usual." Gable smirked.

"Of course!" Buddy laughed and disappeared underneath the counter and retrieved the ageing bottle of Hackenschmidt Whiskey, "For a moment there I really thought you were going to change the habit of a life time."

"Better make it a double!"

He poured a generous double and Gable scooped it up in his large mitt and downed it. He cringed from its heat scorching his throat and then licked the excess from his moustache.

"Sheesh! George, you must be having troubles."

"Of course I am!" He snapped, "Take a look around Buddy, everything has gone to shit and it's all my fault."

"You can't blame yourself for all this George."

"Then who else do I blame, Buddy?"

Buddy had no answer to soothe the Chief's worries, there was nothing to be said, the buck ended with him.

"Fill her up Buddy!" Gable cried and Buddy was about to do just that when the door exploded and in came Deputy Whittaker, his face looked forlorn, a messenger that brought forth information that was really not wanted by his superior.

"Oh God, Darryl, not now for heaven's sake!" Gable groaned and pushed his glass closer to Buddy, indicating that he still wanted a top up, no matter who had just walked in.
Buddy poured him another generous double and Gable pulled the glass back across the bar to him.

"Chief we have some problems." Whittaker announced.

"We've always got fucking problems!" Gable sighed and downed the second double. He slid the glass back towards Buddy and gestured for another. Buddy obliged.

"We've had a phone call from 'Crazy' Kratz." Whittaker said.

"Whoop-de-doo!" Gable cried, twirling his finger in the air sarcastically.

"She said that Denny Lamont and the private detective fella..."

"Jimmy Johnson Junior."

"Yeah, him! Well, she said that they are both headed into Parliament Grove!"

"And?" Gable scoffed as he took the glass again that was swimming in old Whiskey.

"Perhaps they are in cahoots!" Whittaker announced, "The missing kids, maybe these two had something to do with it and they are going back to claim the..."

"Bodies?" Gable finished the sentence that his Deputy

couldn't.

"Well, shouldn't we do something about it?" Whittaker grimaced, it wasn't like him to push himself forward like this, usually what his Chief said was final.

"Probably!" Gable said staring at the whiskey shimmering in the spotlights that hung above the bar, "But I'm starting to think that whatever I do is a waste of my time."

"We need you Chief." Whittaker said quietly, a little embarrassed, but the words were truth, they needed his leadership.

"Do you?" Gable said turning to meet his dark eyes that quivered with worry.

"We do!"

Gable sighed and held aloft the drink, wondering whether he should down this one or not.

"There was something else too, Chief."

Gable turned away from his aged whiskey that seemed to call to him.

"What?"

"Donald Knight!"

"What about him?"

"He's erm...fled."

"What do you mean 'fled'?" Gable growled and slammed the glass down on the bar, some of the succulent whiskey escaping from its confines and onto the bar never to live up to its destiny. Buddy quickly wiped up the mess with his cloth.

"He was supposed to be kept under surveillance."

Gable hissed angrily.

"Well, he ran away."

"Well, couldn't the officer at the scene run after him?" Gable scoffed.

"It was Old Chuck Jaworski, Chief."

"Oh God!" Gable rolled his eyes, "Who put him in charge of this?"

"You did, Chief." Whittaker smiled.

"Well, Goddamn what a stupid idea that was!" He cried, "Remind me to reprimand myself first thing!" He sighed and collapsed on the bar, "How did he escape the old fool? Lure him away with doughnuts?"

"He slit the tyres on his squad car and as he ran, Old Chuck...erm....well he..."

"He got stuck behind the wheel again, didn't he?" Gable sighed.

"Yeah." Whittaker replied, obviously embarrassed for Officer Jaworski's predicament.

"I've told him he needs to watch what he's eating, it's not good for his health and when I catch hold of him I'm not going to be good for his health either!"

"Take it easy on him, Chief. He did leave the big city to wind down..."

"Wind down! What is the old bastard! A Grandfather clock? Where was he seen headed?"
Chief stood and consumed the rest of his whiskey when his Deputy dropped another bombshell.

"He was headed towards the old trailer park, with a

rifle in hand hollering about ending Denny Lamont."

Chief Gable spat the contents of his mouth all over Buddy Race, who didn't move a muscle, he was shocked to the spot as warm whiskey cascaded down his rotund face.

"Jesus Christ, Darryl!" Gable cried grabbing his hat from the bar, "You could have opened with that!" And with that Gable left the bar at speed, quickly followed by his Deputy.

Buddy stood behind the bar letting the whiskey drip from his nose and chin.

"And here's me thinking it was going to be a quiet night." Buddy sighed and dabbed at his face with his cloth.

XXII

Darkness was all that met Agent Wren. Somehow she had slept, but she didn't know how, the crevice that she was crammed into was wet and uncomfortable and the smell of damp and death scratched at the back of her throat. The useless flaps of skin that had once been her eyelids did nothing that she commanded as she tried to open them to see something, anything. It was then that she remembered that she was blind, her eyes taken by whatever that thing was.

The last thing she had remembered was the severe pain of a long slender beak tearing at her sockets. She wanted to scream and shriek but she didn't have it left inside her to do so, she wanted to cry but her tear glands had been destroyed and she was not even allowed such a luxury. So she snivelled in pain weeping only tears of blood and mucus that stained her cheeks. She could hear a pecking sound echoing through what she thought could be a tunnel. She was amazed that there had been so many twists and turns and hidden tunnels from the well that she and her superior Agent Kite had climbed down a few days ago. She believed it was days but she could be wrong, she no longer had any concept of time or awareness of anything.

"Think Lindsey, think!" She murmured to herself, feeling around on the walls of mud, her searching hands occasionally encountering root or rock, which caused her to flinch in apprehension, afraid of what it could be. She needed to turn on her survival mode and remember the things she learnt in the Navy and her training with The Secret Hunters Horde.

"Think damn it!" She growled in annoyance, "Think, or you're gonna die here!"

She managed to stand and found that, although stiff, her limbs were still in working order and she stood, shuffling through what she believed was rock and foliage that the creature had used to make its nest. But her feet instead kicked away bones and limbs of those that had fallen to the beak of the Magpa.

Disturbing such items caused an horrendous rotting smell to circulate around the tunnel and she fought back the urge to vomit.

"Jesus!" She hissed and dropped to her knees to investigate. Her hands felt around brushing flesh and bone until she came across a human skull, her fingers felt it and soon her mind's eye formed a picture of what she was holding. She immediately dropped the skull and leapt to her feet, staggering backwards and falling down. Her landing was comfortable and soft she felt around and felt material and then limbs, her fingers caressing thighs, breasts, fingers and hair.

"No!" She snivelled as she pulled herself away from the bed of corpses that were piled up beneath her, all the bodies in different stages of decay, some belonging to adults, the majority children, their innocent faces fixed forever in the horror of their final moments.

Still she could hear that pecking sound echoing off the damp walls, somewhere near, Magpa was feeding.

She felt through the bodies feverishly as if looking for something important that she had lost.

"Don't be dead, don't you be fucking dead!" She whispered and finally her hands met the thick curls of her superior Agent Kite.

"Goddamn it!" She sighed as she fell back against the wall away from the body of the person that was supposed to be showing her how it's done, teaching her and protecting her.

But she was dead and for that split second Lindsey Lee, AKA 'Agent Wren' from Liverpool, England was glad that she was blind. She was glad that she couldn't see how mutilated the corpse of one of SHH's finest hunters had been left.

She had no time to mourn, she searched around the remains of Agent Kite, the tracking device that all hunters wore on their belts was there she could feel it. She was not yet a hunter and had not yet been bestowed with such gadgets. Her fingertips could feel the design etched in the bronze circle, a stake gripped in a hand, shown in a stabbing motion. She pressed at it frantically, but nothing happened, it had been too severely damaged in the scuffle. She searched her own pockets for her cell phone but nothing, she was met with the same result when she checked her partner's. She felt through the dirt and roots of the nest and felt a cell phone.

She smiled with delight.

She was overwhelmed with hope having found an object that we all seem to take for granted these days, what she heard in her hands now was a lifeline, it could potentially save her life.

"No, shit, no!" She whined as her fingers brushed

across the broken glass of the phone's screen and realising it was useless, she discarded it.

She knew now that she needed to get out of there. There was no hope of finding anyone alive, she decided it was best to arm herself and take her chances. Feeling around the carcasses once more she found a hefty bone that had some weight to it, from its size and length she deduced that it was a human femur. If she got in a lucky swipe at the creature, she believed it would cause some serious damage.

Gripping the femur in her hands she stayed close to the wall of the tunnel and shuffled along following the sound of the cackling and pecking. Suddenly Magpa wailed as if it was in pain or annoyed. Agent Wren froze to the spot, her heels digging into the moist soil, the femur held closely to her chest, all while her empty sockets wept tears of crimson.

The Magpa crouched over her feast, cragged spine coated in thick black feathers, as moonlight glared down the well and illuminated the Bird-Witch.

Her wings quivered with excitement as she fed, dropped over whatever she was devouring and the limb that wore talons reached out from her chest and tore away flesh from bone allowing her beak to pick at the exposed fat and muscle. Magpa's demeanour suddenly changed and her head moved from side to side as if something were attacking her ears. She shrieked and wailed angrily and glanced up at the open well high above her, chattering away angrily. She sensed something, heard something distant, a disturbance in her grove. She stepped back to reveal what she had been feeding on and stared at the little girl that lay with her eyes closed tightly arms wrapped around the dead body of her best friend Abigail Jones. Lucy Knight whimpered but refused to open her eyes, she could not bring herself to look at the witch and what she had done to her. Instead she gripped Abigail's corpse tightly, taking in her familiar smells and praying that it was just a bad dream, a very bad dream.

Magpa shrieked again and staggered away from her prey, she seemed to look on at the child with pity with those human-like eyes and wiped the tears from Lucy's cheeks tenderly with a feathered wing, like a Mother would tend to her babe. She then wailed, the sound was ear splitting and Lucy winched but would not open her eyes and Magpa was gone, clambering up the narrow shaft of dirt and root, mud and rock until she was gone.

Lucy finally opened her eyes and gazed around the pit of the well, she looked at her legs and her lips quivered and tears rolled as she looked away. Her focus resting on the face of her friend, her eyes and mouth frozen wide in dread.

"I'll keep you warm, Abi." Lucy wept and held her tightly, smelling her hair and her skin as she rocked her back and forth, "I'll keep you warm."

"Hello?" Came the voice of Agent Wren echoed around the tunnels as she stepped into the pit of the well, it was lit quite well by the moon, but to Agent Wren everything was black now and forever would be.

Lucy's eyes were wide and focused at this figure staggering out of the shadows, believing that it was some other demon come to feed on her flesh. Lucy tried to hold her breath and remain still, as she saw a woman with no eyes carrying a huge bone staggering towards her.

"Is someone there?" Agent Wren asked, "I can hear you breathing, please answer me."

"Yes." Came a meek reply from Lucy, she didn't even know that she had said it and tears of relief fell down her face.

"Thank goodness!" Agent Wren sighed, finding someone alive in this hellhole was a triumph in her eyes, well her barren sockets of nothingness.

"Are you an angel?" Lucy asked as Agent Wren knelt down to her and felt for her hands that happened to be gripping the corpse of her dead friend.

"I'm afraid not kid." Wren smiled, "My name is Lindsey and I think together we can get out of here."

"My name is Lucy and this is Abi."

Wren realised she was holding someone.

"Is she okay?" Wren asked.

"She's dead." Lucy said bluntly, "But, I'm keeping her warm don't worry."

Wren smiled sadly, her heart sinking in her chest and she stroked the clammy face of Lucy Knight.

"You're very hot, Lucy." Wren said sounding a little worried.

"That's why I'm keeping Abi warm. She doesn't like the winter you see, never even liked playing in the snow."

"Let's get out of here, Lucy."

"I can't."

"Why not?"

"She took my feet. The Bird-Witch took my feet."

"Jesus Christ!" Agent Wren sighed and did the only thing she could think of doing and she held Lucy closely and tightly and the pair of them sobbed.

XXIII

Jimmy had remained rooted to the same spot for what seemed like hours. He had kept himself hidden behind a mass of tired looking brambles, twisting vines that would have once been bejewelled with raspberries and blackberries, succulent, tart fruit long gone, serving their purpose by feeding the wildlife of Parliament Grove. Jimmy's joints were stiff and refused to work, not that he was attempting to move, at this moment in time he was happy to just enjoy another cigarette. He gazed through the contorting vines and watched the well in the middle of the clearing with nervous anticipation. The moon had reared its pale face and illuminated the clearing, giving Jimmy the advantage of not having to use any light that could give away his position.

He waited and absorbed the sweet nicotine, a pastime that gave him so much pleasure, but ultimately he knew that one day he would have to abandon such an unhealthy recreational activity. He glared at the cigarettes that sat pinched between his index and middle fingers and watched as the tip burnt red and amber in the gloom.

"Maybe I should trade you in for a set of golf clubs?" He whispered to himself and smiled as he took another long drag and forgot all about other pastimes that could potentially replace his current vice.

The burning ash consumed the shaft of the cigarette and he

watched almost hypnotised by it, like the sand in an hourglass drifting away, he saw it as a metaphor for his life and asked himself was it worth shortening his time on this mortal coil? He flicked it away into a heap of wet leaves, there was no way that it could continue to burn as the moisture immersed it and he watched as it died.

There was the sound of a distant car engine that interrupted his reverie, an all too familiar sound, the congested engine of his own Volkswagen Beetle, his little Olive. Somewhere close by the car raced through Parliament Grove and Jimmy turned his attentions back to the well, hoping that their plan to lure The Magpa from her sanctuary would work.

"C'mon you bitch, c'mon now." He murmured under his breath, he nervously fidgeted looking for the deep pockets of his raincoat that wasn't there. In many ways his raincoat acted as a comforter, it shrouded him from the elements and kept him warm and kept close all the items he held dear.

But on this occasion he was without it, alone, naked.

The engine gradually became distant and there was no movement from the misshaped pile of rocks that masqueraded as a well.

"Goddamn it you, bitch!" He seethed anxiously, "Take the bait!"

As soon as the words had left his lips The Magpa emerged from the well, as if right on cue. Although Jimmy had already had an up close and personal altercation with the creature he was still awed when he saw her rise from the well's shaft, bathed in the ghostly shimmer of the moonlight. Her wings were folded around her serrated spine, clawed feet gripping the well, the sound of her talons scraping on the rock was sickening. She looked up to the moon and her beak chattered angrily, as the feathers that she did have on the pimpled, leathery flesh of her body seemed to ruffle from the change in temperature and she let out a shriek. The Magpa spread her wings wide revealing those magpie-like feathers, black and white and tipped with mesmerising blue and green tones that seemed to duel against each other for superiority. All of this happened in seconds before she launched herself from her craggy perch and burst silently into the air on those massive wings, drifting off towards the distant sound of the car's engine.

"She took the bait!" Jimmy smiled, he felt his flesh beneath the thick woollen jumper pimple and suddenly it all felt real.

"Denny's done his part," He stopped and took a deep breath that caused him to shudder, "Now it's my turn."

Jimmy moved quickly across the clearing towards the well and peered inside, there was only a thick circle of black that met his eyes.

He saw nothing.

He relieved himself of the burden of the heavy rucksack and removed the hefty length of rope that was coiled around his torso, it was frayed and worn, peppered in greasy marks of mould in places, but beggars cannot be choosers, it was all that was accessible at the time.

He unravelled the rope and moved to a nearby stump that looked sturdy enough to hold his weight and tied the rope around it tightly, giving it several aggressive tugs to make sure it would hold. Everything looked fine, so he moved back towards the well and let the rest of the rope fall down into its maw of darkness. He did not hear any excess rope hit the floor of the well and assumed that it was indeed deeper than either he or Denny had thought, but hopefully he would not be too far from its base and he could jump down safely.

But of course he wouldn't know any of this until he was down there.

He was gearing himself up for the descent when his cell phone chimed and tingled with vibration against his thigh, he removed it from his pocket, the screen flashed up with a text message from his mother asking how he was and complaining that he hadn't been in touch and you know how much she worries... Jimmy rolled his eyes.

"Haven't got time for this Mom." He sighed and slotted it back into his pant pocket.

He unveiled three green light sticks, shook one vigorously and snapped it, unfortunately the liquid inside had sat for too long and had solidified, rendering it useless.

"Shit!" He moaned and snapped another, but sadly had the same outcome.

One remained and he shook it frantically, willing the chemical inside to burst into life.

"C'mon you son of a bitch!" He growled through gritted teeth.

He snapped it and an immediate green glow illuminated from the tube and he breathed a sigh of relief and let it fall down the shaft into the well.

He then retrieved a flashlight from the rucksack and tested it.

It flickered in the darkness and he shined it down into the dark shaft, it lit up rock and dirt and he was alarmed by the misshapen, skeletal fingers that reached for him, it caused him to stagger backwards and refocus. When he did, he realised that they were merely slender roots protruding out from the wall of the well's shaft and he breathed a sigh of relief.

"Get your shit together, Jimmy." He scoffed.

He removed an old revolver and slid it into the rear of his waistband.

"Pop's always said never tuck your piece in the front of you pants unless you want to wave goodbye to your own piece."

His fingers caressed the red slender flare that stared back at him and something told him to leave it there.

"If we get into trouble up here and we need the help of police or, God forbid, paramedics, then they may need to find us."

With that he jammed the flashlight in his pant pocket so that its illuminating head poked out and lit the way as he climbed into the well and gripped the old rope tightly with both hands.

"Do you ever wonder how you get into these predicaments?" Jimmy asked himself as he slowly (and carefully) climbed down the rope, using his feet to guide himself down the craggy shaft, a wall which soon became softer and slippier underfoot.

"One minute your in New York playing choo-choo trains with Pop in the backyard, next minute your graduating police academy, then you're getting shot chasing some drug baron..."

He reminisced as he lowered himself downwards, maybe it was to take his mind of where he was going and what he might find. The faces of Abigail Jones and Lucy Knight flashed before his eyes in the dark, an hallucination for sure, their faces were contorted and twisted by death and fear. His eyelids fluttered to fight back such horrifying images, images that could soon become a reality.

"...then you're in Vancouver police department and life is going well until Pops disappeared. Died in a fire they said. Pah!" He spat with annoyance, "I don't believe that bullshit for a second. The funeral, burying nothing, saying goodbyes that I didn't believe. No, I won't believe it until I find out exactly what happened. I'll find out what happened Pops you see if I don't. You see!"

His feet suddenly had run out of shaft and he swung frantically in the air. Jimmy panicked, the flashlight bouncing of the walls of a vast chamber, illuminating the reaching roots that looked to grab him and feast on his flesh. He gazed down into the glowing green cavern, the flashlight mixing with the light stick's illumination like some psychedelic light show.

"Shit!" He growled, and below him he heard a sound, it sounded like a voice but he couldn't be sure, he took out the flashlight but it trembled erratically in his hand and he dropped it to the floor of the well, beam of light spiralling in the darkness illuminating a screaming face that had no eyes. Jimmy shrieked and he lost his grip on the rope and fell.

The flashlight hit the ground and broke then there was only an eerie green glow before darkness swamped him and in his mind's eye he was falling into the deep, black socket of this screaming harpy.

XXIV

Donald Knight held the rifle close to his chest as he trudged through the sodden foliage of Parliament Grove. There was only darkness to greet him, the moon was being kept at bay by the mass of trees that loomed, menacingly overhead.

Donald was unperturbed by the darkness because that was exactly what filled his head and heart now, darkness. They were now one and the same, his broken heart had been mended by anger and fear, his mind produced nothing but thoughts of loathing and death.

"You will pay for this Denny Lamont!" He growled, spittle dripping from his lips.

His eyes were red raw, lack of sleep and the burden of loss, spurred on by anger and hate and for the need to prove himself right that Denny Lamont was indeed to blame. Maybe just to hold someone accountable for his loss would do, but he could not shake the vision of Denny Lamont and the horrendous things he could be doing or may have already done to his daughter.

He growled as these images danced before his eyes, the hallucinations of a madman perhaps but it fuelled his fire and kept his tired legs moving forward.

Suddenly he stopped dead as he heard the continuous growl of a car engine.

"I must be going mad!" He whimpered, and his wide

eyes flitted around at the dark trees, thick trunks that hid all manner of horrors behind them, bushes that twitched in the darkness causing him to grip the rifle ever closer.

"What is that sound?" He cried, trembling.

He turned on the spot, the sound seemed to echo all-around him, a mechanical grumbling sound. He gazed out all round him, everywhere he saw things, creatures perhaps, peering from behind the trees. He held the rifle out in front of him and aimed it at these imaginary creatures.

"I'll shoot!" He growled, but there was a quiver of fear in his tone, "If you come for me, God help me I'll shoot!"

The rumbling sound filled The Grove again and he shrieked firing the rifle into the darkness. The gunshot echoed forever and then there was nothing, his lips quivered into a smile and his eyes burnt again with anger.

"Got him!" He sneered and moved forward again deeper into The Grove.

"Denny Lamont! Denny Lamont! Denny Lamont! Denny Lamont!" He chanted as he moved, reminiscent of the Witch Finders of the past as they searched The Grove for the witches of Hope Springs.

There was a shriek of a siren and the trees were bathed in flashing lights of red and blue, forming a vibrant purple tone that caressed Donald's frightened face.

"Damn it!" He growled and quickened his pace as he moved deeper into the woods.

XXV

Denny gripped the steering wheel tightly as he weaved in through a labyrinth of tree trunks, shrubs and other overgrown plant life. He stooped forward in his seat, craning his neck and to see through the cracked windshield that was splintered into fragments like a spider web.

"Come on Olive, keep it going, keep it going." He purred to the struggling vehicle seductively, to urge it onwards. His foot was flat out on the peddle and he continued to push it to the limit, it had been years since the poor car had been made to drive like this and even the Volkswagen queried whether it was still capable of this kind of recklessness.

The engine choked, wheezed and hummed, it seemed to mimic Denny's own breathing which was probably asking the same questions of Denny that the car was asking of him, how long can this continue?

The answer was (according to the doctor) not very long.

"We got this, keep going." He wheezed.

But Denny was not alone, far from it, since he made his way into Parliament Grove he had been immediately pursued by a mass of magpies. From time to time Denny looked upwards to see a shroud of feathered demons flying above the car, amazingly keeping speed with the car. Denny grinned a craggy a smile, he had them right where he wanted them.

"Now all we need is for big momma to join the party."

As soon as the sentence had left his lips he heard the infamous shriek of Magpa.

"Right on schedule." He beamed, a crazed look in his eyes.

The magpies parted to allow their Queen to join the chase and Magpa swooped in between them, eyes burning into the compact, yellow car with hatred and purpose. One purpose to rid her delicate ears of such an horrendous cacophony and slaughter whoever was responsible.

"Okay you bitch, see if you can stick with me." Denny cried, as he careened deep into The Grove and fought to keep the vehicle moving over such uneven terrain. He took ridiculous turns throughout and still the Magpa kept with him, but this is exactly what he wanted, Denny was a running distraction in this plan and he had to keep this creature busy for as long as possible.

Magpa swooped down low and her clawed talons scrapped at the roof, but she was unable to settle as the vehicle rocked back and forth making it impossible for her to get a grip. She swirled around in the air, her wingspan was long and strong, they did not falter as she moved into an attacking position and hurtled down towards the car and threw her body up against the driver's side, rocking the car and smashing the windows. Denny almost lost control, but managed to keep the car moving and it skidded over a mass of wet leaves before moving back onto the dirt path that circled The Grove.

"So you wanna play rough, Nancy?" Denny called to

her out of the broken window, mocking her, "That's fine by me."

The Magpa appeared out from the cover of the trees followed closely by hundreds of magpies.

Denny zoomed down the dirt path, the damp tyres kicking up gravel and mud as it skidded and struggled to keep moving, Denny knew if he stopped he was done for and he kept his foot pressed down on the gas the entire time.

She soon caught up and was gliding above him again, looming in the dark sky like some bloodthirsty vampire bat eager to taste Denny's vital fluids. She swooped and again her claws could not gain any purchase and she slipped and skidded on the wet roof, sliding off and down the windshield and onto the hood and looked as if she was about to hit the ground, much to the delight of Denny.

"Eat that, Nancy!" He laughed.

Her claws suddenly sunk into the metal and held on. Denny tried to shake her off but it was no use. The two of them made eye contact through the fractured windshield and it was if she was smiling as she positioned herself on the hood chattering her beak at him.

"Oh shit, oh shit, oh shit!" Denny growled.

With one aggressive strike Magpa's beak shattered the windshield and the clawed hand that protruded from her chest reached into the car towards him, but he managed to move out of the way and turn the wheel from side to side and cause the vehicle to shake almost sending her spilling from the hood once again. He turned back into The Grove and she was suddenly whipped by branches as he drove close to the trees with speed. Magpa retreated back into the air and Denny roared at the top of his lungs with a victory cry.

But a look in the wing mirror soon showed him that she was not yet ready to give up as she returned with a mass of her winged followers flanking her movements as she swooped in closer.

Denny had taken his eye off the ball for a moment and it cost him, as the front wheels ploughed over a fallen tree trunk and stopped all the vehicle's momentum, bringing it to an abrupt halt.

"Shit!"

The engine stalled as Magpa and her followers circled the debilitated vehicle like it was the carcass of a fallen heifer and they were salivating, readying themselves to tear the flesh from its bones. Down came Magpa and she perched on the roof, talons scraping on the metal. Denny watched through the holes that the Bird-Witch had already made it in the vehicle and she glared at him with those eyes, so much like a humans. She peered in through the glassless windshield and chattered at Denny as if telling him that it was finally over and she would have him.

"Well, fuck you!" He growled back at her, "You won't take me without a fight."

Her teeth chattered behind her long slender beak, was she laughing? Who could tell.

Denny continued to try the ignition but nothing, the engine would need the touch of his magic hands if it was to go again and at this time there was no way that was happening. She stretched her neck forward and took a snap at Denny with her beak, but he managed to move out of the way and then revealed his equaliser, his shotgun which he cocked.

"I'll see you in hell!" He screamed and unloaded the first barrel at her that removed several feathers from her wing that caused her to shriek and teeter backward. He was about release the contents of the second when the magpies rained down and attacked the car, thrusting their beaks into the car, the deafening sound like rocks were being hurled at him from all angles. They came in through the broken windows and attacked him, piercing his flesh with their sharp beaks and claws, relentlessly trying to rescue their fallen Queen.

"Little bastards!"

Denny unleashed the other barrel of his shotgun, which now left him empty and vulnerable but it did cause the attacking magpies to disperse. Magpa rose up again, this time with anger in her eyes she stalked him, moving around the car and looking to attack him through the broken driver's window. He suddenly remembered that he had an old revolver stuffed down the front of his waistband and as Magpa crept closer, stalking her prey he aimed the revolver at her but he was met by a swift lurch from the Bird-Witch and her beak knocked the revolver from his loose grip, sending it to the floor of the car and sliding under his seat out of sight.

"Oh shit, No!" He grimaced as he dodged and weaved the thrusts of her serrated beak as if she were heavyweight champion of the world, 'Left Hook' Lewis Johnson.

He unsheathed the hunting knife, but Manga sliced the back of his hand with her talons and he cried out in pain as the knife, tumbled out of the broken windshield and slid down the hood of the car.

His hand felt around under the seat blindly for the revolver, but found nothing.

"Come on, come on, you bastard!" He growled through gritted teeth, the muscles in his shoulders and arms burning at full stretch as he continued to stay out of harms way from her relentless attack. It was too much to ask fate that he could emerge from this onslaught without yet more wounds and her beak sliced him across his face and down his neck. Denny let out a scream and she backed away to revel in her workmanship, just as his fingers met the tip of something extremely sharp. He had no idea what it was but gripped it tightly and as she came for him again, to potentially finish off what she started, he drove the object into her throat. She shrieked and backed away, her claws sliding on the hood of the car, the blade of a Swiss army knife protruding from her throat. She shook her head wildly and the knife fell free, allowing thick red blood to spirt from the wound.

"How'd you like those apples, Nancy!" Denny roared in triumph, but she seemed to shake off the effects and prepared to come for him once again.

Denny slid down to the floor of the beaten Volkswagen and searched for the revolver, cursing himself for not being able to find it, he found himself closing his eyes at one point and praying to whatever deity may have been listening at that time.

He slowly opened his eyes, expecting the attack that would end his life but there was nothing, there was no attack. He found the revolver and hearing nothing but the wind in the trees, he cautiously rose up, peering over the dashboard. Magpa was staring out into the woods, her focus elsewhere and without any warning she leapt into the sky again, immediately followed by her magpies as though they were attached to her very shadow.

Denny left the confines of the car and watched as they flew away, there was the distant sound of a siren and he knew that help may well be on the way, but the distraction was over and Jimmy's time was up.

"I hope you've found what you need Jimmy, because she's heading your way."

Denny ran around to the rear of the Volkswagen and lifted the hatch unveiling a smoking engine and hoped he could get Olive singing again.

XXV

Jimmy's eyelids fluttered and opened slowly, he groaned with pain and discomfort as he instinctively cupped the back of his head. He could feel no blood, but from the humming in his ears and the flicker of stars before his eyes he knew he had a concussion. He rose into a seated position and tried to shake away the cobwebs that clogged his mind, all around him was gloom, highlighted in an eerie green tone from the light stick. Above was a shard of light that came from the gaping hole of the well and brought forth the glow of the full moon. As his eyes adjusted to the damp cavern, he felt as though he were in some kind of psychedelic haze as the light stick's bright green glow blended with the moonlight's subtle caresses of blue. He gazed at his broken flashlight that lay on the damp floor of the well and sighed heavily.

"Shit."

Jimmy adjusted himself cautiously, he did not want to move too quickly and make any injuries he may be harbouring worse, he knew from the discomfort of his lower back that the revolver remained wedged in place and luckily for him had not been triggered in the fall and demolished his tailbone.

"You're one lucky, lucky bastard, Jimmy Johnson Junior." He wheezed as he stood, stretching out his spine and slowly rotating his arms, testing those tender shoulder joints.

He ached, but he was still in one piece.

"Thank God!" He heard a voice whisper in the darkness, "He's alive!"

Jimmy's eyes widened and he turned on the spot, his once fine Italian shoes, spiralling into the mud as though he were a human pile-driver digging for oil.

"Jesus!" He gasped, "Who said that?"

"I did." Came the voice right next to him and he turned to see Agent Wren, her hollow sockets weeping some kind of bodily fluid, appearing like tears down her gaunt and dirty face. Jimmy screamed and fell back to the ground, his rear sinking into a quagmire of mud.

"Please don't be alarmed." She said, she could hear that he had collapsed into the mud from the ugly squelching sound and blindly offered her hand to help him to his feet.

"Who are you?" He asked, "A-And what the hell happened to you?"

"My name is Agent Wren...well, Lindsey if truth be told."

"One of the missing federal agents?"

"No, not a federal agent, I work with a top secret organisation called The Secret Hunters Horde."

"The Secret Hunters Horde?" Jimmy said to himself, something pricked at his brain at the mention of the organisation, he felt he had heard it before.

"Are you going to take my hand or what?" She said.

"Sorry," he replied and he took her hand, she helped haul him out of his muddy resting place.

"What happened to you?" Jimmy asked as he grimaced from the mud seeping into some uncomfortable crevices.

"You know that urban legend about a Bird-Witch in these parts?"

Jimmy nodded and then blushed in his own embarrassment as he realised she couldn't see his response and spluttered a reply, "Yes."

"Well, she happened, that's what!" She said, pointing to her face.

"Jesus!" Jimmy said shaking his head, "What about your partner? I heard there were two of you?"

"I was the lucky one." She said shaking her head.

"Oh!" Was all Jimmy could muster, "I'm very sorry for your loss."

"There's no time for that, we have to get the hell out of here, before the bitch comes back."

"Of course."

"You seem very well informed about us, you knew that we had been here, knew there were two of us and didn't seemed to be fazed when I mentioned the Bird-Witch."

"It's a long story."

"Well, we don't have time for long stories, so just your name will do."

"The name's Jimmy Johnson, Jr!"

"Jesus H. Christ, I am sorry." She scoffed, oozing Liverpudlian sarcasm, "What a bloody mouthful that is."

They both laughed and it seemed to cause the walls to shudder as if the cavern had never heard such a sound before.

"I'm a private investigator working out of Studd City, looking for a missing child, well, I guess it's two missing children now."

"You mean Abigail Jones and Lucy Knight?"

"Yes, but how did you…"

"Because I've found them."

Jimmy's eyes widened like saucers and his heart was filled with pure elation.

"You have!" He gasped, "That is wonderful news! It will be such a great feeling to unite them with their parents…"

"No!" Agent Wren interrupted and then lowered her voice, "It's not good news."

"Oh!" Jimmy sighed, his heart now feeling hollow and void of the elation he had felt only seconds ago. Now a thick sickness seemed to ooze from it and threatened to explode from his throat.

"Abigail Jones is dead." She whispered.

Jimmy dropped his head and sighed, as if his shoulders had just taken on the weight of the cavern's ceiling.

"Then why are you whispering?"

"Because Lucy isn't."

"What?" Jimmy exclaimed and his heart seemed to beat again with love and hope.

"Where is she?" Jimmy asked, "We need to get her out of here."

"I need to tell you…" Agent Wren started but she was interrupted by Lucy's voice that was soft and distant, like the cooing of a frightened dove.

"L-Lindsey?" She whined, "Who are you talking to?"

"Lucy!" Jimmy cried and moved towards the corner of the cavern, following the sound of her voice.

"Wait I have to tell you…" Agent Wren tried again but Jimmy had moved away and she was left feeling around blindly trying to follow him.

"Lucy Knight! My name is Jimmy, I'm here to rescue…" His words dissolved as he laid eyes on the girl sat up against the wall of the cavern, holding onto the corpse of Abigail Jones. She was shivering wildly and two bloodied stumps protruding out of her torn pants where her feet should be.

"Good God!" He murmured and clapped his hand over his mouth, to either suppress his shock or the vomit that was rising in his throat.

"Who is this man, Lindsey?" Lucy whimpered as she cowered close to her best friend's corpse, eyes welling with tears.

"It's okay, Lucy." Agent Wren arrived, "He is going to help us get out of here."

"Really Mister?" Lucy smiled, "You're gonna get us all out of here."

"Yes!" He nodded, removing his hand from his mouth and smiling at her, fighting back the tears that threatened to pour any second. He could not bring himself to look at the child's legs, so he focused on her beautiful dark eyes instead, like two chestnuts, glazed with innocence.

"We need to get out of here as quickly as possible, I have a friend with a car, we can take you back home. Back to your Dad."

"He's going to be so mad at me." Lucy grizzled.

"No, no." Jimmy shook his head as he crouched down in front of her and wiped away her tears with the back of his hand, "I guarantee he won't be mad at you. Not one bit."

"Are you sure?"

"Of course!" Jimmy smiled, "You're one brave little girl you now that? I bet you he'll give you a great big hug."

She smiled.

"Right." Jimmy said standing up, "It's time the three of us got out of here."

"Four!" Lucy said.

"Sorry?"

"We must take Abi." Lucy insisted, gripping her friend's dead body even closer.

"She's not going to leave without Abigail." Lindsey said.

"Okay." Jimmy nodded reluctantly and swallowed hard as he looked into the dead eyes of Abigail Jones.

XXVII

The siren of Chief Gable's 1994 Jeep Cherokee wailed wildly, before being brought to an immediate halt as it rolled into a layaway, not far from the Kratz residence. The red and blue lights dance around, illuminating the trees that surrounded Parliament Grove like a wall around a castle. The net curtains of the Rhonda Kratz's cottage shifted, she was there of course, always watching.

"Kill the lights Darryl." Chief Gable said as he stepped out of the jeep.
The lights died and then there was nothing but the glow from the windows of the Kratz cottage.

"She'll be expecting us to visit, I imagine." Deputy Darryl Whittaker sighed as he joined the Chief.

"She will," Gable replied, but his eyes were focused on the dirt path that led into The Grove itself. "But I haven't got time to deal with her. There's a man in there who is not of his right mind. We need to find him before we do anything else."

"Good! Because I don't think I could stomach any of her cookies at the moment." Whittaker scoffed, trying to make light of the situation, but Gable remained gaunt with distress.

"Now is not the time, Deputy." Gable snapped and Darryl blushed, he knew that the Chief meant business when he referred to him as Deputy.

"Sorry, Chief!" Whittaker apologised and approached the entrance to The Grove, adjusting his belt and zipping up his fur-lined jacket to keep out the chill. He looked up to the clouds that were moving swiftly across the night sky, blocking out the stars and creeping towards the moon the way a great white shark might stalk its prey.

"Looks like we're gonna have some more rain, Chief."

"Yeah, it looks that way," Gable snorted, "but what else is new."

"Do you think Donald is in there?" Whittaker asked.

"I do." Gable replied, "You saw the state of Denny's trailer, someone really did a number on it and it had to be Donald."

"Lucky he wasn't home, I guess."

"I'd say Donald either followed him here or just came here on a hunch."

"According to the call Kratz called in there was no mention of Donald."

"Well, Kratz mentioned a yellow car entering The Grove which also means that Denny and our detective friend are in there somewhere too. You forget that Donald would have come straight through The Grove from the west-side, he wouldn't have needed to use the path."

"Of course. This could get real nasty."

"Exactly! So enough chit-chat and more action."

"Okay, let's do this." Whittaker said with almost excitement in his tone.

"You're staying here, Darryl." The Chief intervened

joining him at the entrance and slipping his hat into place.

"What?" Whittaker exclaimed.

"I want you to stay with the jeep, just in case Donald comes back this way. Well, if any of them come back this way I want them detaining."

"But, Chief, please let me..."

"I can handle this Darryl, just stay with the jeep, please."

Whittaker's shoulders slouched like a petulant child, but he nodded in agreement to his superior's wishes.

"You hear or see anything out of the ordinary and contact me on the radio."

"I will, Chief." Whittaker nodded.

"And if you hear gunshots forget everything I've just said and get your ass in there to help me, okay?"

"Okay Chief," Whittaker laughed, "stay safe."

Gable winked at his Deputy and made his way along the dirt track and into The Grove.

Whittaker watched him walk away, almost envious of how commanding and brave he was, he wished that he could be more assertive like him and it was because he lacked that trait is why he believed that the Chief refused to put his Deputy in harms way.

"He wraps me up in cotton wool." Whittaker sighed and lent up against the jeep, arms folded across his chest in defiance.

"I wish he would just give me a shot, then I could show him what I'm capable of."

The breeze came in with the clouds and disrupted the branches of the trees that loomed over him and the jeep, but he paid no attention, he was too busy feeling hard done by.

"I can handle myself," he scoffed, "maybe I should just go and follow him and show him what I can do."

The remaining leaves flickered in the breeze and a branch creaked uneasily like a heavy weight had just ascended on it.

"No, I couldn't do that." He sighed, "I've never once ignored an order form the Chief."

He heard the snapping of branches from above and several leaves fell around him, he glanced up and still paid no mind to what could be lurking in the shadows above him.

"Maybe that's the problem, maybe I should rebel?"

He drove his fist into a cupped hand and scowled, before laughing to himself and shaking his head, "Who am I kidding?"

He happened to glance over at the Kratz cottage and there standing in the window was Rhonda, her eyes wide and mouthing something to him, terror carved into her round face.

"Oh God, what does she want? Nutty old bat!"

He smiled and waved at her, she gestured with her chubby hand, he believed her gestures meant for him to come inside, but all he did was wave back.

"What's gotten into her?" He said to himself, a look of concern creeping across his brow and then she dived back behind the net curtain and the drapes were drawn quickly.

"Maybe she tried some of her own cookies." He giggled.

The wind picked up and the branches above him quivered again.

"Yeah, let's face facts, Darryl. The Chief always has your best interests at heart and he would never do anything to put you in danger. Maybe I'm better off here."

He was too late to react when Magpa descended silently from the trees above him, his upturned face of shock met her as her beak tore into his chest. Whittaker staggered backwards as Magpa removed her beak and perched on top of the jeep watching on patiently as blood spurted into the air like a fountain. He reached for his gun, as he teetered on the verge of collapse. The gun quivered in his grip, but he had no time to aim and as quick as a hiccup she was on him and had severed his hand from his wrist, it fell to the floor still gripping the handle of the gun. She then gorged herself on his insides before looking up to the moon, viscera and flesh dangling from the tip of her beak as she unleashed a horrendous cry.

XXVIII

Agent Wren had already made it half way up the rope that dangled down the well. She climbed blindly, hand over hand, shimmying up the worn rope liked she had done many times before in her training for the Navy, she could do this with her eyes closed, which was sadly ironic. She took her time, she had to because Lucy Knight was clasped around her torso, eyes closed, afraid to watch with her head buried into Wren's bosom and her arms and legs pinched tightly around her saviour. Wren comforted Lucy with words of positivity and used all her remaining spirit to haul them both up through the shaft of the well.

Jimmy gazed up at them.

"How are you doing?"

"Okay," Wren groaned through the burden of the climb and having a teenage girl wrapped around her. "I'd be doing better if you didn't keep asking me how I'm doing every five seconds!" She snapped, she was frustrated and tired and running on empty.

"Sorry for caring!" Jimmy scoffed, the murmured words carried around the cavern and up to the shaft to meet her ears.

"I heard that!" She snapped again.

Jimmy stared at the decaying half eaten corpse that was once the happy go lucky child, known as Abigail Jones.

He sighed, it was such a sickening sight to see one so young be taken from this world before their time and in such a horrific way made his blood boil and his flesh crawl cold, a strange hypocritical sensation for sure, but that is the feeling that arises when anger meets fear head on.

He had removed his thick red woollen jumper, a Christmas gift from his Auntie that he never thought he would wear, but he had packed it when travelling to Hope Springs during this time of year. He shuddered in a flimsy black t-shirt as he lay the jumper out on the mire and cringed as he lifted her almost weightless corpse and lowered it on top of the jumper and wrapped her in it carefully as if wrapping a fragile Christmas gift. He made sure to cover her horrendous face that had been pecked profusely. He told himself he was covering her face out of respect for the child, but if he was honest with himself he would admit that the sight of her glazed eyes terrified him, it was a sight that would no doubt haunt his dreams for months to come.

"What the hell am I doing with my life?" He asked himself as he stared down at the wrapped bundle at his feet, Abi's legs protruding out from the pulled and frayed red wool.

"We made it!" Wren called down the well, the voice caused Jimmy to jump.

"Are you okay?" Jimmy asked again.

"Yes!" She sighed in annoyance, "Hurry up before she comes back."

"Is Lucy okay?" He called.

"Yeah, I've got her settled, now come on we have to move fast. She'll be back any minute, I can feel it!" She called.

"Calm down, just keep a look out for magpies, if she is close then you'll see them first."

"Oh a comedian!" She snorted, "I can't see shit and he's asking me to go birdwatching!"

Jimmy cringed at his own tactlessness and called up an embarrassed apology.

"Whatever," She scoffed, "just hurry it up!"

Jimmy hoisted the wrapped body of Abigail Jones into the air and somehow managed to tie the excess rope around her body.

"Okay!" He called, "Haul her up."

The rope wriggled from side to side, like the motion of snake, then the body began to lift slowly into the air. Wren tugged on the rope continuously and Jimmy watched on as the wrapped up body went limp under the tautness of the rope that was tied around her torso, her legs dangled in front of his face. Little legs that wore long white socks, now stained with blood and dirt, rising out of two black patent Dolly shoes. Jimmy shuddered as she ascended above his head, eerily lit by the luminous light stick that was rapidly losing its glow. Wren must have been struggling to lift the load after her strenuous ascent or it may have been that a knot in the rope had made it difficult to tug it upwards over the lip of the well, such a menial feat must have been difficult when you were blind to such things.

"Everything okay up there?" Jimmy called and was met by a grunt and the rope quivered causing the body to sway above his head and then start to spin around. Jimmy felt sick to look at her lifeless corpse spinning around like some macabre piñata.

"Bastard!" Wren growled.

"What is it?"

"Rope is stuck on something!" She groaned as she tugged on it vigorously.

"Try lowering her a little and tugging her up again."

The body was lowered gently down, level with Jimmy's eye line again. He couldn't bear it and turned away, staring into a tunnel that led to another cavern, a trail of bones informed him that this was one tunnel he wouldn't be investigating. As far as he was concerned he had to find Abigail Jones and Lucy Knight and that job was over.

Abigail turned around in the air, all the movement had cause her arm to work loose and it fell from its confines falling on Jimmy's head, her ice cold fingertips caressing his cheek. He screamed and the sound flustered Wren so much that she let go of the rope, leaving poor Abigail to fall on top of Jimmy. They both fell to the floor, Jimmy grimacing under the dead body that lay on him.

"Are you alright, Jimmy?" Wren called.

"Y-Yes!" Jimmy stuttered, "Just get her up and out of here for God sakes!"

The rope went taut again and the body moved upwards away from him as he lay there and watched her being lifted up into the shaft of the well, further and further she rose before Jimmy moved, he couldn't bring himself too, he was so shaken up. But he could see now that she had moved up higher than she had been before and stood up wiping the dirt from his clothes.

"Good!" He said, "Be sure to send the rope back down for me when you have untied her."

"I will." Wren growled through the gritted teeth of determination.

Jimmy was amazed at Agent Wren who had shown so much courage and intestinal fortitude, not once even complaining that she had lost her eyesight.

"Whatever kind of organisation the Secret Hunters Horde is, she's one heck of an agent." He said to himself as he waited patiently in the gloom of a dying green light.

XXIX

Jimmy had been waiting for what had seemed to be an eternity for the rope to be lowered back down and he had started to get anxious. He heard nothing from above and his calls had gone unanswered.

Agent Wren lay on the floor crawling backwards through the wet grass and leaves, a hundred magpies circled her pecking at her viciously. She waved her hands at them and occasionally managed to connect with one, sending it sprawling on the floor only for it to shake off the effects, rejoin its horde and continue with the relentless assault.

Lucy dragged herself across the ground through mud and leaves towards Abigail's lifeless body that was still half wrapped in the woollen jumper abandoned next to the well.

"Abi, oh Abi!" Lucy cried, caring not for her exposed wounds that were being heaved through all manner of rottenness, but only for the wellbeing of her best friend. She reached her and removed the rope from around her, exposing her to the cold. Lucy discarded the jumper to one side and then hugged her tightly.

"You're so cold, Abi!" She gasped as she felt her ice cold, decaying flesh, "Why are you so cold? Don't worry, I will keep you warm."

Lucy removed her pink parka which was once a luscious bright colour, almost neon, now it was stained with the grime of all the horrors that made up Magpa's nest. She sat Abi's lifeless body up and put the parka on her zipping it up nicely, as if she were dressing a doll. She seemed oblivious to the magpie attack and the fact that her friend was a corpse.

"There you go, that will keep you snug as a bug in a rug." She smiled and held her friend closely.

"I won't let them hurt you Abi, I won't!" She snivelled and watched on as Agent Wren tried to fight off the mass of magpies that were ganging up on her like schoolyard bullies, cawing and shrieking at her, mocking her for her disability.

"Lindsey!" Lucy cried, fresh tears staining her cheeks.

"It's okay, kid!" She lied, "I've got this covered."

Agent Wren felt around on the floor for something, anything that could act as a shield or weapon to fight back with. She came across an old broken branch, it was thick and heavy and she thought it may well do the job.

"Right then you little wankers," She seethed as she stood cradling the hefty branch in her hands, "let me show you how we do it in Norris Green!"

She launched a frenzied attack with the branch, swiping at the air all around her, taking several magpies out with her propellor like motions. It was enough to cause the birds to back off, but only for them to regroup and attack her from the rear. They pierced her flesh with claw and beak and she cried out in anguish, dropping to her hands and knees in the soaking wet foliage and dirt. Fresh wounds were carved into her head and blood trickled in streaks of red down her matted auburn hair. She refused to surrender, she couldn't bear to think of Lucy being left alone to fend for herself against Magpa, to have her flesh devoured by her and then her bones picked by that despicable horde of hers. Agent Wren was soon back up on her feet, swinging the branch wildly again, using those sordid visions of what might be as motivation and she wailed back at the swooping birds, matching their morbid cries of harassment.

"WHAT'S GOING ON?" Jimmy called from the bottom of the well, still waiting for the rope to drop so he could escape this callous oubliette of death.

Jimmy could hear the high pitch screams of the attacking magpies, the aggressive growls and grunts of Agent Wren and the snivelling of Lucy Knight. All of this met his ears in a cacophony of confusion and he wondered what in God's name was happening above his head.

"Lucy!" Wren called, trying to get her attention, she could sense from her whimpering and incoherent mantra that Lucy was probably going into shock and was no doubt holding the corpse of Abigail Jones again.

She held her so very tightly and rocked back and forth with her in her arms as she cried. Agent Wren's intuition was correct and she didn't need to be a psychiatrist to realise that this kind of behaviour was not healthy for the child, she screamed her name as loud as she could so she could be heard over the whipping of feathers.

"LUCY! GODDAMN IT!" She yelled, slamming the branch into a magpie, flooring it and blindly finding its writhing body with her foot and repeatedly stamping it into the mire.

Lucy gazed at Agent Wren but she was in such a trance she could not make out her words, she was too busy trying to block out the mass of murderous magpies to comprehend what Agent Wren was yelling. Then she caught one word that came through the white noise of wings, 'rope'. Lucy's eyes doubled in size, two dark moist pupils glimmered as understanding gripped her.

"The rope!" Lucy exclaimed and then she could hear Agent Wren's words loud and clear, direction for her to lower the rope down to Jimmy.

Lucy lowered Abi's corpse to the ground and whispered to her comforting words that she would return, encouraging words that fell on the deaf ears of the dead. Lucy pulled herself along the ground, through mud, twigs and foliage until she reached the rope next to the well. She grabbed it and it took a considerable amount of effort for her to rise up to the well on her knees and toss the rope down the dark shaft once again.

"I DID IT!" She called to Agent Wren.

"Good! Now take cover!"

"I..." Lucy began, but then her words choked her, refusing to leave the comfort of her throat as she gazed upon the Magpa, perched on the lip of the well.

Lucy screamed and fell backwards to the ground, instinctively crawling to Abigail Jones' dead body for comfort.

The Magpa shrieked loudly and immediately the magpies left

Agent Wren alone, ascending into the trees. Wren stumbled forwards, ridding herself of the heavy branch and made her way towards the sound of Lucy's screams.

"Lucy? What is it? What's wrong?" Wren said scampering blindly across the clearing before tripping and taking a bad fall next to Lucy and Abigail.

Lucy grabbed hold of her tightly, her fingernails digging into the flesh of her arm and causing the Agent to wince.

"What is it?" She asked again.

"M-Magpa!" She stuttered her reply.

"Oh shit!" Wren murmured, her head instinctively flitting from side to side to search for the creature, but she could not see anything, she would never see anything again.

"Where?" She whispered, thinking that the girl had only spotted the Magpa in a tree or on the outskirts of the clearing.

"There!" Lucy pointed a shaking finger right in front of them, a gesture that was wasted on Agent Wren, but she sensed that the Bird-Witch was very close.

Magpa climbed down from her perch and loudly snapped her beak together rapidly, chattering noisily as her feathers ruffled in the breeze and her talons excavating the mire as she moved towards them.

"Just stay close to me, Lucy." Agent Wren murmured grabbing Lucy and holding her closely.

She could smell the foul stench of death, decay and dampness of Magpa's breath as she loomed over them, breathing on them, inspecting them.

"Stay away from her you fucking bitch!" Agent Wren growled at the creature.

The words did nothing to deter the Bird-Witch and she circled them closely as they huddled together as if them being close could stop this beast's malignant intentions. Magpa chattered again, almost laughing at the agent's empty threats and used her deformed claw that grew from her chest to caress Wren's hair, picking at the blood that was drying in the fibres and causing pain to Wren's scalp.

"Get off me you arsehole! I'll have you, I mean it!"

Magpa tore out the hair from her head causing Wren to screech behind gritted teeth and Magpa snapped her beak at her again in mockery of the blind and helpless agent.

There was a sound from the shaft of the well which caught Magpa's attention and she arched her head to hear what it was. Jimmy's voice came echoing from the shaft as he climbed the rope. Magpa's marbled eyes gleamed with a thirst, a thirst for blood and the eyes smiled sadistically as she turned her intentions to the well.

"NO!" Lucy cried, "Leave him alone!"

The pitch of the child's shriek upset the creature and she turned to caw at the child, her beak a whisker away from the child's face and causing her to burrow her face into the neck of Agent Wren.

"It's okay, it's okay." Wren said soothingly.

But it wasn't okay, far from it.

Magpa seemed to inspect the grounded pair, she considered the empty eye sockets of the Secret Hunters Horde agent and the bloodied stumps of bone and flesh that were Lucy's legs and then chattered loudly before turning away from them and climbing onto the lip of the well, gazing down into the shaft below, waiting for her next meal to come to her.

Agent Wren could no longer smell the foul stench that came from Magpa and asked Lucy, "Where has it gone?"

Lucy glanced up from the agent's neck, tears blurring her vision for a moment.

"She's on the well." Lucy whimpered.

"She's going to ambush Jimmy!"

"Is she going to leave us alone now?" Lucy asked with all the foolish innocence of a child.

"I highly doubt it!" Wren scoffed and could feel Lucy squeeze her tightly.

"Why is she toying with us?"

"She's a sneaky bitch that one, I'll give her that." Wren almost laughed, it was as if she admired the creature for her tactics.

"Why?"

"She knows that a blind woman and a girl with no feet have no chance of escaping."

"Oh!" Lucy sighed, tears forming again.

"If anything we'll be dessert and Jimmy will be the main course."

XXX

Jimmy hauled himself up the rope, almost spent, he had been through so much mentally and physically since arriving in Hope Springs and it was all getting to much as he dangled from a rope in a well.

"I've had the worst day." He grumbled to himself, "It's all just a blur now, so much has happened and I'm getting tired of Hope Springs."

Hand over hand he climbed, his damp, muddy shoes struggling to get purchase on the rope to help push himself upwards.

"And I'm sick to the back teeth of being wet!" He growled, "But it's not raining now and that's promising."

A shadow moved across the opening of the well and it caused him to look up.

"Oh God, no!" He blurted and immediately began to change direction and make his way back down the shaft of the well as the Magpa cackled at him, annoyed that she had been detected and she began to climb into the well to give chase.

"Oh shit, oh shit, oh shit." He whimpered as he clambered to get down the rope as she rapidly gained on him, her wings tucked back as her clawed feet gripped the face of the wall to lower her down quickly.

"Get the hell away from me!" He howled and started to slide down the rope to get away quicker, the rope burnt at his palms and he grimaced with discomfort.

Her large slender beak snapped at him as he ran out of rope and hung in the air above the cavern, instilling an unwanted sense of déjà vu. She lunged at him with that terrifying beak, looking to clamp the aerated edges on his limbs, but she missed again and again. Finally Jimmy let go of the rope, dropping to the moist floor of the well. At least this time his descent was planned and controlled and he knelt in the mud staring at his hands that stung with the heavy burn of friction.

"Okay Jimmy," He asked himself, "What do you do now?"

He gazed up at the entrance to the well and was frozen in awe and horror as she appeared, emerging from the gaping hole in the ceiling of the cavern. The dying light stick was almost spent and it gave off just enough eerie green glow to paint the Magpa gruesomely. It was enough to freeze Jimmy where he stood, her beak and claws gleamed with threat and her eyes displayed heinous desires in radiant green.

She peered into the cavern and unleashed an unholy shriek that could not have come from any being that was created of this world, it was the wail of a banshee from the depths of hell and Jimmy had to pinch himself as he stared into her open maw. His feet sunk slowly into the mud, frozen by pure fear, as if he were a child again playing a friendly game of stuck in the mud and waiting patiently for a friend to run to him and free him from his confines. But it was no childhood game and no friends were coming, that thought alone was grim enough to pull him from his own mind and he clambered backwards gripping at the handle of the revolver that was still stowed in his waistband, the cold muzzle still digging uncomfortably into his spine.

He drew the revolver, his palm sore as it gripped around the handle and positioned a tacky finger on the trigger as he took aim. He had always been a competent shot, as accurate as the rest of them in the police academy, hit the target most of the time. But that was shooting at immobile targets and not bloodthirsty demons from hell that were looming over you at the bottom of wells. His hand trembled violently as he pulled the trigger again and again sending all six bullets speeding towards the oncoming creature. Two of them hit nothing but the cavern ceiling, becoming embedded in the soil, one of them whistled past Magpa and ricocheted off the rocks of the well. Two of them hit their mark, one splintering her limb that acted as her wing, the impact of the bullet, removing several feathers in the process and sending them raining down around the trembling private detective, that held onto the empty revolver for dear life. The final bullet burrowed into her torso and she screamed wildly as she fell from the gaping hole into the mud beside him.

He stood unable to move, he looked down at the mass of feathers lying in heap next to him and he aimed the empty gun at her a habit of a police officer, he kicked the creature gently with the toe end of his shoe.

Magpa didn't move.

Jimmy dropped the empty gun and collapsed to his knees, adrenaline surging through his body.

"I don't believe it!" He sighed, his words quivering with relief, "What just happened?"

He had tears in his eyes and was seemingly unable to move as he began to laugh to himself.

"I don't fucking believe it."

He pulled himself out of the mud and staggered around the cavern until he stood under the well, moisture from the days rain dripped down through the stones and roots and met his face, it was refreshing and he closed his eyes to appreciate the moment. The moment was interrupted when he heard a flurry of wings from above and the shrieking of Agent Wren and Lucy as the magpies descended upon them once more.

"I'm coming!" He called up and grabbed hold of the rope, preparing himself for the climb again. The moment his fingers wrapped themselves around the rope was the moment he heard the ruffling of feathers and the squelching of mud. The chattering of her beak played his spinal-cord like a discordant xylophone, as it seemed to freeze his very soul.

He turned to see the Magpa rise up in the gloom as the light stick died for good and all there was, was the shard of moonlight that illuminated him holding the rope at the bottom of the well.

In the darkness he squinted but he believed she had already moved using the cover of shadow to shroud her movements and he let go of the rope, frantically looking around for her, but he saw nothing, heard nothing.

He swallowed hard and for a second he thought about trying to climb the rope, maybe he could climb fast and make it out, maybe.

In reality he knew that he didn't have a chance at outrunning her, the minute he ascended that rope he would be ripe for the picking and she would have him.

"Where are you?" He called, trying his utmost to be brave, he had to be, where else could he go from here?

He moved around, his eyes everywhere at once, making sure to stay within the circle of light that he stood in. Movement from all around him made him cautious and he staggered around blindly in a circle, losing his bearings. She was circling him, playing with him.

"Don't toy with me you bitch!" He growled, stopping himself from following shadows and clutching at his head to stop it from spinning, he was still suffering from the effects of the concussion and frantically spinning around was not helping matters.

"You think I'm just a ball of yarn and your a big fucking cat! Is that it Nancy?"

There was a shuffle coming from his left and his eyes found the outline of Magpa, her breaths were heavy, and she chattered with annoyance, she couldn't help it and it gave away her position.

"You don't like being called that, do you?" Jimmy smirked, he could see the gleam in her eyes now, her leathery brow had furrowed with irritation.

"That's your true name, you've just forgotten it over all these years."

She stood unmoving, glaring at him, did her brow lose its edge, was it a look of sorrow?

"Does this black magic hang over you like a cloud? Does it block out the memories, of the husband you lost?" He paused to remember his name, "Jonathan."

Her eyes glistened and she seemed to slump down, head and shoulders heavy with remorse.

"Does it control you know? This power that you once called on to save your life? Has it consumed you? Are you more bird than witch now, Nancy?"

Her beak chattered and she stepped forward, her taloned feet squelching in the churned up soil, she remained on the edge of the moon's circle, but now Jimmy could see her and the pain in her moist eyes, was it a tear that he saw slide down that dark length of beak?

"You don't have to live like this, Nancy." He said, stepping towards her, he presumed nobody had ever tried to speak to her before, to find the woman that he believed was still in there somewhere.

"I can help you." He said and smiled at her, she tilted her head to one side and chattered again, as if trying to reply.

"There are people that could help you."

He reached out a hand and her deformed claw cut through the shard of moonlight as if to take his hand, although it was a reluctant gesture.

"It's okay, you can trust me."

Closer the claw came, almost within touching distance, but it waited as she chattered to herself as if she was discussing matters in her own mind.

"Don't listen to it, Nancy."

He had her attention again, her eyes gazing into his.

"Remember all those years ago, remember the good time you had with Jonathan." His fingers touched her claw and she did not recoil from his touch, "Yes, that's it. Unlock those memories of you and your child."

The claw retreated and the eyes that he stared into changed, they burned with fury now, like two flecks of brimstone.

She screamed and lurked towards him again, her wings outstretched and flapping madly.

"Oh shit!" Jimmy cursed and ran backwards, falling over a root and then scrambled backwards blindly towards the tunnel that was the only place open to him. She pursued him, striding with purpose, chattering angrily. Jimmy had stirred memories, but the pain of that day was so great that all it did was fuel her rage and Jimmy would have to pay for picking at a wound that would never heal. He clambered backwards on his rear, his heels churning up the soil beneath as he fled deeper into the tunnel he came to an abrupt end when he felt the pile of bones and flesh behind him and knew that he had gone as far as he could go, as far as he wanted to go.

She hunched down and wrapped her wings around her as she moved into the tunnel.

All of a sudden Jimmy felt claustrophobic, he found it hard to breathe, the air reeked of rotting flesh, dampness and faeces. He felt nauseous, it rose rapidly in his throat and there was no way to suppress it, it came quickly and his gapping maw exploded with thick vomit that singed his throat and the roof of his mouth.

"Oh, Pops is this what death feels like?" He asked as a gentle tear left his eyelid and slid down his face.

Magpa was on him and he had nowhere left go but to join the mountain of corpses that was at his rear. She chattered one last time, a warning or a final word from her serrated beak, whatever it was she said he had no idea and the Bird-Witch moved ever closer to take another victim.

Jimmy's cell phone exploded, the chiming was at such a pitch that it caused the Magpa to shriek and shake her head from side to side in annoyance. Jimmy's face lit up with hope and he scrambled to remove the cell phone from his pocket, immediately the nest was lit by the flashing light of the cell's screen as it rang out loud and proud.

"God bless you, Ma!" Jimmy exclaimed as he looked at the screen and saw a picture of his mother and father smiling back at him, and the words 'Ma Calling' flashing back at him. He held the cell phone out to Magpa who staggered around the nest.

"Answer the call you bitch!" He growled and held it out to her, the light disorientating to her, the sound too much for her to take and she scrambled up onto her nest of bone and flesh. Jimmy was awed when he saw her cowering atop a heap of dead bodies, all of them at very different stages of decomposing. Some were skeletons embedded at the bottom of the pile so old he could not even fathom how long they would have been there. He backed slowly out of the tunnel back into the cavern where the unthinkable happened, the cell phone stopped ringing.

"Oh fuck it!"

Magpa came crashing through the tunnel, fire in her eyes and there seemed no stopping her now as Jimmy willed his phone to ring again.

"Oh, come on Ma, I'll never ignore your calls again ever, I promise!" He screamed, but it wasn't going to ring again and Magpa came ever closer and this time she would not be playing with her food.

He ran into the cavern and jumped towards the rope, with his free hand as the other held the cell phone. Unfortunately his heroic escape was foiled when his own momentum caused him to swing too much and he came tumbling down on the other side face first into the soil. She was on him pecking at his torso. He screamed out in pain and tried to hit her on the temple with the cellphone but it had little to no effect on her and she pecked him again. He jammed his firearm into her beak to stop the pecking, but he could feel her biting down on his arm and slicing at his flesh. He frantically tried to use his thumbprint to unlock his cell phone, which he found very difficult with one hand on the phone, but finally he managed it and as she sliced flesh away from his forearm down to the bone he grimaced and flicked through the application tabs until he found his sounds and ringtones section and selected the first one on the list. He allowed it to play through, the keenness of the chime escaped into the cavern once again, Magpa growled and let go of Jimmy's arm. Blood oozed out from deep wounds that would no doubt leave scars so that he would remember this moment for the rest of his living life, that's if he could survive.

Magpa careened into the wall of the cavern shaking her head as the flashing light dazzled her eyes once again and the ringing echoed around the cavern and sliced her mind like sharpened blades.

Jimmy picked up the cellphone and approached her, she moved away from him quickly, towards the tunnel and to the reassurance of her nest.

"Keep going, keep going." Jimmy chanted under his breath as he pushed her further into the tunnel. When he believed that she was confined in the nest by the earsplitting din he dropped the cell phone in the tunnel. He ran for the rope and worked his way up towards the top, he didn't look back not once all the while the phone chimed loudly and he hoped and prayed that the battery would last.

XXXI

The magpies plummeted from the night sky like dark shards of obsidian, their beaks piercing the flesh of Lindsey and Lucy who sat huddled together, trying to weather the storm of beak and claw. It was all they could do and it was not enough.
It was as if the birds could sense their Queen's angst, feel her pain as though there was a psychic link between Magpa and these feathered reapers of the night.
Lindsey and Lucy continued to cry out as the onslaught continued, but they refused to cease their barrage and relentlessly tore away flesh and hair from the unfortunate pair.
There was a rumbling sound of an engine that suddenly filled the clearing, the magpies were deaf to its spluttering war cry, so immersed in their savage frenzy. The beaten and rusted, yellow Volkswagen Beetle emerged out of the trees and skidded into the clearing, rear wheels spinning rapidly as it looked to gain some traction in the mud and dead leaves. The car slid and span out of control and came to a stop, but still the magpies were not aware of its arrival. Denny thumped down on the horn concealed in the steering wheel and suddenly that had their attention.

"Hey assholes!" He called, hanging out the glassless window, "Why don't you pick on somebody your own size!"
They immediately took him up on his offer and hurtled towards

him, raining down on the car, breaking what was left of the glass in the windows, denting the shell of the poor vehicle and swarming around the open window to get at him. He leaned back and removed a revolver and stuffed it into the nearest magpies beak and pulled the trigger. The bullet exploded as soon as it left the barrel, a spluttering of black and white feathers filled the air and the magpies suddenly dispersed, heading for the safety of the branches, where they remained, watching the group intently, no doubt planning their next move.

"You'll stay where you are if you know what's good for ya!" He yelled to them as he exited the car, wedging the revolver into the waistband of his pants, leaving the door wide open and the keys in the ignition.

"Who is that?" Lindsey called out, relief and trepidation blurring her mind.

"It's okay, I'm a friend of Jimmy's. I'm here to help." He smiled as he moved towards them and crouched down to greet them.

"Thank God." Lindsey exhaled.

"Are you hurt?" He asked and immediately winced with horror and a little bit of embarrassment as he gazed upon her eyeless sockets.

"Erm, just a bit!" Lindsey scoffed.

"Lucy are you okay?" He asked her, she peeled her face out of Lindsey's chest and stared at him.

"Denny Lamont?"

"Yes, it's me, it's Denny."

"They all said you did this, but they were wrong weren't they?"

"Yes, they were." Denny nodded, "I have only ever tried to keep Hope Springs safe."

"I believe you."

Denny smiled.

"That means the world to me Lucy, thank you."

"You're welcome." She said nonchalantly.

"Are you hurt? Can you move?"

She shook her head and started to cry again.

"What's wrong?"

"That bitch took her feet." Lindsey growled.

"Dear God!" Denny gasped and his own eyes were glazed with moisture, he shook his head at the cruelness of this creature. He reached out and took Lucy's hand, "I'm going to get you out of here Lucy."

"You promise?"

"I promise!" He held out his little finger to her, "Pinky promise?" He said, "You know how to pinky promise?"

"Oh sure! Abi and I do it all the time." And with that she hooked her little finger around his and they smiled at each other. It was then Denny realised that Abigail Jones' dead body was lying next to them.

"Abigail!" He whispered.

"Well, this is great and all, but I can't see a fucking thing and if I'm not mistaken the magpies are still watching us and that bitch is down in the well with Jimmy."

"Jimmy's down there with her?" Denny gasped.

"You need to get us the fuck out of here." Wren growled, grabbing hold of his shirt and shaking him.

"Seeing as you asked so nicely." Denny grinned and rose carefully, his breaths were heavy under all the excitement and pressure, he knew in his heart of hearts that he didn't have long left in this world, so if he could save this woman and this child at least people would remember that of him.

"Come on!" He said grabbing her arm and pulling her up to her feet, her wounds were many and weeping eagerly.

"Up you get Lucy." He said and he scooped her up in his arms and lifted her of the ground and started to walk away.

"No!" She screamed.

Denny looked at her dumfounded as she continued to scream in a frenzy, almost to the point of hyperventilating.

"What is it? What's wrong?"

"She won't leave without Abi." Wren added.

"Shit." Denny murmured as he looked back at the corpse of Abigail Jones lying in a lifeless heap.

"Take her!" He said to Lindsey and handed Lucy over, the unexpected weight thrust into her arms almost knocked her off balance.

"What the hell!" Wren called, and then realising it was Lucy in her arms she cradled her and soothed her instinctively by rocking back and forth and stroking her hair.

"Look, I'll get Abi, you get to the car."

"Where the hell's the car?" She scoffed with annoyance.

"Straight ahead about twenty or thirty paces. Now go!"

"You promise you'll get Abi?" Lucy called as Agent

Wren carefully walked towards the car.

"I promise!" Denny called and his attention was shifted to the magpies above them. They were jostling for position on the branches and Denny had seen this many times before, they were about to rain down on them again, hard.

"Not this time!" He growled under his breath, "Not today!" And as Agent Wren and Lucy Knight were half way to the car, unbeknownst to them that the magpies were regrouping and readying themselves for another attack, Denny had moved past the carcass of poor Abigail Jones and dove into Jimmy's rucksack where he removed a flare. The magpies began to descend, aiming primarily for Lucy and Agent Wren as they made their way cautiously to the car.

"Let's see what you can do now, you little bastards."
Denny span the red cylinder in his hands before flicking off the plastic lid, unscrewing the cap and igniting the flare. It immediately spat out a display of fire and then plumes of thick red smoke erupted from it and Denny discarded it to the centre of the clearing. The instant that the clearing was filled with the bright red glow and choking smoke the descending harpies retreated, higher up into the trees, cawing with annoyance. Denny watched them for a while and when he was happy that they weren't going to ambush him he moved towards Abigail, reluctantly scooping her up and holding her closely. The smell of her rotting flesh and the flare smoke was hell on earth to him and his inferior lungs, causing him to wheeze and choke as he moved towards the car as quickly as he could. He saw Agent Wren and Lucy getting into the car, Wren making sure that

Lucy was safely nestled in the backseat and Wren collapsed next to her resting her head worn and frayed headrest.

"I can't see them." Lucy said straining her eyes to see anything through the thick red smog.

"You and me both." Wren sighed, before calling out into the smog. "Is everything okay Denny?"

There was no answer as Denny had to stop to take a knee and rest for a while, his lungs were on fire.

"Rest when you're dead, Denny." He said to himself, "You have to do this. You have to get them out of here."

"Denny?" Wren called again.

"I'm coming." He wheezed.

"I can see them! They're coming." Lucy cried with excitement.

"Thank fuck for that!" Wren sighed as she lent back into the passenger seat, finally feeling relief that this whole ordeal was over.

Denny emerged from the red smoke a proud grin painted on his face, he was hurting inside, his chest felt as though he had swallowed that flare and at any moment it would explode and he would be blown into smithereens. But through all this he felt a sense of achievement, he could finally wipe away the black smudge that had shrouded his name. He cradled Abigail's limp body with care and affection, like he was carrying a child.

"It's okay, I'm here." He whispered to the carcass of the dead child.

The sound of a rifle echoed through the clearing and the bullet ripped through Denny's chest. He staggered back and lost his footing, but somehow managed to stay upright, still gripping Abigail's body tightly in his arms, a look of bewilderment appeared on his face and he glanced down and saw blood trickling from a hole in his fragile chest.

"What?" He murmured to himself.

"What the fuck is happening?" Wren cried, bolting upright, "Who's shooting?"

"Denny's been shot!" Lucy gasped.

Denny dropped to his knees and tears streamed down his face as he tried to come to terms with what was happening. He gazed around into the red clearing, smoke and trees and the black eyes of the watchful magpies that seemed delighted with proceedings.

"No, I won't let it end like this, I won't!" Denny grimaced and somehow made it back to his feet, teetering from side to side and then strode on towards the car, "I will not be blamed for this, I will be remembered for helping to put an end to this."

"Put her down Lamont!" Growled Donald Knight who appeared through the smoke, leading with the business end of his rifle, aimed directly at Denny Lamont.

"No, I have to..." Denny tried to speak, but his lungs were weeping and the effort was becoming too much for him.

"PUT HER DOWN!" Donald roared and pulled the trigger again, sending another bullet hurtling through the air and ploughing through Denny's chest.

Denny dropped to his knees, reluctantly released his grip on Abigail jones and she fell and rolled away from him coming to a halt face down in a pile of dead leaves as Denny collapsed, wavering breathes leaving his body for the last time.

Donald approached Denny and gazed into his glazed eyes, that were busy blinking back tears.

"You were to blame for all of this!" Donald spat, "And now it's all over."

"No…" Denny spluttered, blood and saliva oozed out from the corners of his mouth, "…you're wrong…it was never…me…and…it's not over…yet."

XXXII

Jimmy reached the top of the well, in what seemed like record time, faster than any time he had ever had to climb it in gym class as a teenager, even faster than during his trials in the police academy.

"Maybe they should employ her at the police academy." He scoffed, "The reluctant lardasses would soon be up that damn rope if she was snapping at their heels."

Below him in the depths of the well he could still hear the chiming of his cellphone as Magpa shrieked in agony. He hoped the battery would last, he hoped that she wouldn't figure out that with one peck from her mighty beak she could destroy the handset and rid herself of this foul sound that plagued her delicate ears.

He gripped the craggy rock of the well and lifted himself up, relief pouring out of him in one enormous sigh. It took his eyes a few moments to acclimatise to the glowing red smog that filled the clearing. Through squinting eyes he could just make out the unmistakable slender silhouette of Denny Lamont, and smiled, he wanted to call to him and tell him that he had everything under control. All they would have to do now was seal up the well and leave it for the authorities to clean up, well, this Secret Hunters Horde, they would be the ones to clean up this kind of mess he thought.

But it suddenly dawned on him that something was wrong and his eyes doubled in size as he gazed on in horror to witness a bullet rip through Denny's tender torso, exploding out through his spine in an eruption of crimson droplets.

The moment happened so quickly and was so surreal that Jimmy could do nothing but watch on helplessly as Denny collapsed into the mire.

"DENNY!" Jimmy called and scrambled out of the well, getting a third wind from somewhere and charging across the clearing to the body that lay prone on the floor.

"Denny, Oh God, no!" Jimmy gasped as he reached him, sliding in the mud and leaves before scooping his almost weightless body in his arms and cradling his head on his lap. He gazed down at the two holes in his torso, his flimsy shirt soaking up the blood like a sponge, spreading it out until you would have thought that Denny Lamont's shirt was red when he left his trailer that day.

"What have you done?" Jimmy screamed at Donald Knight who stood holding his rifle in shaking hands.

"I did what had to be done." Donald spat, tears welling up in his eyes, "This has been a long time coming and someone should have had the balls to do it years ago."

"No, you're wrong!" Jimmy growled, he felt so emotional, even though he didn't know Denny Lamont very well, he felt close to him, he knew that he shared the same values as him. He just wanted to help people, something that he had always tried to do.

"He killed them all, all those kids...my Lucy."

"Goddamn you!" Jimmy roared as he leapt from the floor and let Denny's body fall unceremoniously to the ground. He launched himself at Donald, grabbing him by the lapels of his jacket and shaking him vigorously, "Are you so stupid? Are you?"

"What..." Donald spat, as Jimmy shook him erratically, as if to shake some sense into him.

"Look!" Jimmy cried and span him around, pointing him towards the beaten up Volkswagen Beetle to where a watery eyed Lucy Knight stared out of the rear window.

"Lucy!" He gasped, and staggered slowly towards the car, relieving himself of the burden of his rifle as he moved towards her. He placed a hand on her face and she cupped the back of his hand, both of them had matching streams of tears rolling down their cheeks that it could have almost been a reflection.

"Lucy, my baby." Donald murmured and he opened the rear door, the moment of relief and elation was quickly replaced by the horrific sight that met his eyes.

"Daddy," She snivelled, "She took my feet."

"Good God!" Donald cried, collapsing on the back seat crying uncontrollably into his daughter's lap.

"It's okay, Daddy," Lucy said as she held his head tightly, "My friend Lindsey saved my life."

"Lindsey?" Donald said rising up with confusion on his moist face.

Agent Wren appeared from behind his daughter, staring back at him with two deep black sockets, cheeks stained with tears of blood.

Donald screamed and fell back out of the car into the wet cold leaves.

"Don't worry, I get that a lot." Wren scoffed.

"What..." was all that Donald could manage as he sat whimpering.

"Don't worry Daddy, she's on our side."

"Our side?" He whimpered, "Then who is on the other side?" He peered over his shoulder towards the well and finally the realisation hit him like a left cross, that there was in fact something dwelling in its depths. Something not of this world that was to blame for all the pain and suffering in Hope Springs over the years.

Jimmy stood over the corpse of Denny Lamont who suddenly coughed up blood and started to stir.

"Jesus!" Jimmy gasped and knelt to meet him, "Denny, can you hear me?"

"Just...about..." Denny spluttered.

"I don't believe it!" Jimmy shook his head.

"I know...how am I not dead yet..." Denny laughed.

"What can I do? Is there anything I can do for you?" Denny shook his head.

"No, my friend, this...this is it for me...just tell me one...one thing..."

"Of course!"

"Tell me we won..."

Jimmy looked up at the night sky that was filled with red fog, a fog that was slowly disbanding and watched as the mass of magpies jumped around on the branches, preparing themselves for another onslaught as soon as this horrendous red shield had dispersed.

"Tell me...Jimmy."

Jimmy gazed at the well and he could no longer hear the chiming of the cell phone and knew that any minute now that the Magpa would pull herself out of that well in search of yet more blood and destruction.

"We won, Denny." Jimmy smiled and held his hand tightly, "I will see to it that everyone knows what a hero you were."

Denny smiled and held Jimmy's hand tightly before his grip fell loose and Denny murmured his final words. "We...won..."

Denny was gone and as Jimmy stood up, Donald had approached from the rear and placed a hand on his shoulder, Jimmy felt a fire forming in his stomach, he wanted to scream at him to remove his hand, he wanted to punch the bastard right in his face.

But what good what that do anybody?

"I'm sorry." Donald said, "I didn't..."

"Listen?" Jimmy interrupted, spinning to face him, "That's the word you're looking for. None of you listened and now he's dead. That lady in there has no eyes and your daughter will never walk again. All because you didn't listen!"

Donald bowed his head in shame and Jimmy turned away, unable to bring himself to look at him.

Jimmy crouched down and retrieved the revolver that was

tucked in Denny's waistband.

"What are you going to do with that?" Donald stuttered, swallowing hard and looking sorry for himself. "Are you going to shoot me? I guess I deserve that. I can't believe I took his life, oh Jesus! What did I do?" Donald trembled, consumed by his own self pity and guilt.

"Stop feeling sorry for yourself!" Jimmy snapped.

"So what are you going to do?"

"Put and end to all this."

"An end to what? Is it not over?"

"I don't think it ever will be. Just get in the car and comfort your daughter."

Donald nodded and sheepishly walked back towards the car.

Jimmy held the gun in his hand and gazed at Denny, he looked so peaceful now, a beautiful smile caressing his lips, he looked almost angelic.

"I'll end this for you, Denny, I promise." He said and held the revolver up, but before he could take a step towards the well he was halted in his tracks from a familiar, gruff voice.

"Put the gun down, Jimmy."

Jimmy turned around to see Chief Gable standing behind him pointing Old Betsy at him, wearing a look of bewilderment on his ageing face.

"Hi, Chief," Jimmy smiled, "bit late to the party aren't ya?"

"Cut the shit, Jimmy." The Chief snapped, "Did you kill Denny?"

"No." Jimmy replied, calm and nonchalantly.

"Then what the hell happened here? I've just had a peek in your car and there's a lady with no eyes, Lucy Knight has no feet and Donald is quivering like a shitting dog!"

"So, you're all caught up."

"Don't get smart with me, Jimmy!" Gable snapped.

"I'm sorry, Chief, I've had one hell of a day."

"I can only presume she is one of the missing federal agents?"

"Yes, but she's not working for the government."

"No?"

"It's some organisation called The Secret Hunters Horde."

"Never fucking heard of them!" Gable scoffed with defiance.

Jimmy laughed, he liked Chief Gable and even in a moment like this when the Chief was being serious he still made him laugh.

"Don't laugh at me Jimmy, I'm not in the mood for games." Gable growled, his moustache quivering angrily as he moved closer to Jimmy.

"Sorry, Chief."

"And now there's the dead body of Denny and your holding a gun and...who's that?" He nodded to the corpse of Abigail Jones, face first in a pile of leaves.

"That's Abigail Jones, Chief." He sighed as he stared at her through weary eyes, "I guess I found her after all."

"Tell me one thing, Jimmy!"

Jimmy turned to look him square in the eye, paying no attention to the quivering silver barrel of Old Betsy that reflected a glare of pink from the flashing of the red flare back into his eyes, "Did you do this Jimmy?"

"No, Chief."

Chief Gable was a good man and a good Police Chief, but one thing he would pride himself on and that was being a great judge of character. The angry scowl, that contorted his moustache left and he nodded at Jimmy, he read his face, looked into his eyes and knew he was telling the truth. Slowly he holstered Old Betsy and knelt down to inspect Denny's body, he saw the two wounds in Denny's torso and knew immediately that they couldn't have been made by the revolver Jimmy was holding. He saw the rifle lying on the floor and picked it up by its warm barrel, being cautious not to touch the trigger.

"So what happened?"

"The Magpa, that's what happened." Jimmy replied.

"Oh don't give me that horse shit, Jimmy." Gable growled standing back up and cursing his joints that had started to fail him.

"Take a look around Chief!" Jimmy replied, "Does any of this make any sense to you?"

Chief Gable glanced around the clearing, consumed by plumes of red smoke as a mass of magpies fidgeted around anxiously on their branches. He noticed the poor broken-down carcass of Olive the Volkswagen Beetle, its shell filled with holes and not a piece of glass in its windows. Inside the vehicle sat a sobbing middle aged man, a girl without any feet and a woman who had had her eyes scooped out of their sockets. His eyes found two dead bodies on the floor, one of them shot, the other half eaten and starting to rot.

He gazed at Jimmy and shook his head from side to side.

"I can't believe that an urban legend is responsible for all this! In my world there has to be rational explanation for everything."

"Do you know something, Chief," Jimmy chuckled, "Before I came to Hope Springs that's exactly how I looked at the world, but if this town has taught me one thing it's that things aren't always what they appear to be and there isn't always a rational explanation."

Gable shook his head.

"I can't believe it, Jimmy, I won't."

"I understand your reluctance, Chief, and I know you won't believe it until you see it...you probably don't even want to see it because then you'll know that Denny Lamont was right all along and you and the town of Hope Springs ignored his warnings."

"Jimmy," He sighed, "I just want to know what has gone on here so we can move on and start to rebuild. The town's morale is ever so low and it's always left to me to pull them out the mire. If I go back and tell them stories of witches and goblins then they'll laugh me right out of town."

"I don't agree." Jimmy said defiantly shaking his head.

"You don't? Pray tell?"

"I think that deep down they all believe that there is something not quite right about this place. They'll believe."

Gable looked at him dubiously and was about to again try and get to the bottom of what actually happened when he heard something coming from the well that gained his attention.

"What was that?" Gable asked, the sound was a rapid scrapping sound, that increased in speed and volume.

"You know that urban legend that you don't believe in?" Jimmy asked and knew he would not get a reply, so he finished his own question, "Well, you're about to meet her."

The Magpa angrily burst out of the well, Jimmy's broken cell phone gripped in the deformed claw that protruded from her torso. She shrieked loudly and spread her wings, the dying flames of the flare reflected in her eyes making them burn with rage.

"Holy Mary Mother of God!" Gable gasped and remained frozen to the spot as those behind him in the back of the car cowered, holding each other tightly. Donald turned his face away from the creature and couldn't bring himself to look at it.

Magpa discarded the cell phone to the floor, the screen shattered, the handset now dented and scratched.

"I knew I should have taken out the extra warranty on that thing."

She squealed so angrily as she pulled herself out of the well.

"What the hell do we do?" Gable asked.

"Give her hell!" Jimmy growled and aimed the revolver at her, he unloaded, Gable followed suit and instinctively aimed the rifle at the creature and unleashed whatever ammunition was loaded.

The bullets found their mark and each one tore through her leathery flesh, much to the displeasure of the magpies on the branches overhead, they flew around screeching, haphazardly colliding with trees and dropping out of the air to their deaths. She cried out, a sound that was like nothing that they had ever heard before, a cacophony of a human cries and maniacal shrieks. The wailing was such a horrendous sound that neither of them would ever be forget, but if asked to explain it, there would be no way of doing so.

Jimmy and the Chief continued to pull on the triggers long after the guns were empty, both of them lost in the moment and terrified beyond comprehension. Blood burst from her wounds and she fell backwards down the well, her body could be heard colliding with the walls and her wings flapped helplessly as she fell into the dark abyss below.

Jimmy and the Chief lowered their guns and turned to each other, eyes wide, mouths gaping.

"What just happened?" Gable asked, his voice was quiet, as if a raised voice would reawaken whatever it was that just came out of the well.

"I think we got her." Jimmy whispered back and the pair dropped their guns, both firearms spent of ammunition and useless to them now.

The reluctant pair crept towards the well.

"What's going on out there?" Wren asked, Lucy who was cradling her father's head in her lap as he openly cried out loud, riddled with grief and terrified of the scene that had just played out before his eyes.

"Jimmy and the Chief just shot the witch and it fell

down the well."

"Oh!" Wren exclaimed, "Now what's happening?"

"They're headed for the well." Lucy shrugged.

"NO!" She yelled, halting the Chief and Jimmy in their stride. They turned around to face the beaten and weary Volkswagen and saw the eyeless SHH agent screaming at them.

"Don't go near it!" She called.

"It's okay, miss, we have this under control." Gable replied and they continued on their way.

"They're so dead." Wren sighed as she collapsed back into her seat.

Jimmy and Gable cautiously leaned over the lip of the well and stared into the darkness, all that met them was a deep black hole and an eerie silence.

"We should really make sure it's dead." The Chief said.

"Be my guest, Chief!" Jimmy scoffed and gestured for him to descend the well. "I've already been down there once and I don't plan on a second visit."

"What's down there?" Gable asked reluctantly, not really wanting to know.

"The Magpa's nest and the remains of all her victims."

"Good God!"

"It's a graveyard, Chief. All those faces you see staring back at you on that flyer tree? Fifty bucks and my right nut says they're all down there."

"So what's next?" Gable seemed to be in a state of shock that he couldn't function and Jimmy had to take the reins.

"We seal up the well and wait for the Secret Hunters Horde to come and sort it out I guess."

Before another word could be spoken between the two, Magpa exploded from the mouth of the well, her eyes burned with ferocity, her wounds weeping as her talons clawing at the rocks as she heaved herself out of the dark shaft.

Jimmy and Chief Gable seemed to move in slow motion but it all happened so fast, her wings spreading wide and flapping vigorously as she loomed over the horrified private investigator and local Chief of Police.

Those in the confines of the car, gazed on unable to do anything about what was taking place in front of them. Tears ran down Lucy's cheeks freely, without her knowledge, it seemed to be an automatic response now. Her father looked dumfounded and had no coherent words for what he was witnessing. Ironically Agent Wren would have given anything to see what was happening, even if the sight was abominable.

The magpies were riled up into a frenzy, and with the flare rapidly dying, they would look to join their Queen and attack whatever lay before them. Magpa lunged forward and her serrated black beak scythed towards them, looking to decapitate them and have done with it. Jimmy threw himself at the Chief and pushed him out of harms way and they both tumbled to the floor. Magpa's momentum caused her to lose her footing and her claws dislodged several rocks that fell from the well as she clambered onto the mire, her wings wide to keep her upright as she slid on the damp leaves.

She moved cautiously towards the floored pair, trying not to slip in the mulch and sodden foliage beneath her curved talons. Jimmy rose up and span around to face her.

"Nancy, stop this!" He roared and somehow he caught the creature's attention, halting her in her tracks.

"This needs to stop!" He growled again.

Her head tilted to one side trying to comprehend what he was saying to her.

"It's time that you leave the good people of Hope Springs alone, they are not to blame for what happened to you!"

The red smog had all but disappeared and the magpies came swooping down, hatred in their eyes, a thirst for blood on their beaks, but one glance from Magpa's marbled eyes was enough for them to immediately change course and return to their perches.

"Jimmy what's happening?" Chief Gable asked, trying to lift himself out of the pile of wet leaves he had fallen into.

"I think she's listening to me!" Jimmy murmured and smiled at the Bird-Witch that towered over him, bravely he stepped closer to her and she moved her head awkwardly in her surprise of his gesture, it was a rarity to see anyone approach her of their own free will and it made her uncertain.

"It's time to stop terrorising these people," Jimmy added staring into her eyes, observing that she was indeed listening too him, "you cannot blame them any longer, it's not their fault what happened, it was Bittern that took your family, not these innocent people."

Her eyes shimmered as if tears would fall from them any

second, but she twitched at the mention of the old Judge's name and then the eyes returned to those burning, foul balls of fire and it was then that Jimmy realised he could not reason with this creature, the woman that was once Nancy Cartwright had been lost to the magic long ago.

The gruesome, misshapen claw extended from between the empty sacks of flesh that were once her breasts, and grabbed him by his throat, immediately cutting of his air as she squeezed tightly, hoisting him up from the ground, his shoes caked in mud kicking desperately in search of somewhere to tread to take the pressure off his throat. Unfortunately there was nowhere to tread and all he could hear was the muffled voices of Lucy, Donald and Agent Wren calling to him, he could not have told you what the voices had said as it felt as though his eardrums were about to implode. His face turned almost a deep shade of purple as life was ebbing away, saliva bubbled from his gapping maw, blood trickled from his nostrils and the veins of his temples throbbed erratically forcing moisture out from around Jimmy's eye balls. As he gazed into Magpa's face he could see now that she was more bird than human, her bloodthirsty instincts for survival replacing any other emotions and feelings that a normal human being would have instilled. No morals, no compassion, no love.

He tried to speak, say words that he had never wanted to say, an apology to his father, he wanted to say he was sorry that he was not going to be able to find out the truth of what happened to him but she opened up her massive beak and he saw her black tongue, wriggling playfully, calling to him, he knew it was over.

There was a loud noise that erupted nearby, but to Jimmy's ears whatever it was sounded muffled.

The vice-like grip around his neck loosened and he gasped greedily for luscious air as he dropped to the ground and his hearing slowly returned. He rubbed at his throat with his chaffed hands, breaths heavy. He heard several gunshots, the first one caused him to jump out of his skin and he watched as the Magpa screamed, her wings flapping in a frenzy, as blood spurted out into the air. He turned slowly, ears ringing now, he saw Chief Gable standing majestically with Old Betty's muzzle smoking and relief consumed him as he finally felt safe.

The magpies wailed as they all left their perches and hurtled down towards them, the mass of feathers blocking out the moon, but one final bullet left Gable's magnum and burrowed itself between Magpa's eyes, she staggered backwards and fell back down into the well.

The magpies seemed to spasm in the air, convulsing at seeing their Queen fall.

"One for sorrow." Jimmy murmured and then felt himself being hoisted up to his feet, turning to look into the bewildered and stern face of Chief Gable.

"Jimmy? Can you hear me?" Gable asked, Jimmy nodded his response, his throat felt too tender, like raw meat, he couldn't seem to answer.

"Thank God!" Gable sighed and patted him on his shoulder, "Look, I'm so sorry that I didn't believe you, I'm devastated that I didn't listen to Denny when I should have,

I'm..."

Jimmy flung his arms around the Chief and Gable was thrown off by the action that at first he felt uncomfortable, but then as Jimmy's arms grew tighter around him, he relented and hugged him back.

"Thank you, Chief." Jimmy croaked.

The magpies rained down around them hitting the floor recklessly, hundreds of dead twitching carcasses carpeted the clearing as Chief Gable led Jimmy to the battered Volkswagen Beetle.

"Shall I drive?" The Chief asked, but Jimmy shook his head.

"I got this Chief."

Gable squeezed his wide frame into the passenger's seat as the others greeted him with fond encouragement for ridding them of the Bird-Witch.

Jimmy remained solemn, slowly clicking his seatbelt into place, he turned the key and after a few clicks and splutters the engine finely burst into life.

"Where too then, Jimmy?" The Chief asked, "How about we head back to Bobby's for a stiff one!"

Jimmy failed to reply, only stared out of the glassless windshield and clicked his tongue irritatingly.

"That sounds good to me!" Agent Wren scoffed.

"I could do with something." Donald agreed.

"Well, the drinks are on me." Gable cried.

"What about Abi?" Lucy asked and realism seeped back into the car, there were still two bodies sprawled out on the floor.

"I'll come back and sort everything out, my dear." Gable smiled at her, "I promise."

Jimmy put the car into reverse and backed up to the edge of the clearing, he had moved so quickly that it hadn't given any of his passengers the time to manoeuvre themselves.

"Jesus Christ, Jimmy!" Gable choked, "What's gotten into you?"

"You'd best buckle up." Jimmy said, staring at the well in the centre of the clearing and pushing his foot up and down on the accelerator, causing the engine to growl.

"What's going on?" Wren asked.

"I think the detective has lost it." Donald blurted out as he searched frantically for his seatbelt.

"Just put your seatbelts on please." Jimmy said sternly, his eyes almost bulging out of his head as he focused solely on the well.

"What the hell are you thinking?" Gable asked as he heard the scrapping of metal attaching itself into place behind him, he was now the only one that had yet to buckle up.

"We have to seal that well, Chief." Said Jimmy.

"Are you crazy? I just shot her in the head, she's dead!"

"I have to make sure!" Jimmy growled, pushing his foot down again, revving up the engine.

"But..." Gable cried, but it was too late, the wheels had started rolling and Jimmy pushed the Beetle forwards, at top speed, forcing it forward towards the well. Gable realised that Jimmy wasn't going to stop and frantically felt around for his seatbelt, managing to lock it into a place as the neared the well.

"GOD DAMN IT JIMMY!" Chief cried.

"I owe it to Denny, I have to seal it!" Jimmy replied as they approached the well rapidly.

"Wait a minute?" Wren asked, "What are we sealing the well with?"

Just as they neared a claw grabbed ahold of the lip of the well and Magpa pulled herself up, a wing flapping and her beak chattering frantically as the car drove straight into the formation of rocks that made up the well.

Those within the car screamed frantically as Jimmy led them into a surge that destroyed the well, a feat that did not leave a good impression in the hood of the car.

Magpa fell back down into the cavern as rock and dirt rained down around her, the shaft collapsing in on itself and closing up, she called to her birds but there were none to come to her aid this time and the hole disappeared.

Jimmy tugged the gear leaver into reverse and slowly backed out of the rubble, the car wheezing under the strain, its engine hissing, matching the sighs of relief that came from within.

"Brave old Olive." Jimmy sighed and stroke his hand across the steering wheel, before patting it with affection.

Jimmy unbuckled his seatbelt and stepped out of the vehicle he watched on as the well collapsed in on itself, rocks and dirt filling in the hole.

The others stared out of the window, Agent Wren and Lucy held each other tightly, knowing that their ordeal was over.

"It's done now, Lucy." Agent Wren whispered, "She

can't hurt you now."

Donald burst into tears again, guilt and fear constricting his chest, still unable to fathom what had happened here tonight and what he had done.

"Oh, God forgive me!" He whimpered.

Chief Gable looked around at the others in the rear of the Volkswagen Beetle and shook his head in disbelief, turning to watch Jimmy as he stared at the huge divot that was once a well where a unholy creature of hell had dwelled, but now had been smothered by the walls of her own fortress.

Jimmy turned to face those that had fallen, tears rolling down his cheeks as raindrops starting descend on him once again. He gazed up at the sky, staring into the thick dark cloud that always seemed to hang above him. He let the relentless stream of rain soak his face and mix with his tears as if it cleansed him of this whole horrid experience. He turned to the dead bodies of Abigail Jones and Denny Lamont and sighed.

"I'm sorry I was too late, Abi." He whispered before turning to Denny and saying the words that he hoped would help Denny rest in peace.

"It's over now."

XXXIII

    Jimmy believed that it was time for him to leave Hope Springs, he had already spent more time here than he had first assumed he would. He decided to take Chief Gable's offer to stay another week as the town's guest of honour.

Thankfully it's not raining. That makes a refreshing change. I was starting to think that I had become an amphibian and needed the moisture just to survive.

He chortled to himself as he stood at the rear of the crowd that had gathered in the town's square to pay tribute to those that had been lost. He had chosen to stand at the back of the crowd out of sight, he didn't want a fuss.

Chief Gable stood on a small stage behind a podium addressing the good people of Hope Springs, a tall and daunting structure stood behind him, draped in a huge tarpaulin.

Jimmy's name had been mentioned several times throughout the Chief's speech, one about the pain and suffering that the town has been through and spoke of those that had been lost. He did not at any time make reference to the Magpa, this Bird-Witch that tore out the throats of children and pecked out their eyeballs to graze on them like some overindulgent royal. If asked he would just say it was 'something', a word that covered a multiple of sins, he probably could not describe it anyway, even if he tried really hard, that would need him to remember, to cast his mind back to that night and relive the creature clambering out of the well and grasping Jimmy Johnson, Jr. around his scrawny neck and squeezing the life out of him. These were images that already haunted his dreams at night and didn't want to share them with the good people of the town. So his answer to what was responsible for the disappearances...the murders, was simply, 'something'. He was obviously trying to shield the people of his town from such a monstrosity, but it left many to paint their own picture of what had happened and who was responsible. Some made accusations that a mythical creature known as The Blackfoot was responsible, tales of this Sasquatch type creature had spread far and wide but others laughed at such nonsense and believed that it was an escaped lunatic from either the Oakland Institute near Studd City, or Creak-Coast House in Sanctuary City. Whatever they now believed they all knew that Denny Lamont was not responsible.

Chief Gable had paid tribute to Denny and talked about how sorry he was for not believing him, Jimmy had watched on with great interest when the Chief had dropped this bombshell in the congregation's lap and took a little bit of smug satisfaction to watch their faces blush and their heads lower with shame.

He thought of Denny and what an unsung hero he had been, trying with all his might to keep the monster at bay for the past thirty something years and now only in his death did the people of the town appreciate what he did and who he was.

They should feel ashamed.

He had thought and scowled angrily as he did so, but quickly shook it from his mind, this was a day for remembrance not belligerence.

Jimmy thought that it was very strange how death brought people and communities together, especially when the events had been so horrendous.

It's amazing how human beings find comfort in those around them and lean on each other as they instinctively rebuild the walls that have fallen around them. Just a few weeks ago these people were terrified, throwing around accusations and slander and now they stand together united, hand in hand. It gives me hope for humanity that whatever we go through, we can come through the other side.

He gazed around and was happy to see that Rhonda Kratz had been welcomed into the fold, her face beamed just being around people again.

Perhaps that's all that she needed.

Rhonda Kratz stood next to Bertha Colley, two jolly, rotund ladies standing behind a table filled with all manner of cakes and cookies that they had lovingly prepared for the occasion. "Krazy" Kratz and "Big" Bertha united to fill the faces of folk, handing out their treats to a group of children. Jimmy couldn't help but cringe as he saw a young boy biting into one of Kratz's cookies.

Meow. Rather you than me kid!

He saw Rachel Jones, dabbing at her weeping nostrils with a handkerchief, eyes red and raw, as she was consoled by her friend and employer, Elmer Bass. But her eyes glistened with remembrance, not with sadness as Chief Gable talked about her daughter and what she had meant to the community.

The hardest thing I have ever had to do was tell Rachel Jones that her daughter Abigail was dead. You can't quite prepare yourself for something like that, to give such tragic news to someone. But in it all I hope she can find peace and closure and no longer have to live in the shroud of false hope.

Donald Knight stood behind the wheelchair of his Daughter Lucy, dressed in his best three piece suit, that had been neatly pressed for the occasion. His face however was gaunt and strained, creased flesh around the eyes, which was a huge contrast from his immaculate suit.

The guilt. I wish I could tell him that it will one day just disappear, hey maybe it will, but I doubt it. Things like that leave mental scars that never truly heal. The Chief asked me what happened to Denny. Truthfully I can't quite remember. Emerging from the well, squinting through that thick red smoke, hearing a gunshot and seeing Denny fall. Yes, I saw Donald Knight holding that rifle, but did I see him kill him? No, not exactly. Listen, he did kill him, there's no denying that in my eyes, but is it worth dragging it all through the court system and leaving that brave little girl without a loving Father? No, it's not.

He gazed upon Lucy's shining, smiling face, her hands gripping her friends old parka as a thick woollen blanket covered what she wasn't ready for people to see yet, but she looked unfazed by her disability, lost in a moment of pure love and revery for her best friend.

That little girl has been through enough, without my words potentially parting her from her Father. I couldn't do that to her. The Chief had asked me what I had seen and I told him that I couldn't be sure, for all I knew he shot himself. Chief Gable is no idiot, and when I told him my side of things, that thick moustache of his had turned up at one side, the way that it did when he smirked at something. He knew what I was doing and I think he respected me for it. He told me it wouldn't stand up in court, there was no real evidence and the story that they went with was that Denny had struggled with the 'something' and the gun had gone off. Outcome, accidental death.

He gazed up at the Chief as he proudly pulled back the tarpaulin to reveal a large stone monument, topped with a single magpie, the piece had been entitled 'Sorrow' by a local stonemason who had worked effortlessly to carve all the names onto the monument in such a short space of time. Names of loved ones that had disappeared over the years, that the community believed had fallen prey to this 'something'.

The Chief asked me if I was sure and I told him it's what Denny would have wanted. Granted I had only known Denny Lamont for a short time, but I knew him better than anyone that had lived in his town for the past thirty years. Besides Denny gave his whole life to protect this town, he would not of wanted to see that little girl suffer alone.

Jimmy listened to Chief Gable as he read out the names...

"Denny Lamont, Abigail Jones, Max Chambers, Anita Khan, Andrew Bagwell, Sherry Adkisson..."

Many other names continued to leave his lips, but there was a pause and a quiver in his voice when he read out the last name...

"...Deputy Darryl Whittaker."

Gloria Lockwood gazed up at him with teary eyed admiration and it was her that led the emphatic applause.

The Chief climbed down from the stage and wiped at his eyes with the back of his had as people rushed to show their appreciation for his kind words about the lost friends and family members, they all clambered around him, wanting to shake his hand. But Chief Gable looked passed the crowd of people that surrounded him and stared at Jimmy who was left all alone on the outskirts of the indulgence and he smiled back at the Chief.

Gable gestured to Jimmy to join him, to relish in the moment, as he should, for he was the man responsible for all this, but Jimmy shook his head and the pair smiled at each other. Jimmy turned and walked away, Gable attempted to get through the rabble one last time to go and say goodbye to Jimmy properly but he couldn't and sighed, turning his attentions back to shaking hands and listening to the kind words of his people.

Jimmy stuck his hands into the deep pockets of his raincoat and his fingers found all manner of trinkets within, a Swiss army knife, a broken cell phone, two lapel pins. He turned and walked away from the town square just as an announcement was made by Buddy Race that this date would be celebrated yearly and those that had left us too early would be remembered forever, there was a raucous cheer of celebration and then a brass band erupted. He reached his car, which had had some much needed tender loving care spent on it. A gift from Hope Springs, the Chief had said, least they could do, not that Charlie Mendoza would have had any say in the matter, guess he just did what the boss said.

Jimmy wasn't going to complain about the new glass in every window and the patched holes. The car may look like something that just rolled out of Doctor Frankenstein's workshop, but she was his, Olive and he loved her. He slid in through the driver's side and slammed the door behind him, his hands gripped the wheel and he sighed heavily.

"What a ride." He said and then searched his inside pocket for his cigarettes, a brand new pack of Freebird Lights fell into his hands.

"Guess it's time to start easing out of bad habits."

He slid out a cigarette from its pale packaging and placed it between his lips and then searched for his lighter, what he found instead was a twisted piece of metal, silver.

"The silver bullet." He whispered to himself, the cigarette dancing in his lips as his tongue clicked.

"So Pops, where would one get a silver bullet from?"

He dropped the slug back into his inside pocket and removed the lighter, flicked it quickly and lit the tip of the light cigarette, which apparently had 2 milligrams less nicotine than the regular Freebird brand. His face contorted at the unfamiliar taste and he shrugged.

"Best get used to it. Change is needed."

He turned the key in the ignition, the engine hiccuped and spluttered before purring sweetly and Jimmy took off down the road and out of Hope Springs.

XXXIV

Jimmy was heading back West to Studd City, he had a long drive ahead of him and wanted to make good time, taking the route back through Portland, Salem and into Forge City which could take him a good eight or nine hours. He had only just trundled over the Hope Springs border and was surrounded by huge redwoods when he realised he was being followed. He squinted into the rearview mirror and noticed that a sleek black Pontiac Grand Ville was tailing him very closely.

"Hello, what's this?"

There was no way that he could try and outrun or lose his pursuer, not in the bucket of bolts he was lolloping along in. Maybe he was being paranoid, maybe they were just safe drivers that were stuck beyond him and didn't want to over take for fear of being struck by a car moving in the other direction.

"I know Pops," He said to himself, "What's your gut say?"

His gut said they were following him, but to be sure he indicated and pulled off the road and into a clearing next to the towering redwoods where he waited. The Pontiac slid past him coolly at the same pace that it had been keeping all along.

"You see." Jimmy sighed, "Paranoid!"

But then his eyes doubled in size when the Pontiac stopped and then turned into the same clearing, before reversing back in front of Jimmy's car.

"Shit." Jimmy choked and scrambled around in his glove compartment for his revolver, he found it but as he looked up there was a man standing at the window, clad in a black suit, sunglasses and earpiece, he looked ever the federal type. He tapped on the window, hands clad in black leather gloves of course.

Jimmy swallowed hard, and kept the revolver close and slowly wound down the window.

"Can I help you?" Jimmy asked, making sure this mysterious man could see the gun.

"You won't need that, Mr. Johnson." The man said with an arrogant smirk.

"Who are you? What is this?"

"You're to come with me."

"Fuck that!"

"My supervisor wishes to meet with you."

"What?" Jimmy stared at him in bemusement, before he spotted the golden pin that was attached to his lapel. A finch engraved upon it.

"You're with the Secret Hunters Horde aren't you?" Jimmy asked lowering his revolver.

"Please come with me, Mr. Johnson. This shouldn't take long." And with that the Agent walked away.

"A Finch..." Jimmy said to himself, "Agent Wren, Agent Kite, Agent...Finch! Their codenames are birds!"

Jimmy left the revolver on the passengers seat and excitingly clambered out of the car. He straightened up his raincoat as if it would help to make him look more presentable and looked on as Agent Finch, opened the rear door of the Pontiac and gestured for him to join whoever was inside.

Jimmy was apprehensive, but his gut told him everything was going to be okay, these were the good guys, weren't they? With that thought spiralling in his head as he made his way to the important looking car and approached the open door. Jimmy gazed again at Agent Finch who nodded that it was okay to enter.

He was met by a tall, slender man, immaculately dressed, his greying hair slicked back and a thin smile upon a gaunt face that was topped by thick rimmed glasses.

"Good day to you Mr. Johnson." The man said in a very proper English accent.

"Erm, Hi?" Jimmy replied.

"That will be all Finch." The man said and the door was closed, Agent Finch stood by the door with his hands clasped behind his back.

"You've been through the mill haven't you?" The man chuckled and he turned his attentions to a folder in his hands, he flicked through several pages ticked something off and then slotted the papers back into the folder, resting it on his lap.

"So!" The man said cheerily.

"Sorry, but who are you?" Jimmy interrupted, "What do you want?"

"Of course!" He laughed, "Where are my manners. I can understand that this looks very cloak and dagger, but I had to wait until you were out of Hope Springs. Prying eyes and all that."

Jimmy stared at the man in utter bewilderment, his conscience stabbing at his brain making him believe that he had done something wrong and these guys were going to murder him and leave him at the side of the road.

"My name is Mr. Columbidae and I believe you have deducted, I represent the Secret Hunters Horde."

"Thought as much." Jimmy sniffed, "So what laws have I broken?"

"Oh, none whatsoever, Mr. Johnson, Jimmy…can I call you Jimmy?"

Jimmy shrugged.

"Good!" Columbidae smiled, "Jimmy we wanted to take this time to thank you for your help in this matter by ridding the world of another of its gruesome abominations."

"Really?" Jimmy scoffed, "Thanks."

"I am to pass on thank you's and best wishes from Agent Wren. She owes her life to you for getting her out of that well."

"It was nothing." He lied, it was everything and he knew that she played just as big a part in their survival as he did, but he took the praise nonetheless.

"How is Lindsey? Is she coping? It must be very difficult for her?"

"Agent Wren is doing fine, she has taken a leave of absence for the moment. Unfortunately she will not be able to return to the field, but we have a clerical position ready for her when she is fit to return."

"Good, well send her my..." he thought of saying love, but that was preposterous, he hardly knew the girl, "...erm..." He searched for the right words.

"I will pass on your best wishes." Columbidae smiled.

"Thanks."

"And as you may know during all this ghastly business we lost one of our hunters and I wondered whether you had come across any of her apparel?"

Jimmy's hand dove into his inside pocket and retrieved the two pins.

"Splendid!" Columbidae sighed, "May I?" He asked, his hand hovering over them. Jimmy nodded for him to take them and he did, turning them around in his fingertips.

"They are implanted with a small navigation chip you see, so we can track our agents and our hunters in the wild. Wouldn't want these falling into the wrong hands now would we?"

"Hang on!" Jimmy cried, "You knew where they were the whole time and you did nothing to help them?"

Columbidae placed the pins into his inside pocket of his tweed jacket and sighed heavily.

"They know the risks when they enter no mans land Mr. Johnson."

"Yeah, but you could have helped them! You could've help me!" He cried, "I lost a friend back there you know!"

The raised voice had garnered the attention of Agent Finch who turned to look into the window, but was waved away by Mr.

Columbidae.

"I am very sympathetic to the trials you have faced, truly I am, but as a former Police Detective you will fully understand the situation when I tell you that my hands were tied. When orders come from the top for you to stand down, you stand down."

Jimmy was about to fire back with some flippant remark but then stopped and realised that what Mr. Columbidae said was indeed correct, that was the reason he left the Police for the constant bullshit that slithered down from the top.

"Yeah, I understand alright." He sighed.

"Look, I for one am very thankful for your help in this matter and if you are ever looking for a career change then we could use good men like you on our team."

Columbidae held out a card and Jimmy took it, looking at it he saw nothing at first glance, but before he could examine it, Columbidae had wrapped his hand around his and shook it vigorously, telling him how much of a pleasure it was to meet him. The door opened and he was helped out of the car by Agent Finch, who then shut the door and moved around the front entering the car through the driver's side and started the engine.

Jimmy looked on bemused as the window slid down and Columbidae appeared again.

"Thank you again, Mr. Johnson, but a word of warning if I may?"

Jimmy just stared back at him blankly.

"Give up the search for your father, you won't like

where it leads."

"My Father?"

Jimmy was frozen to the spot as the black Pontiac hurtled away leaving him half chasing after it knowing he could never keep up.

"What...what did he mean?"

Jimmy stood in the clearing staring at the empty road and then back down at the blank looking card he had been given, but as he turned it over again and again in his hands he could see that there was indeed wording and a symbol on it, so subtly were the words etched in ivory, tones almost the same colour as the card itself. There was a symbol of a hand holding aloft a stake and an address on the other side that read...

XXXV

It dug itself out from under a mass of rubble and dirt, wings broken and misshapen, throat filled with muck. It coughed and croaked trying to rid its throat of what it choked upon. There was only darkness now, no light from the moon or sun would ever shine on this cavern again, for the well was gone. It clambered out from the thick layering of dirt, and staggered away from what should have been its grave. Its talons tried to grab a hold in the thick ever moving mud that it found itself standing in and then clambered forward to where its nest had been. The Magpa's beak chattered loudly in the darkness as it sniffed out the remains of its past victims, stepping over bones and rotting flesh. It burrowed down into the dead, crunching through brittle old bones and digging out half eaten corpses until it reached a tunnel. The Magpa dropped down into the tunnel, its fragile ankles fracturing from the descent, causing her to shriek in agony and the sound carried along this newly discovered tunnel. The Magpa began to limp its broken carcass through its narrow walls. There was a light at the end of the tunnel, a natural light and the breeze of the outside world caused her feathers to flutter, it sent a chill against her leathery skin, her eyes caught the light and they shimmered with mischief and hatred, eyes like marbles, eyes almost human.

THE END

OTHER WORK AVAILABLE

NOVELS

Hartwaker: The End of Kings
Secret Hunters Horde: Monster Home
Secret Hunters Horde: Finding Condor
Vatican: Angel of Justice
Vatican: Retribution
Vatican: Unholy Alliance
Blood Stained Canvas
Maple Falls Massacre
Dinner Party
Fear Trigger
Welcome to Crimson

COMING SOON

Hartwaker: A Slayer's Quest

Follow author Daniel J.Barnes on social media
@DJBWriter on Facebook, LinkedIn, Instagram & Twitter.

Proud to be part of the Eighty3 Design family.
For all your website and graphic design needs.

www.eighty3.co.uk

Printed in Great Britain
by Amazon